Drunk on All Your Strange New Words

EDDIE ROBSON

Drunk on All Your Strange New Words

A TOM DOHERTY
ASSOCIATES BOOK
NEW YORK

DRUNK ON ALL YOUR STRANGE NEW WORDS

Copyright © 2022 by Edward David Robson

All rights reserved.

Edited by Lee Harris

A Tordotcom Book
Published by Tom Doherty Associates
120 Broadway
New York, NY 10271

www.tor.com

Tor® is a registered trademark of Macmillan Publishing Group, LLC.

The Library of Congress Cataloging-in-Publication Data is available upon request.

ISBN 978-1-250-80734-2 (hardcover)
ISBN 978-1-250-80736-6 (ebook)

Our books may be purchased in bulk for promotional, educational, or business use. Please contact your local bookseller or the Macmillan Corporate and Premium Sales Department at 1-800-221-7945, extension 5442, or by email at MacmillanSpecialMarkets@macmillan.com.

First Edition: 2022

Printed in the United States of America

0 9 8 7 6 5 4 3 2 1

For Catherine, who took the leap

Drunk on All Your Strange New Words

ONE

A THEME PARK VERSION OF ITSELF

The interior of the Broadway theater shifts and blurs in Lydia's vision as the curtain falls for the interval, but she keeps her mental focus long enough to finish translating the last few lines of the first act for the cultural attaché. He calls himself Fitzwilliam and sits to her immediate right in the VIP balcony. (Lydia calls him Fitz, and either he doesn't mind or doesn't register the difference.) Translating while listening to the dialogue is tricky but Lydia can hardly ask the actors to stop for a moment and let her catch up, and she is keen for her employer to have a seamless experience. She is proud of her ability to translate and listen simultaneously—a lot of her old classmates struggled with this aspect of the job, and tonight's play is a perfect chance to show it off—but it's been ninety minutes and there's more to come (Who knew plays were so *long*?), and she's dizzy and needs a break. The cultural attaché thanks Lydia for her work, she tells him it's no problem, then she stands up, trips over her bag and falls backwards over the railing.

By this stage Lydia feels so drunk that, as she plummets towards the stalls, she barely registers that what's happening is bad. She feels little more than sluggish surprise—*Oh, I'm falling off the balcony. Oh dear*—as she hears the cries of alarm from other audience members, some of whom she is about to land on.

And then she stops. Not because she has landed on anything, or anyone. She just stops.

She is upside down. She looks up at her feet.

Fitz has reached out one of his long, slender arms and caught Lydia by her ankle, his flexible fingers clamped tight around the limb. She's heard his people are stronger than they look but until now Lydia has seen little evidence of this because the job of cultural attaché is so genteel. She always wondered if the rumors of their strength were just used by certain groups of humans to justify their own fearmongering but no, apparently not. He's holding Lydia by one hand without straining and she knows she is not the lightest of people.

Lydia stares foolishly down at the crowd of theatergoers staring up at her and feels relieved she didn't wear a dress tonight.

Fitz hauls Lydia back onto the balcony. He doesn't quite lift her high enough and her head glances off the railing on the way. She hears his voice inside her mind: *Sorry.*

No no, you're fine, Lydia replies. *Thanks for catching me.*

She's safely inside the balcony and he indicates for her to sit back down. He seems concerned, although she always finds it hard to read his face, especially behind that translucent wrap he wears over it (the Logi can breathe without these, but find it very difficult). Because his people don't use their mouths to speak, they don't seem to use them for any form of expression, any more than humans communicate their emotional state with their noses. She instinctively interprets his eyes as "surprised" or "curious"—but she knows that's just because they're large and dark.

The audience members still looking up at them from the stalls probably assume Lydia and Fitz are conversing right now. When you have the ability to communicate with someone telepathically, people tend to assume you're talking to them all the time, especially if you're not visibly doing anything else. But Fitz isn't talking to Lydia: anyone who knows him would know that if he's not making expansive hand gestures, he's probably not talking. He knows her brain needs a rest. Lydia should have known it too: taken more care, and not stood up so quickly. Now everyone will think she can't cope with the demands of her job, just because she fell off a balcony.

Eventually Fitz does speak. He says: *We can skip the rest of the play if you're too tired.* He always says "tired," never "drunk," because he's polite like that.

Part of Lydia would very much like to duck out of this. But it's the closing event on the last night of the seventeenth annual

Plugout NY Festival, a very busy week in the cultural attaché's calendar, and this is the first time she's done it, and she doesn't want to wimp out so close to the end. There's also the reception afterwards, which is kind of a big deal.

Can we get some air? she says.

They walk down to the lobby, his hand discreetly but firmly placed on her shoulder to make sure she doesn't fall down the stairs.

When Lydia was a kid, of course she'd heard that communicating with the Logi made you drunk—everyone heard that—but she honestly wasn't sure if it was just a stupid urban myth. On her first day at the London School of Thought Language (LSTL) they told her that processing the language in your brain didn't make you drunk but it did make you *feel* drunk, a distinction Lydia found hard to grasp: drunkenness is a feeling, so what's the difference between feeling drunk and *being* drunk? They explained that from a biological perspective it was very different because your body wasn't dealing with toxins, and the process didn't damage your body in the same way alcohol did. So it was like getting drunk with no downside? Awesome.

At least, that was what she thought at the time.

As part of their education, pupils at LSTL were given weekly sessions where they had to complete tasks while "drunk." These were not nearly as much fun as everyone imagined they'd be. They weren't allowed to have real alcohol (they did ask, of course), and were instead given a nasal spray which (apparently) more accurately reflected the type of intoxication they would feel while working. They were then given basic comprehension and memory tests, or they'd be told to prepare a meal from a recipe or issue a complex set of instructions to a service terminal, that sort of thing. Lydia had plenty of practice at doing things drunk from when she lived in Halifax (the one in Yorkshire, not Nova Scotia, as she explains to New Yorkers on a regular basis). But it was different when you were being watched by humorless tutors assessing your performance, rather than sitting on the floor of a kebab shop at 3:00 A.M. with chili sauce in your hair while your mates laughed at you.

Towards the end of Lydia's time at LSTL this training progressed past basic competence while intoxicated and focused on the trickier skill of appearing sober. Lydia asked why this was necessary since everyone would know they weren't, what with drunkenness being an inevitable consequence of the job. But the tutors just told her it was important for those in service to maintain a "professional" manner at all times. The problem with being intensively trained to act like you're not drunk is it leads you to do things you shouldn't do when you're drunk, such as standing up too quickly on a balcony.

Lydia stands on the sidewalk outside the Shubert Theatre sipping from a bottle of Coke Lo! she bought from the machine on the way down. The evening air is like a warm bath. A security drone hovers at her left shoulder, Fitz stands at her right. She looks up at the drone to see which one it is: When she started in this job she dubbed them Arthur and Martha (they are not coded male or female—Lydia chose the names arbitrarily). The one with them right now is Martha, a slightly newer model than Arthur, the most obvious difference being her Taser is top-mounted rather than side-mounted, and her spherical surface has more of a matte finish. Arthur must be guarding their seats.

Lydia doffs her jacket and hangs it on one of Martha's coathooks, then rolls up her shirtsleeves.

Like all the Logi stationed on Earth, Fitz chose a name for himself that humans can actually speak. Their names simply don't translate: they are effectively a separate language, unconnected to the words they attach to objects, concepts, actions, etc., and while Lydia could describe what she thinks of when she hears his name (pale violet; ice slowly cracking over the surface of a pond; the scent of lemon; and then just a bunch of numbers), that's not actually his name, and also it would take ages to say.

Fitz is still saying nothing, leaving her to recover. His huge hands are plunged into the pockets of his dark blue coat as he stares across the street. He always wears stuff like that—very tailored and plush, with a distinct Earth influence. Most of the other Logi she's met don't dress like him, they wear clothing with a more meshy look to it—but they all cover up, all the time, regardless of the heat. And hats, they all wear hats: Fitz has a wool cap that matches his coat. The small, narrow spikes that cover the top of his head poke out through the weave.

The Logi's bodies are long and slim, evidently not built to retain warmth because their natural habitats don't require it, and even in weather like this they're capable of feeling cold. Lydia has rarely seen Fitz—or any Logi—without their face wrap, but she's seen pictures, obviously, because at LSTL they did modules on being able to tell them apart, to avoid causing offense. Lydia always enjoyed that, it was like a puzzle game. She latches on to certain elements of appearance—for instance Fitz has a more pronounced nose than most Logi (which still means it's barely there at all) and a slimmer, whiter face. Many Logi have more rounded, cream-colored faces which put Lydia in mind of a cartoon she used to watch about a guy with a skull for a head who worked in an office. She used to love that show, but it's a good thing Fitz doesn't remind her of it, it's quite distracting.

Of course, Lydia knows him well enough now that she doesn't need to make an effort to recognize him. She knows his mind, and can tell when he's there even if her eyes are closed.

The theater district is one of Lydia's favorite parts of the city. She's seen old photos and it's not much changed from how it was a hundred years ago, though that's true of most of Manhattan. Mrs. Kloves, their neighbor at the cultural attaché's residence on the Upper West Side, has many, many opinions on how the area has changed. She told Lydia that when they put up the sea barriers the mayor's office started slapping protection orders on everything and turned Manhattan into a theme-park version of itself: no life, no change, no danger, just *heritage*. When Lydia heard this she felt a little bad for liking it here, as if this meant she had really basic taste, but she can't get on board with the idea it's such a terrible thing if a place stops being dangerous. Were any of your childhood friends stabbed to death, Mrs. Kloves? Because that gives you a different perspective on the appeal of dangerous places.

Even so, Lydia often finds herself in quiet moments like this searching the city for evidence of this decline, that a once great and vital place is now hollowed out and trying too hard to be itself, like a rock star who's done too much coke for too many years.

The streets are lively tonight, filled with pop-ups and stalls and corporate sponsor zones. It's been like this throughout the festival, which was devised to bring physical tourism to the city and boost the flagging arts scene during the often unbearably hot summer months. Fitz is attracting more curious glances from passersby than usual—maybe they're coming from the tourists? New Yorkers are usually cooler and more relaxed about Logi walking around, unlike people in Halifax. Even though her hometown's industry is entirely based around the Logi these days, none of them ever go there, so most people have never seen one in the flesh.

"Ambassador!" says a voice from behind them, and Lydia turns to see a young man emerging from the theater and heading their way. Fitz doesn't react, because he doesn't register the noise as being aimed at him, so Lydia gets his attention and points to the approaching figure. The young man has a light beard and wild, dark, curly hair and wears a shapeless pair of overalls with a dress shirt underneath. His attention is fixed only on Fitz: he doesn't seem to see Lydia at all.

"He's not the ambassador," Lydia tells the young man.

"What?" the young man asks, seeming surprised she's speaking directly to him as herself, rather than translating for Fitz. Or maybe he's just surprised by her accent.

"He's the cultural attaché." Lydia over-enunciates this and is aware her words are coming out with a leery, aggressive edge. She *really* needs to use this interval to sober up and wishes this guy would go away, but she needs to be pro about this.

"OK," the young man says with a tone to his voice that says: *same difference.* "I want to ask him about—" He stops addressing Lydia and turns to Fitz instead. "My name's Anders Lewton—

hi—and I'd really like to talk to you about—" He seems to realize he needs more pleasantries and chitchat before launching into his sales pitch and pulls back, saying, "How're you enjoying the play so far?"

Wearily, Lydia translates what Anders has just said for Fitz. He listens, then replies.

"The play is excellent," Lydia conveys to Anders. "I find the intricacies of the character dynamics fascinating." She knows a large part of the credit here belongs to Henrik Ibsen for writing the play, and to the theater company for staging it so well, but she also feels there's a compliment in this for her. She prepared for this extensively by reading *Hedda Gabler* twice and watching two (very old) TV adaptations and a film, so she wouldn't be thrown by anything on the night. She didn't want to be desperately looking up references on her glasses in the middle of the play: multitasking has its limits.

"Great," says Anders. "Listen, I need to talk to you about a live cross-portal event I'm raising funding for—my background's in devised theater, I don't know if you know what that is but it's an ideal medium for intercultural collaboration, and I really want—"

Before Lydia has even started to translate this for Fitz, she hears his voice in her head. She suppresses a smirk as she tells Anders what Fitz has just told her: "Could you make an appointment to come to my office later in the week? My translator has been working hard interpreting the play for me, and she needs rest so we can enjoy the second half."

Anders stares at Lydia for a moment. He doesn't fully trust what she's just told him, and suspects she has modified Fitz's words to suit herself. This is all written clearly on his face. He opens his mouth to speak to her; then he closes it; then he smiles at Fitz, says, "Thank you, I will," and walks back into the theater.

Prior to retaking her seat in the VIP balcony, Lydia goes into the bathroom, powers her glasses down for a moment (the agency doesn't like their employees doing this, but reluctantly accepts they must have *some* privacy) and takes a small bump of &amp. Lydia usually prefers not to use drugs while working, partly because it contravenes the terms of her contract, but mostly because she worries it will make her say things she shouldn't. But if she's just translating the play for Fitz it (hopefully) shouldn't be a problem.

To an extent it works and she feels sharp throughout, but the problem is that &amp is not a drug you take to watch a play about repressed emotions and thwarted lives set in a drawing room. It's a considerable effort for Lydia just to sit still and pay attention to what's happening onstage: she keeps up with translating the play, but grows impatient that the actors won't speak faster, and any poignant silences, which before the interval she regarded as a welcome opportunity to rest, have become *unbearable* to her now. She chews gum furiously, jiggles her leg and fiddles with the buttons on her jacket until one of them comes clean off. Fitz notices this and Lydia tries to keep it in check. Never mind falling from the balcony, now she's having to fight the urge to *leap* off.

When the play is over and Lydia has faithfully related every word of it to Fitz, she jumps to her feet and applauds wildly and maybe whoops a bit, not *that* loudly, though a few people look up to the balcony to see who's making all the noise, but most of them are focused on the stage, it's fine. No one ever really notices her: they're always looking at Fitz.

WORKING THE ROOM

The function after the play—effectively, the after-party for the entire festival—is being held in the upstairs room of a restaurant across the street from the theater. Half of New York's arts and literary community seem to be here, as well as various sponsors and patrons and hangers-on: the ceiling is low and the noise is overwhelming. Lydia tells her glasses to scan the room and identify people she's met before and in what context. Within a minute they've identified fifty-three, and there may be others she can't see or who haven't arrived yet.

Deep breath.

First Fitz is brought over to meet the cast and director of the play. Fitz talks to them about his interpretation of it and asks about the social context in which it was written, but the director seems more interested in telling him that nearly the entire set and props were handmade and *not printed,* which she felt was important because at the time the play was written and set, printing didn't exist (the director says this as if Fitz might not know) and it helps the actors feel their way into the *world* of the play if their surroundings are authentic, although naturally the backdrop outside the windows was done with digispective. Fitz politely agrees with everything she says.

Lydia's &amp is wearing off and she's just wondering if it would be *such* a terrible idea to do another bump when the actress who played Hedda, who has an incredibly striking face and a high musical voice that makes you shiver, speaks directly to Lydia. Now, Lydia isn't meant to have conversations of her own while working. She's allowed to be polite and helpful (provided the people she's talking to are sufficiently important—no chatting to waiters, etc.) but every second she spends talking to someone else is a second when Fitz is frozen out of the conversation. On the other hand, Lydia really wants to talk to the actress.

"Are you OK?" the actress is saying. Her accent sounds like Minnesota or maybe North Dakota: Lydia's fascinated by all the different American accents; she stores sound clips of the people she talks to, with the ultimate aim of collecting at least one from each state. She has seventeen so far.

"Fine, thanks," says Lydia, unsure why the actress is concerned for her well-being.

"After your fall, I mean? In the interval?"

"Oh! Yes." Lydia has almost forgotten about the fall. When she's drunk from translating, her memories take on a dreamlike quality and she can easily feel like they didn't happen. The agency says this is why they urge their translators to keep recordings of everything they do, so they can check back later and clarify their memories. While that aspect of recording everything can be useful, it clearly isn't the *real* reason the agency wants them to do it. "How did you see it?"

"Oh, a whole bunch of people took grabs of it," says the actress, "so it's everywhere now."

"Shit." Lydia turned her notes off during the play so she could concentrate and hasn't turned them back on yet. She should've guessed it'd go online. The agency will have words with her over this.

The actress finds the clip on her scroll and holds it so Lydia can see. Lydia is dismayed that she looks even more foolish than she felt at the time, her large eyes staring gormlessly like a cartoon character. Also she needs a haircut, it's down around her shoulders and looking messy. She considers changing the color so people won't recognize her from this clip: the electric blue is more memorable than she would wish.

"What happened?" says the actress, stroking Lydia's upper arm. Actors are often tactile people, she's learned in recent months, and it doesn't necessarily mean anything.

"I just felt . . . tired," says Lydia. She's conscious of freezing Fitz out and failing at her job, so she includes him in the conversation, which means it becomes a conversation between Fitz and the actress. Lydia does this reluctantly but at least retains the actress's attention. (What's her name? Lydia thought she had the Playbill stacked on her glasstop but can't find it now. Surely facerec can find her online?) When Lydia is speaking the actress looks at her, not Fitz, and her gaze is magnetic. Maybe it's just because she's got that charisma you need to play a leading role on Broadway but Lydia feels like she and the actress might get on well if they could stand by the bar and enjoy a few drinks and a proper conversation. If she ever got to go to things like this on her own.

But if she was at this party on her own, she'd be out of her depth, wouldn't she? She doesn't know how to talk to these people, she doesn't come from their world—even if she used social crib-notes she'd be struggling to keep up. At least with Fitz around all she has to do is say his words and people listen to her and she belongs here, more or less.

The actress sees someone else she knows, tells Fitz and Lydia it was *so* nice to meet them and moves off into the crowd.

Fitz has just been introduced to one of the festival's key patrons when Anders barges in on the conversation and makes a show of greeting the patron warmly as if he and she are terrific friends, taking her hand and cradling it as if he's going to kiss it. Lydia gives Fitz her interpretation of the situation, which is that Anders and the patron have met once, twice at most, and the patron barely remembers him. Fitz seems to appreciate her commentary: the Logi don't do laughter, but he does that psychic quiver that denotes amusement.

The patron says she's just *raced* back from Montreal to catch the last night of the festival, and asks Anders if he's ever been.

Anders shakes his head. "I haven't left Manhattan in eight years."

The patron is astonished. "Eight *years*?"

"Everything I need is here. It's a wasteland out there, isn't it?"

"Do you mean culturally or literally?"

"Uh, both, I think."

The patron laughs. "It's not all like *Florida,* dear boy. The Montreal scene is so much more *vibrant* than here. You should go."

"No thanks. I met a guy at a mixer last week who said his cousin decided to do Route 66 last summer, and their car got stingered and stripped in Oklahoma."

"Montreal and Oklahoma," she explains patiently, "are different places."

"What I mean is, *everyone* out there hates New Yorkers. Everyone knows that." Anders considers this the final word on the matter. Lydia wonders what he'd make of Halifax.

"What did you think of the show tonight?" says the patron.

Anders' lip twists into an unimpressed curl. "Revivals aren't my thing. I feel like this slot should have gone to some bold new *experimental* work. As I said, my background is in devised theater . . ." And he moves on to talking about his event, aiming his pitch more at the patron than Fitz: evidently her patronage is worth more than Fitz's. (Lydia facerecs her and yes, her wealth puts her in the top 0.5 percent globally.) The patron keeps trying to steer the conversation in another direction and Anders keeps steering it back, and they both speak over Lydia. Despite Lydia's skill at simultaneous translation, situations like this are beyond her and she's relieved when Fitz politely bows out of the conversation as soon as someone else joins it.

Fitz has to speak to lots of people from publishers, as usual. His dispatches are influential back on Logia, and though the market there for books from Earth is relatively niche, the market overall is huge, so it's still lucrative if a title breaks through. Ideally these publishers want Fitz to request a translation of their books for his personal use. It helps if he also reads it and likes it, but even if he doesn't, the fact it's already translated removes a significant cost and makes it easier for the publisher to sell the book extraterrestrially. If only these publishers knew their efforts would be equally well directed at Lydia herself, since if Fitz is interested in a book, he'll give it to her to read first and then ask if it's worth translating.

As Lydia translates Fitz's conversations with these people, the language takes its toll on her sobriety and she feels increasingly loose-tongued. The editor-at-large of a major litcast doesn't look at her at all when Fitz is talking to him, and she has to stop herself from saying *You have no fucking respect for me at all, do you. You think I'm just some pond scum they've dredged up and put in a shirt. Well, you can fuck right off because*—

Are you alright? Fitz says, directly to her, and Lydia realizes some of her thoughts have been leaking through to him. That's embarrassing.

Bit tired, she replies.

Likewise. Shall we leave?

Lydia tells him yes, just as soon as she's used the bathroom, and she moves through the throng to the door at the far end of the room. It's cooler and quieter in the corridor that leads to the bathroom, which is lined with ornately framed loops of the restaurant's most famous customers down the years.

Before she took this job, Lydia never knew she would value time spent on the toilet so much. It's not that she doesn't like Fitz—on the contrary, she's lucked out working for him, many of her classmates ended up in positions that are much more demanding and far less interesting—but when she's at his side she has no control over what's happening and just has to react constantly to what others do. One of the few times she can legitimately be away from him is when she goes to the bathroom, and accordingly she always spends longer there than she needs to. Either Fitz is too polite to mention this, or he just thinks this is how long it takes. Maybe Lydia's predecessor did the same thing? Everyone always says how sharp and efficient she was, so probably not.

Lydia slumps against the wall of the cubicle, rolling her head back and forth, humming tunelessly and very quietly. She closes her eyes.

Her head snaps up. Bloody hell, Lydia, don't fall asleep on the toilet.

When she leaves the cubicle she splashes some water on her face and looks at herself in the mirror, forcing her slack facial muscles into a smile. She just needs to hold herself together long enough to walk back through the function room, find Fitz, then go downstairs to the car and *bosh,* that's the festival *done.* She steps into the corridor—

And Anders is there, leaning against the wall outside the bathroom. "Hey," he says.

This *fucking* guy. "Alright," Lydia replies; doesn't stop, keeps walking back to the function room.

"Listen, I didn't get a chance to properly talk to your boss earlier—"

"Because you got distracted by someone more important, yeah, I noticed."

He laughs lightly. "But seriously, I really do think he'd be interested in the concept I'm working on—"

"Oh right, she didn't agree to back your devised theater event thing," she says flatly, "so you're coming back to Fitz. Got it."

"So what would be cool," he continues, undeterred, "is if you and me and him could find a quiet place downstairs, and then maybe—"

At this moment Lydia walks through the door to the function room and almost collides with the actress who played Hedda, who's walking through in the other direction. "There you are," the actress says, her face lighting up in a way that pleases Lydia greatly.

"Yeah," she replies stupidly. "Here I am."

The actress jerks a thumb over her shoulder. "I just saw Fitzwilliam over there all on his lonesome and I wondered—"

"Shit," says Lydia, peering across the room, "sorry, did you want to talk to him? I was just—"

"No, I was hoping to talk to you actually."

Lydia is thrilled to hear this. But—bugger, what's her *name*? Facerec did eventually pop up with it, after the actress had gone to talk to someone else, but Lydia's forgotten it now. She tries to retrieve the search—

"Excuse me," Anders says to the actress, annoyingly *not* using her name, "I loved you in the play—"

"Thank you," the actress replies.

"But this young lady and I were in the middle of a conversation and—"

"No," says Lydia, "actually we were done."

"I was midsentence."

"Yes, but I'd stopped listening," says Lydia, walking away across the room. The actress walks with her, trying not to laugh.

"Look," says Anders, following, "I don't get why you're being so obstructive—"

"Because I don't bloody like you and I want you to go away."

The actress is no longer suppressing her laughter.

"Right," says Anders, "you *fat fucking bitch,* tomorrow I'm getting in touch with your employers and I'm reporting you—"

"Oh, report *this.*" Lydia wheels around and punches him in the face, sending him flying. His head smacks into the table where the free wine is, jolting it backwards and knocking over glasses, and then he drops to the floor. Luckily it's well past midnight and most of the free wine has already been drunk, so very little is spilled.

Lydia turns back to the actress, who's gawping at the scene in alarm, and *finally* her name comes up in Lydia's glasses. It's Neve. Of *course* it is. She knew that.

IN-FLIGHT ENTERTAINMENT

On the hopper from New York to Manchester Lydia listlessly flicks through her feed, not opening anything, just looking at an endless stream of headers, previews and images.

@JUICELINE / Why Gen ((O)) Teens think your favorite Transformers film is problematically cyberphobic / TR91
@SKINNYDIP / We got a sneak peek at the new G17 human rights reform bill! SPOILERS AHOY / TR86
@DEADPLANET / What the fuck lives at the heart of Australia, and why? This zoologist has answers that may surprise you / TR77

What's that last one doing there? Her truthiness filter is meant to be set at 80, regardless of whether a post has a good Chime score. The bloody thing always resets to default if you don't keep an eye on it. She corrects her settings and then flicks to her personals.

@Dubi80Du / Got a hyperwave nutrient bath installed in my bed and it has CHANGED MY LIFE / TR82 / SPONSORED
@Agger4nn / Disappointed by the reaction to my apology yesterday so yeah I'll be closing down this identity and opening a new circle / TR84
@NemoZemo62 / making a cinnamon babka LIVE here in 20 mins, mirroring it on the veearr if you want to try some for yourself! / TR94

She hasn't seen anything about the Anders incident since yesterday, which means either no one is talking about it anymore or the filters she set up are working: she doesn't care which. As she scrolls she wonders when she last saw anything from someone she's met in hardspace. Back home she really valued her hardspace connections on account of her interface nausea syndrome—those were the people who'd remember to include her and not do everything in veearr. But she's not made any friends like that in NYC (she can't even find any INS support groups, which seems nuts), and her friends from back home have drifted to the edges of her circle and rarely get pushed at her anymore. The other connections she's accumulated are people she can happily talk to on main, but doesn't feel she could ask any of them to talk on private. And if she doesn't feel like talking on main, she doesn't exist—so her interactions have become very superficial.

The feeds aren't giving her the distraction she craves, so she tries books, vids, pods, actives—she even attempts to lose herself in that cube-stacking puzzle game she wasted whole days on as a kid. (Once she placed #4 on the daily global leaderboard. She was eleven years old, and nothing has ever felt as satisfying since.) But her brain is still snagged on going over the events repeatedly as if this will change them. This is a waste of time and energy, because it will not change them, but try telling her brain that.

So she attempts to get drunk—*properly* drunk, on complimentary booze. She only has to double-tap the armrest and the runner comes down the aisle with the tray: the perks of going first class. Fitz paid and she didn't ask how much it cost. She never knew anyone who could afford intercontinental travel when she was growing up. She'd known a few who'd *come* from the tropical deadzones—but none of them could afford to go back, or would have wanted to.

She can't remember the last time she got drunk—when she gets a night off, she prefers to spend it sober—so she expects her tolerance for alcohol to be very low. Yet she feels barely anything. She wonders if something in her biology has changed in the course of her work and she can no longer get drunk. But then, she also heard something once about how the hopper companies put a sobering drug in the air-conditioning to stop you getting lairy. So you can down as many free drinks as you like but after a point it stops having any effect.

Lydia tries to sleep, but cannot. Her brain goes through the events again in the hope they'll turn out differently this time.

The day after the Anders incident Lydia had a *horrendous* hangover, naturally. Translation hangovers are different from alcohol ones. It feels more like having a mild flu—drained of energy and full of weird aches. Also the body doesn't know how to react, because human bodies were never meant to do any of this, so it produces excesses of various chemicals in an effort to cope, and you have to deal with all that going through your system too. On top of this she'd been doing &amp. This was the state Lydia was in while trying to come to terms with what she'd done at the reception.

Surprisingly there was no note from the agency about it when she woke up. She expected one to arrive sometime in the morning, but it didn't. She blocked all her other feeds without looking at them, a display of extraordinary willpower on her part: news of the incident was bound to be doing the rounds to some degree. She decided to pretend it was one of those hazy dreamlike memories, adopting the demeanor of a child who wasn't really aware of having done anything wrong. Perhaps everyone else wanted to forget about it too. Perhaps no one would mention it, and if they did she could act all surprised before going *Wait, it's starting to come back to me . . . oh god, I can't believe I did that!* Etc, etc.

In fact she remembered the incident vividly. The moment *before* she punched Anders she felt very drunk, but when her fist connected everything jolted into crystal clarity. And while she felt bad for having embarrassed herself and Fitz and caused a scene, she didn't feel bad about the act itself because Anders was totally asking for it. If she'd punched him on the street at night and no one had seen, she'd have felt satisfied and gotten on with her life.

In the immediate aftermath Lydia was ushered away and the haze of drunkenness slid over her perceptions again, leaving the punch as a point of perfect focus in her impressionistic mental image of the evening. She dimly remembered telling one of the staff what a lovely event it had been as she and Fitz left the restaurant. She didn't much recall arriving back at the residence.

Lydia lay in her room at the residence throughout the morning and into the afternoon, afraid to get up and face whatever awaited her. Around two o'clock, three people—two human, one Logi— arrived at the residence. She recognized one of the humans, who was from the local branch of the translation agency. The Logi was a member of embassy staff, the other human was her translator: Lydia had met them both before but couldn't remember either of their names. The translator was called . . . she wanted to say Ben? She'd failed to make friends among the other translators. Lydia sensed some resentment, like they all preferred her predecessor and blamed Lydia for her absence, though none of them ever said this or even implied it. Some said her predecessor was the best student the New York School of Thought Language ever had, so Lydia avoided raising the subject because it made her feel a total fraud, a mediocrity stepping into the shoes of genius. She couldn't *imagine* how disappointed everyone must be in her after this incident.

Lydia waited to be summoned downstairs to explain herself.

But the call never came and she realized they weren't interested in hearing her explain herself. There was nothing she could say. The meeting went on for quite some time, which surprised Lydia because if they were discussing her dismissal she'd expected it to be a short conversation. Eventually they left and Lydia watched them go from the window, trying vainly to read the outcome of the meeting from their body language.

At this point she accepted she was going to be sacked. She deserved it. She'd spent much of the day trying to put a positive spin on the situation, but the plain truth was she'd screwed up very badly. When she accepted this she actually felt better. It simplified everything because she didn't have to make any decisions. She ordered in some pancakes, figuring it was her last chance to do so before she got booted out of this town for good: they were droned direct to her window and she ate them lying on her bed.

Shortly before four o'clock, Fitz sent a message up. Like all his messages it was written on premium-weight, headed notepaper and delivered by the domestic, a robot roughly the size and shape of an upturned wastepaper basket: It held the note in one of its white-gloved, eerily human-looking hands. The message requested Lydia's presence in the downstairs study at her earliest convenience.

Well, this was it.

Lydia changed out of her pajamas and into a dark gray skirt and white blouse, because that outfit went with her favorite boots, the ones with the black and white spirals coming up from the ankles. She went down to the hallway, where she found the study door closed as always. Fitz never left the study door open: if he was inside on his own, he'd be working; if he was inside with someone else, he'd want privacy; if he wasn't inside, he'd keep it closed to stop dust getting in.

She mentally pinged Fitz through the study door to let him know she'd arrived. (The proper term, which she'd learned at LSTL, was *presenting,* but Lydia hated it for some reason and always thought of it as "pinging.")

Yes, please enter, came the reply.

Fitz's study was one of the largest rooms in the old brownstone house, all done out with fitted mahogany bookcases that had been here long before the building had been acquired for use as the cultural attaché's residence. Many of the shelves didn't fit his books, because Logi books tended to be taller and wider than books made on Earth, but he'd filled the smaller shelves with books accumulated while living here: books in English, Mandarin, Spanish, French, Japanese, Urdu, Portuguese, Russian, German and more. (The concept of one species on one planet speaking so many different languages fascinated him—the Logi's own language had slipped into standardization long ago—and his lack of progress with learning to read human languages was due to his inability to focus on one at a time.) He had a desk by the window and a long, deep sofa against the back wall. There was little space for pictures, but the area above the sofa was filled with a morphing canvas he'd brought with him from Logia, which generated images based on the mood of the room—it responded to Logi, but also to humans who could speak

Logisi. At that moment it displayed a sunrise on Logia. Sometimes it showed Fitz's family and friends back home, sometimes spectacular vistas, sometimes phrases in Logisi which Lydia couldn't read but suspected might be motivational slogans. One time she entered the study looking for him and he wasn't there and the canvas was displaying what looked very much like erotica. She was too embarrassed to mention it and could never decide whether it had anything to do with Fitz or if whatever intelligence drove the canvas had a mischievous side. Lydia knew little about their technology—not through ignorance on her part, the Logi were careful not to bring too much of it to Earth or explain how it worked, and had complicated protocols about this—but she understood much of it was organic and could, in some sense, think.

Fitz was on the sofa, reading a coffee-table book of Scandinavian landscapes, holding it easily in one huge hand, fingers splayed to support its four corners. He closed the book, put it to one side and gestured for Lydia to sit in the high-backed padded chair. It was designed for someone of Fitz's height and Lydia always found her legs dangled down, making her feel like a small child sitting in Daddy's office (not that she had ever actually done that). She sat on it cross-legged in the hope this would make her look very slightly less foolish.

Lydia was going to start by apologizing to him. But then he apologized to her instead. He'd put her under too much strain, he said. Expecting her to translate the entire play for him *and* cope with the reception afterwards, at the end of such a busy week, was too much. He should have scheduled more time off during the festival and departed the reception earlier.

No no, Lydia replied. *I was totally up for it and I—*

But Fitz just held up a hand and said, *I've taken full responsibility for what happened.*

Lydia wasn't sure he could do that, legally, if Anders pressed charges. *What about the bloke I punched? Is he happy with that?*

I've told him I'll sponsor his event.

His devised theater thing?

Yes.

Oh. Sorry.

It's fine. It sounds quite worthwhile.

So he's not going to take it any—

No.

This was all being presented to her very lightly, but Lydia knew Fitz had put himself on the line for her and she wasn't sure she deserved it. But he genuinely wasn't angry: She'd have known if he was. It was impossible for him to outright lie to her in that way, and vice versa for that matter: their true feelings would always filter through.

I saw someone from the embassy was here, she said.

Yes. Her name's Madison. When Fitz said this, Lydia realized he'd mentioned her before—possibly not by name, but there was a tang of animosity she definitely recognized from previous conversations about his dealings with a colleague. He didn't always have to use someone's name for Lydia to know who he was talking about.

Was she very cross?

Fitz flexed his fingers in what Lydia had come to recognize as a dismissive gesture. *Madison and I have never got on. She thinks I let myself be influenced too much; I think being influenced is an essential part of my job. She's using this incident to lobby for me to be reassigned. This isn't really about you.*

This made Lydia feel worse. *You mean I could have got you fired?*

His fingers flexed again, faster this time. *No no. There was never any danger of that.*

Lydia looked up at the canvas. It had changed to an abstract piece in yellows and greens: It often did this when she was in here, especially if she was having some work-related stress, and she didn't like it. There used to be a print exactly like that in her tutor's office at LSTL, and Lydia always found it irritatingly distracting, and the canvas must have taken that image from *her* memory, picking up on how she associated it with feeling inadequate.

I think you need a holiday, Fitz said.

But we just had a holiday. In May they'd spent three weeks in East Asia, first staying with the cultural attaché for that region, who was based in Shanghai, before moving on to Incheon, Seoul, Kyoto and Tokyo. It was an extraordinary trip but exhausting. At

LSTL they had explained to Lydia she'd feel like this: having spent the first two decades of her life barely moving outside the town where she grew up, she'd find new places and experiences tiring. At the time Lydia felt this patronizing, but annoyingly it turned out to be accurate—during her first couple of months living in New York she spent a lot of her downtime just staring into space, too exhausted to process anything else.

Our trips aren't holidays, Fitz replied.

This was true. All his holidays were working holidays, since he was always absorbing new aspects of human culture, and if she was with him she was working too.

You haven't been home since you started working for me, he went on. *Maybe that would do you good?*

She told him her bag was already packed.

SQUARE ONE

Lydia takes a train from Manchester Terminal to Halifax and puts it on work expenses: Fitz told her this was fine because the whole trip is being classed as "research," and if pressed he will claim he wanted to know more about the Halifax inkworks and how it influences the local culture. His confidence that this will all be signed off by the embassy makes Lydia uneasy—she's clearly not the embassy's favorite person right now—but she literally can't afford to turn the offer down. Mum's flat, Lydia's former home, is on the south side near the inkworks, so she takes the tram through town. Be nice to see the old place. Well, probably not *nice,* but, y'know: interesting.

Lydia finds a seat on the tram that's empty except for a discarded paperback—a history of the organic food movement. It looks quite intriguing, so she sticks it in her pocket and sits down. The accents around her are warmly familiar, yet also make her melancholy and uncomfortable. At LSTL they urged her to speak more "neutrally," and for half an hour every day she had to wear a collar that used low-level sound waves to put pressure on her larynx. When she had the collar on she *did* sound dead posh, it made her laugh—but she loathed the idea of sounding like that permanently, and quietly fought against it by playing up her accent when the collar was off. She always sounded different from the other pupils and reveled in it—but she knows her accent has faded, and hearing the voices of the other passengers makes her realize just how much.

There's no need for her to speak while she's on the tram. She can just listen to music and look out of the window. See what's closed down since she was last here, that's always a fun game.

The sun has just set and the light is bad, but at a glance it looks like there are even more of those printed lean-to shacks in the out-of-town retail park than there used to be. Charities give them out for free and they usually last a year or so before they fall apart, assuming no one kicks them down first. Nobody builds houses for the people who use these. Most of them'll have come in from Lancashire, from homes that are underwater now. Nobody felt it was worth building a sea barrier in Morecambe like the one around Manhattan.

If you lined up all those printed shacks around the coast, you'd probably have a sea barrier. If only someone had bothered to do it at the time. Too late now.

The tram dips down into the underpass. The whole bloody thing is lined with those shacks, there's barely any room to walk down the pavement—

Another passenger is waving at the corner of her vision. Someone she knows from school? One of her brother's mates? No—just some random lad. He's sat down next to her and wants her attention.

Lydia turns to him, shakes her head and goes back to looking out of the window. She glances down to check her suitcase is still clamped between her feet, and reminds herself he's not going to rob or stab her on a tram, it's well lit and the tram's ayaie is good at recognizing crimes. Once she was on a tram going through town when a guy pulled a gun on another guy: the tram automatically diverted and continued to the nearest police station, where the one with the gun got picked up. Everyone knows trams are stupid places to start some shit. But on the other hand, some people *are* stupid.

Just then the music in Lydia's ears is replaced by a deliberately primitive, singsong, robotic voice intoning *JUST WANT TO TALK TO YOU LOVE WHAT'S YOUR PROBLEM?* while an image flashes in her glasses: the lad grinning, looking well pleased with himself. He's hacked into the link between her glasses and scroll. This rarely happens to her in Manhattan and she's been lax about updating her blockers. In a minute or so her scroll will learn how he got in and shut him out, but a minute or so of this is more than she can bear. She takes off her glasses and turns to the lad: a skinny guy, younger than she is, thin mustache, no shirt, tattoos down his jawline to make his face look like it's been riveted on. A lot of people these days have tats to make themselves look like machines, and Lydia gets the point but feels it's a bit much to make your face into a permanent ironic joke. The guy's running his tongue over his teeth and Lydia wishes she had Arthur and Martha with her so she could just wave her hand and they'd tase him. She glances at his mates, who are sitting on the backseat, watching how this plays out, snickering to one another. She'd like to tase all of them too, but as this isn't an option, maybe she'll throw that book about organic food at them.

Playing up her old accent as much as possible, she asks the lad what the fuck he wants.

"You got fancy clothes," he says.

Lydia's wearing her gold blazer, the one that strobes when the sun gets low in the sky—it's not particularly fancy, that's why she wore it. She's too warm in it but she was wearing it on the hopper and couldn't be arsed to cram it into her suitcase after she got off. The air-conditioning on the hoppers is always fierce because people associate cold with luxury—and it's only *now* that Lydia realizes the blazer makes her look like a rich person, regardless of how fancy it is. Fuck's sake. That's not a mistake she'd have made before she left Halifax.

"You new in town?" the lad asks.

"No," she replies.

"What you doing here?"

"They made me take time off from my job because I punched a lad for being a cunt."

Over on the backseat, his mates all laugh.

The lad grins. "Good thing I'm not a cunt then, isn't it?"

"Oh mate," Lydia says, putting on a mock-sympathetic face. "I've got some bad news."

His mates all laugh again, and in spite of herself Lydia feels satisfied she's got the better of him in their eyes. She shouldn't care what they think. She shouldn't care what *anyone* around here thinks.

The lad leans in towards Lydia. "Seriously though—"

By now Lydia's scroll is able to lock him out, but his channel is still open, so before locking it she brings up POV footage of herself punching Anders and pushes it right into his eyes.

The lad raises his eyebrows. "Alright, princess. Just being friendly." He stands and walks back to his mates.

When Lydia gets to Mum's flat (fourteenth floor of Wainwright House, thank god the elevator's working), Mum moans about Lydia arriving on such short notice and how she's had no time to get anything ready and there isn't even really anywhere for her to stay what with Mikhaila living in her old room now.

They'd managed to hang on to Lydia's bedroom while she was studying at LSTL, arguing that she still used it when she came back during the holidays, but now that she'd graduated and moved to another continent that argument didn't wash anymore. The council told Mum it was either let someone else have the room or move to a two-bed flat. They didn't even give her a choice about who took the room, so she ended up with Mikhaila, a pale woman with a demeanor like an anxious cat: before she moved here she lived in one of those printed shacks. Mum and Gil seem to like her well enough.

Lydia parks her case in the corner of the living room, almost knocking over a meter-high stack of paperbacks that's been left on the floor, and takes off her blazer. Mum looks her up and down.

"Glad to see they're feeding you," Mum says.

Lydia sighs: She knew a remark of this nature was coming. People assume she's put on weight because she goes to loads of fancy dinners and buffets as part of her job. But it's nothing to do with that. The chemical fluctuations caused by the translation process include an overproduction of insulin, and however carefully you eat and no matter how much time you spend working out (Lydia does at least an hour a day in the gym in the residence's basement and hates every second of it), you're still liable to gain. She gets a lot of comments about this when fronting the (barely watched) English-language version of Fitz's feed, but thankfully her sweeper automatically deletes most of them.

"I *have* explained about this, Mum," Lydia says.

"I know, I don't mean anything by it."

"Then why'd you say it?"

Mum sighs. "I can't say *anything* to you these days."

"Actually you can. You can say *It's nice to see you, Lydia*."

"Of course it's nice to see you, I just wish you wouldn't drop in from nowhere and—"

"I can go to a hotel if it's too much trouble. D'you want me to go to a hotel?"

"Don't be daft—"

"I can afford it, you know. I'm making good money now so you don't have to—" And without warning, Lydia breaks into tears.

Mum steps over, puts her arms around Lydia's shoulders, pulls her in close. "I'm sorry, love. Of course it's nice to see you."

"I've really fucked up, Mum."

"I'm sure it's not that bad."

"It really is—you saw the footage of me?"

"Well, yes. So have they fired you?"

"No."

"Why not?"

Lydia can't help but laugh. "I don't know. They should have done. I think they wanted to and Fitz stopped them."

Mum raises her eyebrows. "Why would he do that?"

"Because he likes me? Maybe? And thinks I'm good at my job?"

"You can never tell what they're thinking, them lot. I know *you* can, but—"

"I can't read their minds, Mum. I only hear what they want me to hear."

"There you go then, even *you* don't know."

"He's a nice fella. I don't want to make trouble for him."

"Don't worry about him, worry about yourself."

Lydia waits a moment before saying this next part. "I dunno if I'm gonna go back."

"What?"

"I was thinking, I might just . . . not go back at all."

Mum looks puzzled, gives a little shake of her head. "But why?"

"It happened once, it'll happen again. I do daft things when I'm drunk."

"Mm," says Mum, unsure if she ought to agree.

Lydia sighs. "It never used to matter if I did daft things, so I never used to worry. But these days I'm really trying to do things right, and I *still* can't . . . what if I'm just not cut out for all this business?"

"Don't be silly. Do you want a cup of tea?"

Lydia says yes and goes along with the change of subject. She'll bring it up again another time, when she's not so tired and can argue her corner. Because now she's got some distance on it all, it feels a lot easier to be here, away from all that. Nobody can *make* her go back.

THE HIGH LIFE

Lydia's sleeping on the sofa when Gil rolls in from the pub, waking her up. He flops in the armchair: he's done a late shift at the ink-works and that metallic smell permeates his clothes. He asks how her flight was. All he wants to hear about is the flight, he doesn't ask about work: maybe he's steering clear of work deliberately, figuring she won't want to talk about it. So she gives him what he wants and tells him about the flight in as much detail as she can recall. Gil has always wanted to take a hopper. He doesn't even seem that interested in going to other countries, he just loves the idea of seeing Earth from orbit while getting served free drinks. He's jealous Lydia got to go at all, and he's *insanely* jealous she got to go first class.

"Here," Lydia says, reaching into her bag. "I wasn't hungry when they brought this round so I saved it for you." She hands him a tube of sushi with the hopper logo on it.

Gil is thrilled, tells her she's the *best,* and unwraps and noisily eats the sushi. Lydia wonders if she used to eat like that. They always told her at LSTL she needed to improve her table manners, which annoyed her because she never thought she had a problem with it. But maybe she did.

She asks Gil if he's picked up or fixed up any cars lately—if she's honest that's all *she* wants to hear about from *him*—but he just shakes his head. "No time. Working like a bastard at the moment. We're short staffed."

"How can you be short staffed? There's tons of people out of work."

"Turnover's bad. They're not training people properly. You should tell your boss about it."

The inkworks was founded, when Lydia was a kid, specifically to produce books for export to Logia. This is the foundation of

Earth's trade with the planet: the Logi have an awkward relationship with digital, which they regard as chaotic compared with the clarity of mind-to-mind communication. Coding is anathema to them, and their technology is altogether more organic, operated via direct mental commands. They do use imported digital technology in a limited way, but few of them really understand it, and so the vast majority prefer physical books. After making contact with Earth, the Logi were fairly cool on the relationship until they discovered how much cheaper it is to make books here: the plant matter usually used for this purpose on Logia is trickier, and slower, to cultivate. The rougher texture of Earthmade paper has taken some getting used to, but the Logi put up with it for the sake of the huge cost savings. (Lydia knew a lot of this already, and the rest she learned when helping Fitz research a paper about the parallel development of the book in different cultures.)

This activity has led to a minor resurgence in printed books on Earth, which means the inkworks does make some home market material. But this is really only an offshoot of the business they get from the Logi, so Gil blames his working conditions on them, saying that as they're the major customers, they ought to insist on better standards.

"He's not in charge of that stuff, Gil," says Lydia wearily. "It's not like they all know each other." In fact Fitz probably *does* have the influence to bring such issues to the attention of someone who could potentially do something about it, but (a) she doesn't want to speak out of turn and (b) she's quitting. "You want to go out for a drive tomorrow?"

"I've not got a car at the moment."

"Not even the Umu?"

"Sold it."

"No!" Lydia is horrified. "You should've told me—I'd have bought it off you and kept it here, you could've gone on using it—"

"That's the problem, nowhere to keep it. Jadon won't let me use his garage anymore. Only a matter of time before someone nicked it off the street."

"That's what I was looking forward to most—it's been *ages* since I've had a drive."

"Sorry. I can ask around, see if anyone'll give you a lend of theirs—"

"What will you do?"

"What d'you mean, what will I do?"

"If you've not got one either? What will you do about driving?"

"I told you, I've no time for it. Taking all the shifts they can give me. And I worry, y'know—if I broke my leg or ended up in a coma or whatever, I worry what'd happen to Mum."

"She earns alright from her streams, doesn't she?"

He sticks out his lip. "Al*right,* but it's pin money really. Barely more than she'd get from the Credit Office. So I shouldn't take stupid risks."

"Well, if you're not driving there's no point me going anyway."

"Sorry."

Lydia sinks back into the sofa. "I *loved* that Umu. You taught me to drive in that car."

"I remember."

Since Lydia was twelve she and Gil had been modding old cars: removing the Smartsteer, fitting decent manual steering and transmission, adding other funky touches. After a while Gil left the modding to her because she was better at it, while he focused on finding cars and sourcing parts—he didn't have a job back then. It could've been a proper business if there was more of a market for it: only rarely did they make a decent profit when selling a car onto another manualer. But even though she was able to strip an engine and put it back together by the age of sixteen, Lydia couldn't actually drive.

Gil could have taught her but Mum would've thrown him out of the house: She didn't approve of manualing, said it was dangerous, said there wasn't a person alive who could drive better than a Smartsteer. Mum wouldn't get in a car with Gil under any circumstances. One time she fractured a wrist at home and needed to go to hospital, and Gil insisted he could get her there quicker than an ambulance: Mum turned him down, saying that was exactly what she was afraid of.

But Mum finally accepted she couldn't stop Lydia learning forever, and she'd be as well to do it with Gil. So that summer after Lydia turned sixteen, every day for a month, he took her out in that dark maroon Umu to the crumbling retail park on the edge of town (which wasn't a village for the homeless then) and taught her everything he knew. They tried not to get into traffic because other cars would instantly detect the slightest infraction of road regulations and report it: instead they stuck to deserted areas, of which there were plenty. Gil taught her emergency maneuvers, cornering, stopping distances. He taught her doughnuts, handbrake turns, drifting.

Eventually Lydia was good enough to race with Gil's mates, usually out at one of the abandoned villages like Todmorden, where no one would see them. It was technically illegal but no one ever did anything about it: they weren't endangering anyone except themselves, and as they were unemployed, no one cared if they died. Lydia did the Longfield run in under forty seconds once, taking the big corner at fifty miles per hour. Those days in the Umu when Gil taught her to drive might be the happiest she's ever had.

Lydia's set her presence to dark, so she doesn't register on any of her old friends' feeds and they won't know she's in town. She's not sure they'd look her up even if they knew. During her first couple of years at LSTL, whenever she came home she'd do a blitz on her presence and make an effort to see everyone. She was keen to show them (and herself) she was the same person she always was, until it started to become clear she wasn't. They'd comment mockingly on her clothes and how she talked and the things she knew, and she would try to laugh along self-deprecatingly, because what else can you do? Over time it started to feel like more and more of an effort, and the outcome didn't seem to justify the effort, and it became easier not to bother.

The most awkward one was Emma, who—five years ago now—had been the one who suggested they go along when the translation agency sent their mobile testing center around. It didn't come here; they had to go to Sheffield. Lydia felt sure she wouldn't be suitable: she'd seen the list of common indicators (good at art *and* maths, able to focus on one person talking in a noisy room, synaesthesiac) and none of them applied to her apart from the one about having INS (prolonged veearr use does her head in after about an hour, which is how come she developed an interest in fixing cars instead). But Emma assured her they'd test anyone, and you got to go to the language school for free and there were great jobs at the end of it, much better than anything around *here,* and Emma didn't want to go on her own. The test indicated Emma was unsuitable, and she just shrugged and laughed: it was a long shot, about one in a hundred thousand. Lydia lied and told Emma she'd failed the test too.

A week later Lydia secretly traveled down to London for the next round of testing, figuring she was bound to fail *that* one so there was no point upsetting Emma by telling her. When she was offered a place at LSTL she told Mum and Gil straightaway but didn't put it on her stream for ages, because she was putting off telling Emma. When she finally did, Emma pretended to be pleased for her, and Lydia made a weak attempt at softening the blow by telling her the school wasn't *really* free, you had to pay it all back when you got a job at the end.

"Oh," Emma replied. "Yeah, that's not so great." Then she asked if Lydia was going to accept the offer.

"Probably, yeah," Lydia said. She'd already accepted three weeks ago.

Lydia wants to get a sense of the local mood, so while Mum cuts her hair in the late morning, she tells her glasses to narrow her feed's geo range. But nothing much comes up, so she tries lowering truthiness and raising Chime:

@DALEDIGGER / City councilman found dead at home, AI had been attending meetings on his behalf "for months"—did it PLOT to KILL him? / TR62

@LONGVOICE / Firefighters respond to criticism of satellite heatmap tech, saying it's cut fake callouts by 88%: "We were getting swamped" / TR76

@FEEDCHURNER / Barnsley: The new global capital of Scientology? We go beyond the walls of their compound / TR51

Bloody hell, who reads this garbage? Some of her old friends used to set their filters low, saying they didn't really believe the junk, it was just entertainment—but bits of it seeped into their conversation anyway. Some didn't trust the truthiness ratings and inevitably claimed it was all just a way of suppressing inconvenient information. Lydia sometimes worries it's naive of her to set so much store by the TRs, and yeah they probably are manipulating her to some extent, but she needs *some* way to make the whirlwind of crap manageable. The world has enabled so many bullshitters. It's exhausting.

Lydia closes her feed and goes back to working out how she can manage her future while Mum tells her to hold still so she can check if the sides of her hair are even. If she quits the agency she'll still owe them most of the money for her education. She currently pays it back at the rate of 8.5 percent of her salary, and she's been in the job for only ten months: she still has six years to go. The terms state she has to pay it off only when she's earning, and if she gives up translation and moves back here she doesn't expect ever to earn again—the assessment process at the inkworks classed her as having medium to low suitability for any of the roles there, and there's sod all else.

So she's looking at living in debt, in Halifax, for the rest of her life. But that's fine. She'll go back to watching old vids on her scroll and reading whatever books Gil brings home: the inkworks realized years ago they lost fewer books to theft if employees were allowed to take as many as they liked, killing the illicit thrill. She could get back to fixing up cars, maybe convince Gil to get back into it. Mikhaila would have to move out, of course. That might be tricky.

She's stared this in the face before. There was that time at LSTL when everyone was talking about the new translation technology that was being developed in California. Lydia remembers gathering around a scroll with her fellow pupils to watch a demo. The device looked rough and unfinished, but a Logi was wearing it like a helmet, loose cables connecting one part to another, and one of the dev team was speaking into a mic. The helmet could receive the speaker's words and, via an organic component made of cloned tissue from the brain of a translator, reprocess them into a signal the Logi could understand. It worked both ways: the helmet could receive the Logi's thoughts and a speech prog spoke them aloud. The demonstration was very impressive.

Lydia was distraught. They all were. They were due to graduate soon and it was all for nothing: this helmet would come on the market and all the Logi would get one and no one would need translators anymore. They were no longer special or useful and they'd all be in tons of debt. Some of them cried. Others watched the demo over and over, trying to convince one another (and themselves) that the thing didn't really work, that it had all been faked in order to raise investment, or something.

Their tutors told them not to worry about it and to continue their education. Lydia couldn't see the point, but she had nothing else to do.

A few months later it emerged that during subsequent tests the helmet had created a feedback loop, causing the wearer to uncontrollably repeat what they heard, effectively turning them into a transmitter. This proved a most unpleasant experience for any Logi who used it, filling their mind to the exclusion of all other thoughts. The developers insisted they could eliminate this malfunction but the damage was done: The Logi insisted emphatically they would not use the helmet, it would be commercially nonviable, and they took a dim view of any further development. The project was abandoned.

The LSTL pupils had a party in the dormitory the night they

heard: they got drunk (properly, on actual booze) and Lydia had clumsy sex with Maybelline, the girl from the room next door. In retrospect that was the closest she ever felt to her fellow pupils.

Gil's friend Jank calls around before work and sits and chats to Lydia while Gil hauls himself out of bed. Lydia doesn't want to chat: she's trying to color her hair. Jank has already told her he dislikes the new color, an opinion he was not asked for. He's one of those people—she runs into them quite often—who asks questions about her job with a tone of bemusement and *rather you than me*.

"People say they don't really need translators, the aliens," he says.

"Who says that?"

"Apparently it's all a big grooming ring."

"What?"

"Yeah," Jank says with a leer. He used to send Lydia nasty messages back when she lived around here, until Gil told him to stop it. He'd deepfake vids of them fucking, stuff like that, the most basic sex trolling you could imagine. He's not changed much.

"You must've seen them using translators on the feeds though."

Jank shrugs. "Yeah. So?"

"So . . . that's obviously bollocks, isn't it."

"Maybe not *everyone* who went to your school got a posh job like yours though. Maybe the ones who don't *get* jobs end up doing *other* stuff."

"You don't know what the fuck you're talking about."

For a few blissful seconds Lydia thinks Jank might shut up, but then he asks: "What sort of stuff do they think about then?"

"It's not like that."

"What is it like, then?"

Lydia sighs. "There's stuff he says to me, which I can hear, and there's stuff he just thinks, which I can't. And he doesn't know what I'm thinking either."

"Probably just as well you don't know what he thinks. You probably don't *want* to know."

"You're a fucking idiot, Jank."

Why did she come back home? She could have told Fitz she wanted to visit London for a few days. He'd have agreed to that. Probably booked her a nice hotel. She could've looked up Leif or Tregan, or one of her friends outside LSTL like Esme. Or even Maybelline. Like, it's nice to see Mum and Gil, but she'll have loads of time to see them when she moves back. This might have been her last chance to be somewhere other than here, and she's pissed it away.

HIDDEN PALACE

Lydia falls asleep in the late afternoon and everyone leaves her alone until she wakes up around 10:00 P.M. She idly remarks to Mum that the antilag shot she bought at the hopper terminal was rubbish and didn't work, and her glasses ask her if she wants to post that as a product review. She says yes.

Facing the prospect of being wide awake all night, Lydia decides to go out. *Out* out. Not with old friends, or Gil (who won't be back for hours anyway): on her own. She digs out some old clothes from a vacuum box Mum has stashed in the hallway cupboard, but of course they no longer fit her, so she'll have to go in some work clothes. She adjusts her outfit in the long mirror by the front door while Mum sits with her feet up on the coffee table and plays a strategy game set in a cod-medieval fantasy world. (Lydia can't help but notice the evil army of wraiths in the game bear more than a passing resemblance to the Logi.)

"You look nice," says Mum while her stream is temporarily muted so she can sip her tea.

"Yeah," says Lydia: the gray-and-black striped suit goes well with her new dark green hair, and she's absolutely nailed the eyeshadow. "Who cares if I look massively out of place?"

"Exactly."

"Doesn't matter, because I'm an international deluxe bitch."

Mum frowns. "That's not how I'd put it."

"Well," says Lydia, straightening her silver tie, "you're not me, are you, Mum."

"Have fun," says Mum, unmuting her stream and going back to her game.

"I will."

———

Lydia goes to Hidden Palace, a club she's been to precisely once before, on her eighteenth birthday. Back then it was rare her friends ever felt rich enough to go hardspace clubbing (the only kind Lydia could join in with) and when they did they went somewhere cheaper than Hidden Palace. The club seemed impossibly luxurious back then but now seems shabby and dated. Or maybe it was never that nice, and she just sees it differently now.

She easily scores some &amp and has a dance, but after an hour or so she still feels wound up and frustrated and she's just starting to think this was a waste of time when her gaze momentarily settles on a cleanskin guy with long dark hair and flowers sewn into his shirt staring down at the bar and she thinks, *Christ, he's fit*.

He looks up at her. She glances away but he's already seen her looking. He walks over.

His name is Hari and he's younger than she is, early twenties at the oldest, maybe even late teens. He tells her she doesn't look like anyone else in the club, and she tells him he doesn't either—but it turns out this isn't true because his friends join them and they're rocking the same look he has. Hari introduces her to them—Chukka and Fionn. They're cleanskins too—they don't even have piercings—and Chukka is heavily bearded, like Lydia's granddad in old images. They want to know who she is and where she's from and what she's doing here and are amazed to learn she's originally from Halifax. They ask a lot of questions and buy her drinks. They chatter eagerly and offer some of what they're on, which is some vape-chamber thing—she doesn't catch the name but accepts it anyway because they seem to think she's cool and she doesn't want to break the spell. It gives her a mild, not entirely pleasant buzz which gives way to a jittery rush, on top of the &amp, and she hopes it wasn't a terrible idea to take it.

Fearing she's being rude by talking about herself, she asks them questions (Hari's an on-call cybersecurity patcher; Fionn's a colleague of his who specializes in data analysis; Chukka makes and sells bespoke hash pipes). But they don't really want to talk about themselves, they want to know about life in Manhattan and all the places she's seen with her own eyes. They ask, is it really different when you're really there? And they want to hear her say yes, which is good because it's true.

As they're leaving Hidden Palace, Hari sheepishly tells Lydia he shares a bedroom with his younger brother so going to his flat's not really an option. No problem, says Lydia: she looks up the nearest Quickrooms on her glasses and requests an open-ended short stay, because booking a hotel room on a whim is what an international deluxe bitch would do. The hotel itself is not deluxe—it's a spartan crash house for seasonal workers—but it's all there is. Minutes later they breeze through the doors of the hotel and kiss in the elevator. The room, when they reach it, is tiny and barely accommodates a double bed—but a double bed is all they need.

His body is sleek and solid and full of energy, and after sex they engage in excitable chatter. He laughs at her jokes. There's a moment when he holds her gaze and she feels like she might tell him about why she's back in town, because she glossed over that part when she met him in the club.

But the moment passes and they fuck again instead.

It's after 9:00 A.M. when he finally falls asleep. She could just leave him here, tell him the room is paid for and he can check out when he wakes up. But she stays. Her thoughts go back and forth, like a conversation. She thinks how relieved she was last night to see herself through the eyes of Hari and his friends. They were properly impressed with her. She misses Manhattan. So what if it's become a theme park? She likes theme parks. And she wants to make up for her mistake: she's afraid of failure and the associated humiliation, but she's already suffered that, so what does she have to lose?

Above all she misses the focus and certainty she gets from Fitz, that when she's with him she knows exactly what she's meant to be doing, and that he's not just bullshitting her.

The other voice in this conversation Lydia's having in her head belongs to Fitz. The voice doesn't say exactly what Fitz would say, but says it how he'd say it. They told her at LSTL this was normal, that after a while she'd hear the voice of her assigned Logi in her head even when they weren't around, and it's become so commonplace she rarely thinks about it. But suddenly, perhaps because she hasn't spoken to him in a few days, it strikes her how weird it is.

"What's weird?" says Hari sleepily, turning his head on the pillow and looking up at her.

Lydia realizes she spoke that rather than thinking it. She's embarrassed, then decides not to be, and just explains what she was thinking.

"That *is* weird," he says. "Having him in your head all the time."

Lydia agrees. But she doesn't mind. She likes the weird.

NEW LYDIA

When Lydia gets back to Manhattan she draws a thick line in her consciousness between Old Lydia and New Lydia. All the mistakes of the past belong to Old Lydia. New Lydia doesn't make those kind of mistakes. New Lydia:

- is slick
- is polite to the point of blandness
- doesn't punch people (at least, not when she's working).

Fitz seems delighted to have her back, saying the temp tried his best but simply wasn't as good. *He needed everything explained,* he tells Lydia. *He didn't anticipate things like you do.* This wasn't something Lydia had realized she was good at, and she's pleased but now feels under pressure to keep it up. *And I assumed you all had a basic level of knowledge about literature, geography and so on. Your predecessor did, as do you, so I thought they taught you all that at the school. But the temp really didn't know anything. He didn't seem very bright.*

Lydia laughs, remembering the LSTL pupils who'd come there from expensive schools and coasted through the core subjects, getting creditable grades before forgetting it all. Whereas no one ever expected Lydia to know things, but the ignorance was theirs, not hers: They didn't know what it was like to grow up in an ink-works town with random books in every home, in the corner of every pub, even piled up in the veebars. You found stuff in books that was almost certainly online somewhere but you'd never see it unless you were looking for it. Whenever there was a run of a new English-language book being inked there'd be people talking about it on local feeds, in pubs, on street corners. Not everyone, but if you did it wasn't seen as odd, people didn't give you grief about it. They gave you grief about other stuff, but not that.

Then Lydia picks up on something Fitz said a moment ago. Having just seriously considered quitting, Lydia finds herself curious to know why her predecessor left, so she asks Fitz.

Burnt out, he replies in a bland tone. *It was just time for her to move on.*

The following week Fitz and Lydia are onstage in a lecture theater at NYU. There's a conference on the subject of the alien in literature and how this has changed over the years Earth and Logia have been in contact. Fitz is giving a keynote paper on what the human has represented in Logi texts, and Lydia is giving it simultaneously. To save strain on her, they've prepared her translation in advance so she can simply read it from her glasses rather than translating as she goes along. Looking out across the audience now, she's surprised how many of them are in hardspace. With this being an international conference she'd expected most of them to plug in. Either a lot of them are locals, or the kind of people who go to these things are wealthier than she realized.

During the early part of the paper Lydia is nervous, but reminds herself most people in the audience aren't looking at her anyway, and if they do look at her she's wearing an *excellent* new outfit (dark purple crushed velvet trousers and a light blue shirt with white pinstripes). Her delivery grows more confident and authoritative: she tells herself there's no reason not to be because after all she understands everything she's saying; she and Fitz talked through the ideas thoroughly, she's not just learned it parrot-fashion. By the end, Lydia's nerves have gone and she feels she deserves the applause she—and Fitz—receive.

But next she has to translate the audience's questions, the first of which comes from a smartly dressed, middle-aged woman and concerns a Logi work of fiction whose title roughly translates as *The Edge Pieces.* "Have you read it?" the woman asks Fitz.

Fitz admits he hasn't. Lydia hasn't either, so she can't help.

"I have to say I found it deeply patronizing," the woman says, testily. "You can talk about the enriching effect of cultural dialogue all you like but I find it deeply worrying that your people are reading it and thinking it represents us. I think it says far more about *you*."

Lydia relates this to Fitz, adding *Which was exactly what the bloody paper was about. Shall I point that out to her?*

Just tell her I'll read the book, and thank her for bringing it to my attention.

Lydia does so, but the questioner isn't satisfied and keeps talking. Fitz is too polite to intervene, so Lydia eventually does it for him. The woman looks most disgruntled, and for a moment Lydia thinks she's going to kick off and security will have to escort her from the building. Lydia hastily moves on to the next question, which comes from an elderly man.

"I see very little of religion in your literature," he says, "and you must forgive my ignorance, but is that because there's no plurality in such matters, and hence no conflict to write about? Or because there's no religion?"

Lydia translates this and Fitz thinks about it for a moment. *Such matters are discussed in our literature,* he replies. *But those works don't translate well, so almost no one here has read them.*

The questioner asks what the basis of their religious and/or spiritual beliefs are.

It's a complex subject, I don't feel I can adequately explain it in the time we have. Someone else would be better qualified. On the other hand, I find your own depictions of religion deeply fascinating . . . And he talks about this with great enthusiasm until they run out of time.

The keynote is just the start of a long day. Fitz commissioned written translations of the papers in advance and has already read them all, so he sits in on them and pretends to listen out of respect, while Lydia just listens without translating for him. But merely concentrating on papers all day is tiring, and she also has to translate the discussions at the end of each paper, and in the gaps between panels there are people they must speak to. When the attendees gather for the closing remarks Lydia is exhausted and tipsy and sneaks off to take a small bump of &amp.

At the evening banquet she's a dynamo, hopping from conversation to conversation and translating smoothly and at speed, placing Fitz at the center of the proceedings as befits his status as keynote speaker. After dessert has been served Fitz asks Lydia if she wants to go home and she genuinely doesn't. It's not just the &amp, it's natural adrenaline. Doing her job well is a buzz, it's like a game she keeps on winning, and she can't believe she almost quit.

Right, says Fitz. *Just tell me when you get tired and we'll go.*

Absolutely, Lydia replies.

She doesn't remember much after that.

She wakes the next morning and feels like fucking death. She's still wearing her shirt from last night but not the trousers. She has a desperate craving for sugar and caffeine but getting either of those things will involve moving, which hurts. It also hurts to open her eyes. She feels like her brain has been pumped full of junk thoughts and is collapsing under its own bloated weight.

She reaches for one of the cans of Coke Lo! she keeps in her bedside table, tears off the strip and waits for it to chill. Once it's cold enough she opens it and reluctantly pulls herself up into a sitting position so she can drink the contents without pouring them into her nose. She tells the curtains to slowly switch to fifty percent opacity. It looks like a sweltering gray day out there, with storms on the way. That's not going to help her headache.

She searches for her glasses so she can check her feed and make sure she didn't do anything last night that's going to get her fired. But she can't find her glasses anywhere. She usually leaves them on the bedside cabinet to charge, and the magnetized surface stops them falling on the floor, so she can't have knocked them off in her sleep. Maybe she left them in her bag.

OK, where is her bag?

Lydia opens the cabinet and gets out her spare glasses, the ones that aren't agency-issued, that she wears when she's not working. To her relief there are no alarming notes. She's been tagged into some clips of the paper.

@jairzin70 / Interesting issues raised in this paper from CA Fitzwilliam and @Lydl_Wordz / humbled to find the roundtable discussion I hosted in January is cited! / TR94

@Sansalee[=/=] / So proud of my beautiful friend @Lydl_Wordz smashing it HARD hard with this key note!! / TRUSTED FRIEND

Lydia wonders if it would be vain to share these to her feed, then she says sod it and does so. Looking down farther she finds images of herself at the banquet, not looking too messy—a little wild-eyed in some of them, but you could argue she just looks like she's . . . listening intently? Yes, you could argue it looks like that. She doesn't share these to her feed.

As her mind stops screeching with paranoia and settles into just a normal hangover, she notices Fitz doesn't seem to be in the house. She's familiar with his psychic footprint or whatever you want to call it, and can usually sense when he's here: if she strains she can talk to him even if she's up here and he's in the study. Strange. He very rarely goes anywhere without her. He doesn't take walks in the park. Whenever she's resting or using the basement gym, he usually just sits in his study and works.

Maybe he got lucky with one of the Logi attending the conference and didn't come home, the sly dog. Lydia amuses herself with this thought as she hauls herself out of bed, even though something at the back of her bruised consciousness tells her that's not what's happened, and this drives her to get up and investigate when all she really wants to do is lie back and order pastries to be droned to her window.

She descends the stairs and in her head she calls Fitz's name, hoping for a reply and not getting one. Tentatively she peers into his bedroom, establishes he's not in there and quickly retreats.

He's just gone out, she tells herself. That's all.

She goes down to the ground floor—and look, *there's* her bag leaning against the wall in the hallway. She must have dumped it there when she came in last—

The study door is open.

As Lydia approaches, there's a faint smell she can't identify. She looks through the doorway of the study and can tell the sofa is occupied, her eyes can detect the shape of Fitz lying on it in his usual fashion, but she doesn't want to look directly at him because she can see his dark greenish-purple blood pooling on the rug and the hardwood floor, and that's what she can smell, and if he's right in front of her but she can't sense him in her mind there's only one possible explanation.

TWO

MURDER AND MARSHMALLOW FLUFF

During her lifetime thus far Lydia has been very successful at avoiding contact with the police. She's had some automated spot fines, the kind of thing where you get a message telling you a drone saw you breaking the law and you can either pay the fine or contest it. Contesting it rarely works and costs more in the long run, so you take the fine and the points on your record. The fine gets taken directly out of your support wages, so if you don't appeal, you have no contact with anyone in authority. There's rarely any human intervention in the process, and no one even knows you did anything unless they check your record.

From her driving escapades with Gil, Lydia had learned how to keep off the radar, spot trouble brewing and duck out before the police arrived. This proved useful in other situations: for instance, one time when Lydia was at her block's book group, someone told Melia Grace her interpretation of *Gravity's Rainbow* was "overly literal" and Melia *kicked off.* Lydia saw which way the wind was blowing, quietly slipped out and went up to her flat. The fight escalated and eight people were arrested. Mum told Lydia she should've stuck around and streamed it: She could've got a few thousand views and earned a bit of pocket money off the affiliates. People love watching that stuff. But Lydia never thought it was worth the risk.

Now as Lydia stands in front of Fitz's corpse slumped on the luxurious sofa, her glasses take in the scene, read her emotional state and a window pops up with *911?* in it. Lydia answers *yes* while still trying to get her head around the situation. She tells the operator

"Someone's dead" and her glasses attach images of the scene. The operator tells her to wait there and cuts the call, and Lydia realizes she's just called the police for the first time ever. It was barely even a decision.

She has instinctively read this as a murder, because everything about it looks like a murder, but she can't take in the enormity of it. Stupidly she looks around as if the murderer might still be in the room and she's just failed to notice—but no, she's alone. There's a particular type of alone you feel when in a room with someone who's no longer alive, she's discovering now, and it is the worst kind.

But what *happened*? If she could access the house data she could find out, but she doesn't have those permissions. She'll just have to work out what she can from what she can see.

Lydia forces herself to look at Fitz. She learned the basics about Logi biology and some first aid at LSTL, so she knows stuff like what their blood looks like and roughly where their vital organs are. It looks like he died of a gunshot to the chest and either died instantly or bled out: surely the former, otherwise he'd have tried to get help, or at least moved from the sofa. Her eyes travel upwards and for the first time she notices the canvas above his sofa is blank: a crack spreads out across its glassy surface from a hole slightly off-center. At least two shots were fired, hitting Fitz and the canvas, all while Lydia was asleep upstairs. How did they get in? Where was security? What were Arthur and Martha doing?

Lydia leaves the study, opens the front door and looks out. The morning air is already hot and sticky. Arthur is stationed to the left of the doorway, where he always is. Martha is presumably in the backyard.

The street looks so normal. How can it look normal when Fitz is dead in there? Even though they walked around every day accompanied by drones specifically tasked with protecting Fitz from harm, even though she was aware of the hostility many people felt towards the Logi, Lydia never felt like she lived in a world where harm might actually come to him.

"Can I help you with anything this morning?" says a voice behind Lydia, making her jump. She turns and sees the domestic has silently trundled up behind her.

"Did you see what happened?" Lydia replies.

"Can you be more specific?"

"Who killed him? What happened? How did they get in?"

"Sorry, I can't answer that. Would you like some breakfast?"

Lydia blinks.

The first thing Lydia needs to do, she realizes in a panic, is dispose of any &amp she still has in her possession. There's a small amount in a vial in her bag, which she briefly considers taking in one go before deciding, correctly, that this is the worst idea ever. She then washes out the vial and pushes it down to the bottom of the waste bin in the kitchen. Is it well hidden enough? The cops won't be thinking about that sort of thing, surely?

At this point she's hit by the reality that she's going to have to *talk* to the *police*.

Lydia calms herself down. Everything is fucked and she cannot control that, but she *can* address her hangover, and if she does that she will be more able to deal with everything being fucked. The domestic has made some coffee so she drinks it and asks it to make toast. "And put some extra coffee on. The police are coming."

"I know," says the domestic: it's patched into all that stuff.

"I mean they might want some coffee."

"Yes. I understood this."

Lydia waits for her toast while she rues the fact there are no baked beans in the house: her ideal hangover breakfast would be beans on toast with a glug of maple syrup on top, a meal that covers all bases. Fitz would probably order some in for her if she asked but she can't do that because he's dead. She wishes she could stop thinking about this in terms of what it means for her. This is not about her. But she has no idea what she's going to do now. LSTL didn't prepare her for this. If he was killed there were supposed to be people around to deal with it.

She's spreading marshmallow fluff over her first slice of toast when the police arrive and let themselves in: an emergency call registered from this address gives them automatic permission to enter. She remains at the kitchen table as a cop drone hovers in to ascertain whether she is armed and dangerous.

"Put down the knife," the drone tells her.

"It's not sharp," she says, holding up a knife slathered in marshmallow fluff, a drip of which runs down the side of the knife and over her fingers.

"Put down the knife," the drone repeats.

Lydia puts down the knife and licks her fingers. The drone emits a loud chime that indicates it's safe to enter the kitchen, and two uniformed officers do so. They take in the scene—Lydia in her pajamas, sitting at the table and licking marshmallow fluff from her fingers—and she feels the marshmallow fluff was an error. It seems a frivolous thing to eat after discovering a murder victim, the kind of thing a sociopath would eat in such a situation. She wants to explain to them that high-sugar foods are the most effective thing for a translation hangover because of the insulin imbalance. But at the same time she doesn't want to draw more attention to the marshmallow fluff. So she says nothing.

"Your name is Lydia Southwell?" one of the cops asks, reading the information from his glasses. The standard-issue police glasses are aviator-style reaction shades and make all the cops look like utter dicks, without exception.

"Yeah, that's me."

"You worked for the victim?"

Victim. "Yeah."

"What happened?"

Lydia tells them she found the body and immediately called the police, and that's all she knows. Did she touch anything, they ask? No, she says, she touched nothing. She checks her glasses for stats on which rooms she's spent time in so far today, and it says she was in the study for one minute and forty-one seconds. She tells them this, and at their request bounces her full footage of her time in that room over to them.

The cops mutter something to each other, tell her to stay in the kitchen, then leave. Lydia realizes she forgot to offer them coffee and calls down the hallway to them, but they don't seem to hear. She sits back and eats her marshmallow fluff on toast, under the watchful eye of the cop drone.

Lydia listens to the police come and go while she refreshes her feeds over and over and over, watching the news start to break via her neighbors.

@McLean&Evans67 / Police arriving in our street . . . very odd for a Sunday . . . gone into the Logi embassy house? Live now / TR97
@Swingleton1604 / Picked up cop chatter—homicide detectives have arrived, treating it as murder, no word on victim yet / TR96

These, and several others, have set up streams and Lydia finds herself watching the outside of the building she's currently inside. More police arrive all the time, pouring in resources commensurate with the importance of the victim: a huge CSI truck pulls up and a dozen drones stream from the back. A pop tunnel is erected between the front door and the road, frustrating the growing crowd who stand behind the barriers erected across the street, peering in the hope of seeing Fitz's body being carried out. Whoever puts the first shot of it online will be able to megamonetize it.

In the absence of any official statement from the police, distortions of the story begin to spread. Many people leap to the most obvious and straightforward conclusion—that Fitz has died and there are suspicious circumstances—but that's not the juiciest version:

@SKINNYDIP / Logi cultural attaché COMMITS SUICIDE in shocking development—take short survey or medical scan to view pictures / TR23
@FACTS4FRIENDS / Assassination of high-ranking Logi LATEST—who's next? We rank ten most likely targets, number four will surprise you! / TR15
@EVERYTHING_FOCUS / Embassy covers up death of cultural attaché in SEX GAME GONE WRONG—FULL REALDEF recon for premium subscribers AVAILABLE NOW / TR19

There's a picture of Lydia on the last one, with her old blue hair. It's nice to know some of the spinners and contengines who generate this stuff are aware of who she is—although when she clicks through to the "tributes" she finds none of it is accurate and none of her "colleagues and friends" are real people, just stock images with generic quotes attached. Until some actual facts push these stories down they'll float around the feeds regardless of their junk TRs, and people will be looking at them, just as she is. The temptation to dip into this stuff is annoyingly strong, and she tries to resist it.

Lydia knows she could send out the truth herself—the truth-ometers would recognize her connection to Fitz and her stream's solid record and score it highly—but she suspects that would antagonize the cops, and anyway she doesn't want to make this story about her. She takes off her glasses to force herself to look away, and notices a bunch of pap drones at the kitchen window, grabbing footage of her. She goes to dim the panes—but then Martha deals with it by unleashing a crackle like a discharge of static and fritzing the paps. It's almost comical how they drop out of the air, making a series of *clonks* as they hit the patio.

Lydia dims the panes anyway.

Messages are arriving from the agency and the embassy, and she wonders if she was expected to contact them herself. She replies to tell them she's fine and is cooperating with the police and she doesn't know what happened. Her connections have seen the news and are messaging her, but she can't bring herself to reply to those. Maybe she should set up a triple-O: Hi! Thanks for the reachout! My boss has been murdered and I may be slow to respond.

Another cop comes in. Lydia remembers to offer him coffee this time, but he declines.

"Where were you at the time of the murder?" he asks.

"When was the time of the murder?" Lydia replies.

"Two fourteen a.m."

"I was asleep upstairs."

"You didn't hear anything, or come down at any point?"

"No. But you'll be able to see all that in the house data, there's cameras in all the hallways."

The cop runs his tongue over his top teeth and nods. "We'll need you to come to the station to give a statement."

"Can we not just do it here?"

"Protocol is to do it at the station, miss," he says impatiently, and escorts her to the front door. (Lydia takes an involuntary glance through the study door and notices Fitz's body has been removed.) She emerges into the pop tunnel, which leads down to a secure car. Lydia gets in the back; no one gets in the front. The windows are blacked out. She can hear a commotion as the car pulls away—the crowds speculating on who's inside—and over this an ayaie formally warns her that all her actions and speech will be recorded until further notice.

ON MY LAWYER'S ADVICE

Nobody's there to see Lydia get out of the car at the police station except for an actual human cop who escorts her inside, takes a DNA sample from her, then brings her to an interview room and tells her to wait. She sits at the table and checks her feed again, though everyone knows the police can legally intercept all data inside the station, so she's careful what she looks at.

@MILLIONPAGE / CONFIRMED: Logi "Fitzwilliam" found dead of gunshot wound at home in Manhattan—police investigation in progress / TR94

This story is repeatedly duplicated across every outlet that might conceivably run it, obliterating the junk stories—for now, at least. That picture of herself she saw earlier is proliferating, and is being linked to the clips of her falling off the balcony at the theater. Great.

Lydia checks her personals and then takes her glasses off. She'll put them back on when the police come to talk to her, but she needs a moment of quiet—and she hears Fitz's voice in her head telling her that's a good idea. But of course it's not him, it's just her inner monologue again. She wonders how long that'll take to fade. Maybe not until she's reassigned to another Logi and has their voice inside her head instead.

That'll be a shame, when his voice has gone. Maybe after a while she'll forget what it even sounded like. There are no recordings of it, after all.

Lydia has been here half an hour when someone she's never met arrives, introduces themselves as her lawyer and scolds her for not wearing her glasses.

"Nothing's happened while I've had my glasses off," Lydia protests.

"According to *you*," the lawyer tells her. "But if you'd kept them on we'd have a record to *prove* it, wouldn't we?" The lawyer is slender and elegant with swept-back ash-gray hair, and they're dressed in a suit of deep purple. They introduce themselves as Alinn and take a seat next to Lydia.

"I'm just giving a statement," Lydia says: she feels like having a lawyer here makes it seem like she's got something to hide.

"I know."

"I haven't been charged with anything, is what I'm saying."

"Good. Let's keep it that way." Alinn produces a scroll from their pocket, unfurls it and places it on the table in front of them. It's a maxiscroll, the size of a coffee-table book. A number of folders appear on the scrollface and Alinn moves them around, hides some, brings others up to the top. "Keep it simple," they tell Lydia while doing this. "Don't answer questions you haven't been asked."

Lydia wants to ask exactly what this means but Alinn holds up a hand to silence her. A moment later, a plainclothes officer walks in and introduces himself as Lieutenant Rollo. He's a smallish man, a little older than Lydia, unimposing and friendly, with a neat beard.

"Glasses," mutters Alinn.

Lydia hurriedly reaches for her glasses and puts them on.

"Those aren't your agency-issue glasses," says Alinn quietly but firmly.

"I know, I couldn't find—"

"Tell me later."

Rollo sits down opposite Lydia and asks her how she's doing.

"OK," says Lydia.

"So you've been through something pretty rough, huh."

Lydia's about to answer when Alinn holds up their hand again. "Is this being recorded?"

"Yes."

"Has my client been made aware of that?"

"Yeah, I have," says Lydia.

Alinn nods and addresses Rollo again. "Could you please

proceed with *relevant* questions, my client's emotional state is not important."

"I was just trying to be nice."

A tight smile from Alinn. "And it was a fine attempt, Lieutenant."

Rollo shrugs and asks Lydia to go through what happened, which she does, again. Was anyone else in the building? Not that she knew of. Does anyone else have access to the building? Apart from herself and Fitz, just some of the embassy staff. Did she notice anything out of place? Only that the door to the study was open. When Lydia finishes she sees Alinn out the corner of her eye, nodding and making notes, and she feels pleased to have done well so far.

"And when did you last see the deceased alive?" says Rollo.

"Last night."

"What time?"

"I can't remember."

"We don't need an exact time, just roughly."

Lydia tries to remember. "We were working last night, you see, at a banquet—"

"Banquet?"

"Yeah, at an academic conference, and you know how it is with my job, and I don't remember anything much after about nine o'clock—no wait, I remember I was talking to a poet who wouldn't stop banging on about soil types in his vineyard, and I checked the time and it was nine thirteen, and that's the last time I was aware of what time it was."

Alinn is not nodding now.

"And you were there with Mr. Fitzwilliam," says Rollo.

"Yeah—working, as I say."

"Do you often use &amp while working?"

Lydia swallows her first reaction, which probably would have been "What?!?! *No!*" or something along those lines. She needs to be very, very careful what she says here. (She certainly shouldn't correct his pronunciation—cops always say "and-amp" whereas users just say "namp.") She glances at Alinn.

"I fail to see the relevance of that," Alinn says without looking up.

"Traces of &amp," says Rollo, "were found in Ms. Southwell's system when she arrived at the station today, consistent with having taken the substance early yesterday evening."

Bollocks. The DNA test. She should have realized it wasn't *just* a DNA test. But then, she could hardly have turned it down.

"The relevance isn't becoming any clearer," says Alinn.

"It affects her reliability as a witness."

"I don't accept that, and truthfully I don't think you do either, otherwise you wouldn't be talking to her—please proceed with questions related to the investigation."

Rollo turns back to Lydia. "Do you remember how you got home?"

"No." Lydia doesn't have to look at Alinn to know they're grimacing. "But we'd have gone back to the residence in a diplomatic car, together, and there'll be a record of the car and who was in it, won't there?" This is exactly what Alinn meant by answering questions she hasn't been asked, isn't it. Lydia can hear herself and knows she sounds desperate, maybe a little guilty. Why? She hasn't done anything. *Get a fucking grip, Lydia.*

Rollo glances to one side, into the middle distance. "Can we check that please, guys?" he says to someone who must be listening, somewhere.

"Why is this necessary?" Alinn asks. "Surely you've checked the residence's security data and you know exactly when they arrived home and who else was there and what time Mr. Fitzwilliam died?"

"Data's been tampered with," Rollo says. Lydia can see he's been putting off telling them this, because he wanted to see if she let slip that she knew anything about it. "Everything from eight p.m. to eight a.m. is gone."

"What?" says Lydia. "But surely it's all clouded?"

"Also gone."

"Is that possible?"

"If you know what you're doing."

Lydia wants to tell him she wouldn't know how to do that, but that would be an answer to a question she hasn't been asked. "What about street cams?"

"There's a gap on those too. Same period."

"Hacked?"

"Presumably."

"Bloody hell." Lydia sits back. She wants to ask how they got past Arthur and Martha too, but again she refrains. She's very aware the simplest answer to that is the killer was already inside the house.

Rollo points at her eyes. "Were you wearing your glasses last night?"

"Not these ones," says Lydia, sensing she's losing control of the narrative. "I had my work ones on."

"Do you have those with you?"

"I don't know where they are."

The room is quiet and Lydia can hear Alinn chewing their lip.

"You've lost them?" says Rollo.

"They must be in my bag back at the residence." She meant to get them from her bag at the same time she removed the &amp but she had other things on her mind. "But I had them on last night, definitely, and I always sync, so it'll all be in my niche."

"Can you share that with us?"

Lydia turns to Alinn, who clearly doesn't want to say yes to this, but also feels it will look bad if they say no. "Go ahead," Alinn says.

Lydia takes Alinn's scroll and uses it to access her niche. She never clears out her niche, everything is clouded here—but the most recent video file is easy to access and that's the one she needs. She opens it and skips to the end.

The last thirty seconds of the video show a view from the edge of a high balcony, at least fifteen floors up. Lydia has never liked heights, and is astonished and sickened that she appears to have stood on this balcony when she was so drunk, and so soon after falling from the one at the theater. Irrationally she worries she might actually have fallen off and forgotten it, before telling herself that if this had happened she would be dead, and if she'd somehow survived she would certainly not have forgotten.

Then the wearer of the glasses leans over the railing at the edge of the balcony—

And the ground starts rushing up towards the camera. Lydia panics. Is she in fact dead, and this is how she finds out about it? Maybe nothing that's happened since she woke up this morning has actually been real, and it's all just a flight of fancy as her dying brain burbles through its last moments of consciousness? It would explain why it's all been so strange and nightmarish. Maybe she'll look up and the lawyer and the cop will lead her out of this room and on the other side of the door will be the afterlife, whatever form that might take—

Then the glasses hit the ground and the sound that accompanies it is wrong. It's a light *tink,* not the sickening wet *crunch* and hideous cry of pain you'd expect if the glasses were still attached to a person. The picture breaks up and the video stops, and Lydia understands she did not fall off the balcony: the *glasses* fell off her *face*. What a relief.

But this relief is short-lived, because this means she has no record of events from this point onward. And she is not a witness, but a suspect, and she has been all along.

HISTORY OF VIOLENCE

The footage from the diplomatic car that carried Lydia and Fitz back to the residence last night makes for an uneventful eight minutes and seventeen seconds' viewing, apart from the bit halfway through where Lydia can be seen to wind the window down and scream "ANNE BRONTE COULD KICK EMILY'S ARSE" at Fifth Avenue, before Fitz reaches out an arm and guides her gently back to her seat. Lydia's feelings when she sees this are a mix of embarrassment and fondness, because Fitz never seemed perturbed when she behaved like that: just accepted it as part of the job. Either he was very tolerant, or she amused him, or maybe he just didn't have a concept of embarrassment.

At the end of the video they get out of the car. Lydia sees herself fumbling at the door, increasingly frustrated by her inability to open it. Fitz comes around the other side and opens it for her, then guides her out, ensuring she doesn't step into traffic, not that there is any—the timestamp shows 12:52 A.M. and the street is quiet. This seems to be the last footage of Fitz alive.

"That doesn't tell us much," says Rollo.

"It doesn't tell us anything," says Alinn.

None of it jogs Lydia's memory. It could all be a deepfake for all she knows. She's rarely drawn this much of a blank before. She pushed herself too hard at that conference, and so soon after the festival debacle: Why didn't she learn? Why didn't she listen to Fitz? Maybe if she had, he wouldn't be dead.

Rollo sits back and folds his arms. "In the absence of other data, the only other person in that house—"

"That's conjecture," says Alinn. "You don't *know*—"

Rollo's eyes roll behind his glasses. "The only other person we can *place* at the scene of the murder is *you,* Lydia."

Lydia revises her earlier opinion of Rollo: he's not that friendly after all. But the thing is, he's right. She has no memory of what happened, no alibi, and the surviving security data doesn't exonerate her. She has no motive, cannot understand why or how she might have done it, but the simplest explanation is that she killed Fitz, and the worst part is she cannot say for certain that she didn't.

"This is bad, isn't it?" Lydia tells Alinn when they finally get a chance to speak alone.

"It's not great."

"Oh god." Lydia buries her face in her hands. She's barely managed to absorb Fitz's murder: she can't believe she might be *accused* of it.

"But look—it's all circumstantial at the moment. Forensic data means nothing—you live in the building, you were in and out of that room all the time, plus you found the body. They need a weapon."

"Where would I get a gun?"

"You could've printed one."

"Seriously? If I was printing off guns, the network would've flagged it and the cops would've been round like a shot."

"Embassy properties have privacy privileges."

Lydia scoffs. "Yeah right, the cops *say* that but we all know—"

Alinn glares at her, reminding her where she is, and she stops and changes tack.

"The embassy is strict about what you can do with the connection," Lydia says. "They'd get an alert, and there'd be a download record."

"In theory, but we seem to be dealing with someone with a real talent for covering their tracks."

"Which I definitely don't have—"

"*But,*" says Alinn, holding up a hand, "what they need is to find the weapon itself, or evidence of you leaving the residence to dispose of it."

"There isn't a weapon, I swear—"

"Which means they won't find one, and they *have* to find it or they don't have a case. They're searching the house for it now."

"Christ." So they'll be going through all her stuff. They'll find the empty vial in the kitchen bin, but they already know about that anyway.

"They're leaning on you because you're all they have. The embassy will be leaning on them, so will the mayor's office, they need a result. It's still very early days. Other stuff will come to light."

"Would they plant a gun? If they really need a result?"

Alinn raises their voice. "Absolutely not," they say in a performative tone that makes clear they'd give a different answer if they were not in a police station.

"I had no reason to kill him. Why would I kill him? I was happy in my job—in fact I would've been fired if it wasn't for—"

Alinn holds up a hand. "Don't *look* for reasons you might've done it, that's their job, don't do it for them. Look for reasons *someone else* might want to kill him. Did he have enemies? If we can give them something else to think about—"

"There's Madison."

"Who is that?"

"I think she's like the chief of staff at the embassy or something?"

"OK, great—and?"

"Well, they had a *massive* argument over him wanting to keep me on and her wanting me to be fired, after that business at the festival."

"Your history of violence might not be the best thing to bring up."

Lydia rolls her eyes. "I punched a lad, it's hardly a 'history of violence.' Don't tell me *you've* never punched anyone."

"I'm not the one suspected of murder here. So this person from the embassy—"

"Madison, yeah—Fitz told me she was trying to get him removed from his job. And she'd have had access to the residence, and the security—"

"Could she have deleted the street cam too?"

"Dunno, maybe?"

"And you really think she might have killed him?"

This pulls Lydia up short, because she doesn't, actually. "Well, her campaign to get him fired didn't come off, so if she got desperate . . . maybe she secretly had another, more important reason for wanting him out of the way?"

"You want to tell them you think she might be a suspect?"

Lydia doesn't hold out much hope for this, but she desperately wants the heat off her. "Yeah."

Alinn nods. "The agency won't like you pointing the finger at someone from the embassy."

"They won't like me being charged with murdering my boss either, so swings and roundabouts."

"What does that mean?"

"Doesn't matter."

PERSON OF INTEREST

Lydia has been left alone in the interview room for almost an hour. She wishes she'd brought a book: she resists the temptation to use her scroll or glasses because the police will be watching her activity. Although she's (almost) sure she isn't guilty, she *feels* guilty and is worried this will make her *act* guilty. She knows they've got all kinds of bioanalytics and body-language readers, and that stuff isn't evidence but it can strongly influence an investigation. So she sits and does nothing. Then she worries *that* will be interpreted as guilty.

Suddenly she knows Madison is walking down the corridor outside the interview room. Can't hear her thoughts, of course, but there's a buzz at the edge of Lydia's skull that tells her Madison is very close and conversing with somebody—possibly her own translator but more likely a police one, since the cops wouldn't trust anything they were told by a suspect's employee. When Lydia was at LSTL they took a careers module that included a visit from some cops, inviting them to consider a career in police translation. Fuck that, if she wanted to be a cop she could've stayed in Halifax.

Bloody hell though—they took Lydia's accusation seriously. Lydia's not sure she takes her *own* accusation seriously.

The door of the interview room opens and Lydia jumps—but it's just a desk sergeant bringing her a burrito. When Lydia's alone again the sense of Madison's presence has faded. She must have been taken to a room farther away, out of Lydia's range. While Lydia eats her burrito she imagines Madison in one of the other interview rooms, breaking down under questioning, unable to bear up against the guilt, confessing in tears or whatever their equivalent is (she's pretty sure she never saw Fitz cry). She imagines the cops commending her for supplying this vital lead, the embassy thanking her for identifying the culprit before she killed again . . .

Then Rollo returns with a cop she hasn't seen before. Alinn enters behind them. Lydia shoots Alinn a questioning glance and receives an uneasy one in return. She senses they have not come to tell her Madison has confessed and she is free to go.

The new cop—a middle-aged guy in a uniform, chunkily built and handsome, with an incongruously boyish fringe—introduces himself as Inspector Sturges, warmly shakes Lydia's hand and sits down. The others also take seats around the table. Lydia wonders what it signifies that a more senior officer has turned up. Probably nothing good.

"I'd like to make clear," says Sturges, "how grateful the NYPD is for your cooperation in this matter. I know this must have been a deeply traumatic day for you, and Lieutenant Rollo here tells me you've been nothing but helpful."

Lydia glances at Rollo: she finds it hard to imagine him saying that, but she's not about to contradict Sturges. "Well yeah," she replies. "I want you to find who killed him, of course I do."

"Of course." Sturges removes a scroll from his pocket and unfurls it. "You recently visited the UK, is that correct?"

"Yes. That's where I'm from."

Sturges smiles. "Who did you have contact with, while you were there?"

"My mum. My brother. The woman who lives in my old room. Some people in a club. What does this have to do with—"

"Did you speak to a man named Mark Jankovic?"

Lydia shakes her head. "Was he that lad who hassled me on the tram?"

Sturges looks around the table. "What's a tram?"

"Like a bus but—I think you call them trolleys?"

Sturges brings up a picture on his scroll of a young man holding a bottle of beer and leering at the camera. "This is Mark Jankovic."

"Oh! You mean Jank."

"Right. Then you did meet him."

"He's a mate of my brother's. No one calls him Mark, that's what confused me."

"Gotcha. What'd you talk about?"

"I spoke to him for like *two minutes*—I don't know him, I don't *like* him, he's just—"

"Did he ask you about work?"

Lydia wonders where this is going. "Yeah . . ."

"And what did he want to know?"

"He didn't so much ask me about my work as imply I was a, what's the word, a sort of live-in prostitute? Courtesan, is that what I mean? Or is it concubine?"

Sturges raises his eyebrows. Alinn suppresses a laugh.

"And what did you tell him?" Rollo says, entirely impassive.

"That I wasn't."

"You tell him anything else?" asks Sturges.

"I told him he was a fucking idiot, and that was pretty much the end of the conversation."

"And he didn't give you anything to take back to New York with you?"

"Like what?"

"Anything."

"No, and I wouldn't have taken it if he had, I'd have probably caught something off it."

"Did you give him anything?"

"No."

"Did he put you in touch with anyone?"

"No."

"Why is this relevant?" says Alinn.

"Were you aware," says Sturges, still focusing on Lydia, "that Mr. Jankovic is a member of an organization known as Illogic Alliance?"

"Known as what?"

Sturges repeats the name of the organization more slowly, leaving more of a gap between the two words.

"That's a terrible name," Lydia says. "When you say it out loud it sounds like Illogical Irons. Or Illogical Lions?"

"I think the Lions thing is deliberate," says Alinn, "like a symbol of power."

Lydia wrinkles her nose. "Really? It's not very good."

"They're a pressure group campaigning against Logi influence," says Sturges. "You didn't know Mr. Jankovic was a member?"

"No, but I'm not surprised."

"My client will not answer any more questions along these lines," says Alinn, "unless you explain what this has to do with the murder of Fitzwilliam."

"It's a line of inquiry we're pursuing," says Sturges, "and we're not saying Ms. Southwell led anyone to Fitzwilliam consciously or deliberately, we just think it's coincidental that she made this trip so soon before his death. She may have . . . *inspired* someone to seek out Fitzwilliam as a target."

"Inspired?" says Lydia. "Like I'm a murderer's muse?"

"Do you have a recording of this conversation with Mr. Jankovic?"

"Probably. But nobody would involve Jank in something like this anyway, he's an idiot and I'm willing to testify to that in court."

"These people you met in the club, who were they?"

"Just some cleanskin kids."

"Cleanskin?"

"No tattoos or piercings." Lydia brings up one of the pictures she took of herself with the cleanskins on her glasses and pings it over to Alinn, who checks it and pings it to Sturges, who asks their names. Lydia noted all their first names, but of the surnames she caught only Hari's: Dessai. Sturges tells Rollo to run a check.

"Did you talk to them about your work?" Sturges asks Lydia.

"They were interested," says Lydia stiffly. "If you live in Halifax you don't meet a lot of people who work in New York."

"Do you recall the conversation," says Rollo, "or were you drunk then as well?"

Sturges holds up a hand to Rollo and says quietly but firmly, "Just run that check, please."

"I do remember the conversation," Lydia says, stopping herself from addressing the part about her being drunk.

"And?"

"They mostly wanted to know what it was like living here, and what sort of events I go to. They weren't really interested in Fitz. William. I hardly mentioned him."

"Did you have any contact with them after leaving the club?"

"Yes, I took one of them back to a hotel and had sex with him."

Rollo suddenly looks up from his scroll.

"No need to look so surprised," Lydia says. "You think he must have had an ulterior motive for shagging me?"

"Why go to a hotel?" says Sturges.

"Neither of us had any privacy at home. For the sex, I mean," she adds hastily.

"Did you and he talk any further about work?"

"A little bit—no sensitive information though. They do train us in this stuff at school, you know."

"I'm aware."

"He was just sort of interested in what it's like to have someone else's voice in your head."

"What sort of view did he take on that? Did he think it was bad, impure, degrading?"

Good grief, says a voice in Lydia's head: it sounds like Fitz's. "No, he just thought it was a bit . . . odd."

"And since the hotel, have you had any contact—" Sturges stops because Rollo's brought something to his attention. "Huh," he says. "That's interesting." He looks up at Lydia. "Were you aware Mr. Dessai arrived in New York yesterday evening?"

The NYPD swiftly throw everything into searching for Hari. All they know at the moment is he was on a hopper that landed at LaGuardia just after 9:00 P.M. yesterday. He traveled on his own passport and the scan at control confirms it was him . . . and then he dropped off the radar, which is suspicious in itself. They've got bots trawling footage from every cam in the city, looking for where he went next.

When Lydia gets to talk to Alinn privately again, she asks what all this means for her.

"It means they have another credible suspect," Alinn replies, "which is very good. He's connected to you, which is less good. The inspector seems prepared to believe you didn't lead him here deliberately, but we'll have to watch that."

"I just . . . can't believe Hari would do this," says Lydia, fully aware of how lame it sounds. She likes to think she's a good judge of people. But who doesn't? Maybe it *was* all a plot on Hari's part. Maybe he knew she was in town, followed her to the club, zeroed in on her. She tries to remember if he spoke to her first or if she spoke to him. Maybe he scraped her scroll while she was taking a shower at the hotel. Maybe he copied her DNA from one of her hairs and used it to fool the systems at the residence. Maybe it's *all* been constructed to set her up.

"Seems strange he didn't tell you he was coming."

"I know it does."

"You said he's a cybersecurity patcher," Alinn replies. "Good enough to cover his tracks?"

"I didn't ask him for a demonstration. He wasn't a hard case though, you know. He seemed more the type who gets robbed straight off the hopper than the type who commits an undetected murder within hours of landing."

"Well, Sturges says you can go."

This takes Lydia by surprise. "As in, leave the police station?"

Alinn nods. "They've swept the residence top to bottom and haven't found a weapon, so they can't charge you."

"And I can go back there?"

"The forensics team have capped the whole ground floor of the house and the immediate area, so they shouldn't need access again."

Lydia hadn't anticipated this but it makes sense: things at the actual location can decay or be tampered with. Better to have a comprehensive, frozen-in-time model, and refer to that.

"I'm afraid they've already confiscated your passport, and you won't be allowed to leave Manhattan."

Lydia laughs shortly. "Where else would I go?"

A VOICE IN AN EMPTY ROOM

It's another warm evening: there was torrential rain while Lydia was in the station, but it's passed on and the streets are almost dry already. She's been in there about eleven hours. In some ways that's a long time, but when she considers how much has changed since she entered the building, it's hardly any time at all.

The street around the corner from the police station is lively, its bars and stagewalks doing good business—summer-season tourists often sleep most of the day and come out at night when the heat's more bearable, especially those from the north country who aren't used to it. She calls a diplomatic car (to her relief, she hasn't been struck off the access list), and rides it up towards the Upper West Side. She checks her notes, and among all the ones from her connections she finds a fretful one from Mum and a more measured, but still concerned, one from Gil. She dashes off replies to assure them she's fine and hasn't been arrested and to ignore all news that doesn't come from an official police source, and onto Gil's message she tags a stream of her progress through the streets of Manhattan because she knows he'll enjoy it. She taps the dashboard, idly flicking a finger against the catch that releases the emergency steering wheel, tempted to pull it and just drive the car right out of town. They'd pick her up at the tunnel of course, but it's fun to think about. She wonders what these diplomatic cars are like to drive. She imagines driving with Gil through these big old wide streets, taking the right-angled corners at speed. They could have *such* a laugh.

She's struck by how few other people she feels the need to reply to. Her friends from home mean little to her now, she never made any good friends at the language school, she hasn't made a single hardspace friend since she got to New York and her INS means she really depends on her hardspace friends in a way typicals just don't understand. Maybe that's why she got overly invested in her relationship with Fitz.

When Lydia reaches the street where the residence is and gets out of the car, it feels like the noise of the city has been placed under glass. She can sense the shock, people still trying to take it in. Or maybe she's projecting that onto the scene. Maybe people are just getting on with their lives. Maybe they're excited by it. Maybe Mrs. Kloves is delighted some danger has returned to Manhattan at last, and even now is thrilling at the possibility of someone else being murdered in their own home tonight.

A uniformed NYPD officer is stationed outside the residence, with a drone. They told her someone would be there in case Hari turned up, but of course it's also to keep an eye on her. Alinn pointed out part of the reason they've allowed her to come back to the residence is that if she's hidden the murder weapon in the building, they hope she'll try to dispose of it and lead them right to it in the process.

But what if they've planted a weapon in there and are waiting for her to find it, put her prints and DNA all over it? What if *that's* why she's been allowed back?

She resolves not to poke into too many corners.

The drone idees her and the cop waves her inside.

The residence is quiet. This is no different to how it usually is— Fitz never made much noise—but the silence means something now, which it didn't before. The study door is shut, as it would have been if he was alive, and Lydia doesn't want to open it. She doesn't want to see the room without him in it, and she certainly doesn't want to see the bloodstain on the carpet, assuming they haven't taken the carpet away as evidence.

It's a relief to be out of the police station, no longer second-guessing herself. At one point she felt an overwhelming urge to blurt out *Maybe I did kill him I don't know I can't remember,* and had to fight it down. But she had terrible visions of being presented with incontrovertible evidence of her guilt—a matching gun covered in her prints, microscopic splatters of his blood on her clothes—and having to just accept it.

Lydia automatically closes the door behind herself when she enters her room, then remembers there's no one to shut out: she's the only person who lives here now. But then again, it offers an extra line of defense. She goes back to the door and locks it.

She lies on the bed and, even though she's so exhausted it hurts (it's wild how sitting in a small room for most of a day and talking to people can be *so tiring*), she has to ping Mum before it gets too late. It's almost 3:00 A.M. back home and Lydia's activity array indicates Mum is deep in a match of *Mighty Fleets,* the popular game of oceangoing conflict, but she doesn't seem to be streaming right now, so Lydia pings her to ask if she can put the game on pause and talk.

The conversation with Mum is necessary but in no way useful. "Are you OK?" says Mum, then barely listens to Lydia's reply, instead launching into a sort of ramshackle ted entitled Why I Have Always Believed New York Isn't Safe. There are murders happening on every street corner, she says, and everyone has these smartshooters that give you elite sniper skills, and she backs this up with mediocre-truthiness vidclips from a folder she seems to keep for exactly this purpose. Above all she keeps telling Lydia to come home, no matter how many times Lydia explains she can't, she literally can't, the police have explicitly banned her from doing so.

"You can't blame me for worrying," Mum says.

"Mum, if whoever killed Fitz wanted to kill me they'd have popped upstairs afterwards and got me too while I was asleep."

"What if they didn't get a chance? What if they come back for you?"

"Why would they do that? I'm not important."

"Maybe you know too much."

"I don't know *anything*. I don't deal with government secrets, we just go to operas and stuff."

"Why couldn't they have sent you somewhere nice and safe and *nearer*?"

"Halifax isn't that safe, Mum."

And so on and so on. Mum doesn't want to let her go off the line but there's nothing else to say. At least she doesn't ask Lydia if she killed Fitz. That might just be because it would be a very foolish thing to say over a ping channel—but it genuinely doesn't seem to occur to her.

"Look," Lydia says wearily, "the police are guarding the residence round the clock. Nothing's going to happen to me, I'm safer than ever."

Mum makes an unconvinced noise.

"I have to go," says Lydia.

"Why? What's happening?"

"Nothing, I'm just tired and I need to eat something before I go to bed—why, what did you think was happening?"

"The way you said it sounded like someone had come to take you away."

Once again Lydia can't sleep because her mind is snagged on what might have been. What if she'd woken up last night and heard the killer breaking in? Could she have stopped it, or at least identified the killer? Or would she have been killed too? What if she'd gone along with Fitz's suggestion of leaving the banquet early? Would the killer have had their opportunity? At least Lydia might have been more alert and remembered what happened.

What if she'd never come back from Halifax at all? That's the kicker. Because she so nearly didn't. And who knows, Fitz might still have died, but at least she'd be lying on Mum's sofa right now reading about it and it would have nothing to do with her.

A little after 1:00 A.M. a voice that sounds like Fitz says, *You didn't kill me.* Her inner monologue always sounds most like him when she's trying to be very rational about things.

I know, she replies, drifting into that state where those chemicals that make you dream are seeping into your brain but you're not quite asleep yet.

The voice keeps insisting: *You didn't kill me. You didn't kill me.* It sounds *so* like Fitz. She's going to dream about hearing his voice.

She'll probably dream about it for years. His voice has filled up all the corners of her brain she doesn't use.

As her brain trips away into unconsciousness, the last thing she does is tell the voice to be quiet.

You didn't kill me, Lydia.

A LITTLE CALM LOGIC

Lydia is awoken by a knock at the door of her bedroom.

Why is someone on the other side of her bedroom door?

Suddenly she's very, very awake. She sits upright in bed, her heart accelerating, and looks around for something to defend herself with. She grabs her bedside lamp, which is actually quite light, and wonders if she could smash the bulb and use it as a kind of makeshift cattle prod? It's probably too low-powered for that.

"Who is it?" she shouts.

"It's Marat."

Lydia relaxes and puts the lamp down. A killer would probably not knock, she tells herself. She gets out of bed, pulls her dressing gown on and opens the door.

Marat runs the agency's local branch. He's a tallish, middle-aged man with broad shoulders and graying hair: he has the look of a retired athlete but in fact he's a retired translator who never lost his manic penchant for working out. Lydia has met him only a couple of times: he didn't even get involved in the Anders incident. She resists the temptation to say *Wow, this must be serious, then.*

"Why was your door locked?" Marat asks.

"Because there was a murder in this house last night."

"For a moment there I thought you'd killed yourself."

"Why?"

"I've been knocking on the door for several minutes and you didn't answer."

"I was just asleep."

"It's ten fifteen," Marat says. It takes Lydia a moment to realize she's being criticized. Her work with Fitz often involves—*involved* going to evening events, and Fitz was always fine about her sleeping late the next day.

"I slept badly last night. I don't know if you heard but I've had a pretty grim experience."

"Of course," says Marat mechanically. "How are you feeling?"

"Fucking dreadful."

"That's to be expected."

"I didn't think there was any reason I needed to be up and about this morning."

"We need to talk to you."

"Who's we?"

"Madison from the embassy, your line manager, a rep from HR, and some others—they're downstairs."

Even though the embassy owns this building, Lydia still feels like it's a liberty for them to all let themselves in while she's asleep upstairs. She wonders if Madison knows Lydia is responsible for her being hauled in for questioning by the police. Maybe that's why she's here. Maybe Lydia will be called upon to explain herself.

"Can I have a shower first?"

While Lydia is in the shower, she remembers how Fitz's voice was in her head last night when she was trying to sleep. There was a moment, just before she dropped off, when she could almost have believed it was actually him.

It was me, Lydia, says the voice.

Lydia stops washing herself and focuses on her thoughts, the white noise of the shower in her ears. She's clearly still very, very tired and mentally fragile, and she needs to just clear her head and—

Lydia, please—it's me.

No it's not, Lydia replies. *You're dead.*

I know I am.

Lydia is unsure whether this is progress. *You're just a voice my inner monologue puts on sometimes. It happens all the time. No reason it should stop just because you're dead.*

A brief silence. Then: *Does it really happen all the time?*

Yes, she says and then feels annoyed with herself for answering.

That's not what this is, though. This is me, the real me.

The real Fitz would never have talked to me in the shower.

I'm sorry, but it's urgent. I need to speak to you before you see those people downstairs.

This is definitely not sounding like her internal monologue now. Either something has broken inside her brain, or . . . something else is going on.

How are you talking to me if you're dead? she asks: a reasonable enough question.

She doesn't get an answer for a few seconds, and she thinks maybe this question has quelled the voice. A little calm logic has dealt with it. She just needed to get a grip. She turns off the shower, steps out of it and reaches for a towel.

There are things about my people, the voice says, *that are not widely known among yours.*

It's like when you've got hiccups and you think they've gone away and you relax and then they come back. She wonders whether to tell the agency this is happening. They might be able to help. They might go easy on her in this looming inquiry. Or they might dismiss her as damaged goods and throw her out of service.

Death for us is not the end, the voice continues. *Our . . . essence, if you like, remains in the place where we died.*

You're haunting this house, you mean?

You make it sound malign. I'm simply here.

So your soul has sort of glommed on to the house then, says Lydia, shaking her toothbrush to charge it and then squeezing toothpaste onto the bristles.

You seem skeptical.

Yeah, that's because I don't believe you. The good thing about carrying on a conversation with a phantom voice projected by some fragment of your shattered subconscious is, you can brush your teeth at the same time.

Why don't you believe me?

Why should I?

Because I'm talking to you.

Yeah, but I hear your voice in my head all the time when you're not there, like I told you.

But not like this.

No, not like this. But I've been through a lot.

You have. But this is real, I assure you.

Lydia stops a moment, looks in the mirror. *You do sound just like him.*

I am him. Why do you find this so hard to accept?

I don't believe in ghosts.

I'm not a ghost.

Essence, spirit, soul, call it whatever you like—I don't believe in life after death.

Don't you?

You sound surprised.

I didn't realize you didn't believe. I suppose we never spoke of such things.

Lydia tries to remember if this is true. She doesn't think they ever did.

I suppose that, with humans not being able to communicate telepathically with each other, you've never had any real proof.

Lydia laughs and has to stop and spit out her toothpaste.

What? says the voice.

Sorry, you said it so lightly. Like a rich guy who's never really thought about why normal people don't live in a massive house.

It's not something I'm ignorant of, says the voice, a little offended. *I have studied your notions of the afterlife quite extensively, it's a subject that greatly interests me.*

Lydia remembers how he spoke on this subject after the keynote. She also remembers how evasive he was about the nature of Logi religious beliefs. *There's a lot of disagreement between us about what happens,* she tells him.

So I've gathered. I sort of envy you the mystery. A lot of your most interesting thinking centers around this question.

Lydia returns to her bedroom and starts getting dressed. *Should I wear black?* she asks. *Will they expect it?*

Your boss might. But Madison won't care, or even notice.

Lydia nods, telling herself she hasn't really just taken sartorial advice from a dead person, she's just working through the question in her head. She'll wear something low-key, but not full-on Victorian widow in mourning. *So what, your people all just hang around in the building where they died, forever?*

Not forever. We're like echoes. Eventually we fade away.

Lydia is picking out some underwear and this stops her in her tracks. Strangely this idea strikes her as impossibly sad, more than the idea of just dying. *How long do you last?*

It varies. Sometimes a few weeks. Sometimes many years.

And then what happens? You're just . . . gone?

There's some debate about that. Some think we're gone. Some think we're still there, but people just can't hear us anymore. Or that we've just chosen to stop talking. Some think we move on elsewhere.

What do you think?

I've always believed we stop being heard when no one needs to hear us.

Gosh.

That's a fairly mainstream view, to be honest.

Lydia snaps out of this weird reverie and picks out a white shirt and a dark gray jacket and trousers. She suspects her employers currently don't see her in the most professional light, so she wants to look smart.

So who do you think still needs to hear you? she asks. *Me?*

Actually it's more that I need you to hear me.

Why? Is there something you never said to me in life that you desperately need to say to me now?

No, he says, sounding uncharacteristically impatient. *I need you to find who killed me. I would have thought that was obvious.*

Lydia has kept everyone waiting long enough, and she needs to break off her conversation with . . . whatever it is she's talking to and go downstairs.

Please, the voice tells Lydia as she pulls her shoes on, *under no circumstances let them know you're still speaking to me.*

God no, I had no intention of doing that. In fact I was about to ask you not to speak to me while I'm having this meeting with them. Applying Occam's Razor to this situation, she is simply having a breakdown, and while that's worrying in itself, there seems a good chance it's down to shock, or PTSD or whatever, and it will pass before long. At the meeting she'll say she needs some time off to get over Fitz's death, and afterwards see if there are any meds which will help, and probably she can recover without having to tell the agency she was suffering from any serious problems. Because the agency has a weird thing about mental health: At LSTL she was screened regularly and thoroughly for disorders. Almost like they think you might infect the Logi with them.

You see, the voice continues, *they'd regard it as something like sacrilege, for me to talk to a human after death. This kind of communication is viewed as deeply personal, only to be shared with those who were close to you in life. We certainly don't talk about such things with outsiders.*

So you and I doing this would be, like, frowned upon?

I fear your safety would be at risk.

Fucking hell. She wants to ask from whom. But then she reminds herself this probably isn't real anyway.

Just don't tell anyone and you'll be fine. There's no way they can find out unless you tell them.

Or if you tell them.

I won't be talking to them.

Why not? says Lydia, lingering on the second-floor landing. She can hear the people down there waiting for her and she knows they can hear her coming. She takes off her shoe and pretends to remove a microscopic pebble from it. *One of your own people could do a much better job of this than I could.*

I don't know who I can trust.

What, seriously?

Very much so. Internal politics.

But you trust me?

Yes.

Lydia feels a thrill in being told someone she deeply respects trusts her and *only* her to investigate his murder. However, she worries this is a sign she is succumbing to the madness.

So don't tell them I've spoken to you, the voice says. *The other Logi will wonder if my consciousness has remained here, it'll be a point of interest among them—but they won't talk to you or any other human about it.*

Right.

And it's vitally important you continue to live here. Don't let them force you into other lodgings.

How am I supposed to stop them doing that? This house belongs to the embassy.

I don't know. But it's essential we keep in contact.

Lydia can't stall any longer. *I need to go. Anything else?*

I wish I could tell them you didn't do it.

But you don't know who did?

No. It was dark, they were masked.

Then how do you know it wasn't me?

I'd have sensed the intent in your mind. Of course it wasn't you.

As Lydia heads down the stairs, she sways and has to grip the handrail to steady herself. She's starting to feel a little drunk.

Listening to her own inner monologue doesn't make her feel drunk. Only talking to a real Logi does that.

LEAVE TO REMAIN

Everyone in the reception room is looking at Lydia like all of this is her fault. There are eight of them in there: Madison and her translator, another Logi called Valli and his translator, plus another four humans, including Marat. Madison wears a long hooded robe made of that meshy stuff, but it's in bright orange, yellow and blue, giving her a flame-like appearance. It's a strong look, Lydia has to admit.

Lydia puts on her best shell-shocked face as she sits in the chair that's been left for her at the other side of the room. There are a few token inquiries into her well-being, then Lydia is required to repeat her version of events *afuckinggain*. Lydia points out the police asked her all this yesterday.

With respect to the competence of the human authorities, says Madison, *we think it prudent to carry out our own investigation, as our priorities may differ from theirs.*

Lydia actually can't argue with this: the Logi are right to be concerned the murder might be part of a broader campaign against them, and they're right to seek information themselves rather than wait for the police to bring it to them. If only they would all just bugger off, Lydia could ask Fitz if *he* has any ideas who might have killed him.

Then Marat says, "The police told us there were traces of &amp in your system."

Lydia wants to say this is an absurd thing to focus on in the circumstances. She also wants to say if he thinks his staff aren't using drugs to help them do their jobs then he's genuinely an idiot, but she doesn't, not least because she doesn't want to be quizzed over who else is using them, or where she got the stuff (a retired translator called Candice who Lydia is disappointed not to have forged a proper friendship with, because she seems really cool). So she just nods. "I used some to keep me going at the conference."

"Did Fitzwilliam know you were using it?"

"Of course not."

"We take drug abuse very seriously, Lydia."

Abuse? Use, surely. She was using it exactly as intended. "Yes, I know."

"That'll go on your record, and we'll have to consider it in the investigation."

"Investigation?"

Into your conduct, says Madison.

What does my conduct have to do with Fitz's murder?

A delegation of monitors has left Logia yesterday. They're on their way here to address the situation. We need to provide them with as much information as we can before they arrive.

Which will be in about five days, Lydia reckons, depending on how stable the gate is. And the embassy wants everything to look as tidy and under control as possible . . . which may well involve finding someone to blame. And of all the people in this room, it's clear who the top candidate is.

Why did Fitzwilliam defend you over that assault incident? Madison asks.

That was weeks ago.

This is to be a wide-ranging investigation, as befits an incident of this gravity. Now please cooperate and answer the question.

I don't know why Fitz defended me. I expected to be fired.

Did you think you should have been fired?

I . . . felt I made a mistake while working under difficult circumstances.

Did you in any way attempt to influence Fitzwilliam's decision to retain you?

No.

No? A skeptical note enters Madison's voice.

I didn't get a chance. When you met with him I hadn't spoken to him at all that day. Madison thinks Lydia had some kind of sinister hold on Fitz? That's hilarious.

Marat wants to know about Hari and anyone else Lydia met when she was back in Halifax—the agency always hate it when you go outside their jurisdiction, and they especially seem to hate

Lydia having gone back home, as if she might slip back to being the person she was before they remolded her. He asks about Fitz's state of mind when Lydia returned from Halifax; about the content of the keynote speech; about who else was at the conference; and the events of the evening prior to the murder.

Valli, a particularly tall and pale Logi who works as a liaison officer at the embassy, wants to know if Lydia ever saw anything that led her to believe Fitz had enemies. Lydia is very tempted to answer *Apart from Madison, you mean?* But this would not be well received, and might lead Madison to realize who put the cops onto her. Lydia wonders how that went: clearly she hasn't been removed from her duties. Fitz's remark about whom he could and couldn't trust is playing on Lydia's mind. Maybe she wasn't so far off the mark after all?

Or, she reminds herself, Fitz's remark might just be her own subconscious feeding her suspicions back to her. It could all be meaningless.

I never saw anything like that, Lydia tells Valli. *He was just really nice.* She directs this last sentence at Madison and feels the slight resistance from her mind as the words go in, like pins into a cushion: Madison hears it, but doesn't want to.

You and he had quite a rapport, then, says Valli.

We got on well. I liked him. Lydia looks around at everyone and speaks aloud: "You're not going to tell me he was talking shit about me behind my back, are you? Because I thought we had a good working relationship."

Marat starts to answer but Madison traces a circle in the air in the direction of his face—a gesture that means be quiet; Lydia thinks it's a polite gesture but she's not entirely sure. *Your working relationship,* she says, *is less of a concern for me than the clear lapses of security that have occurred.*

You mean the records being wiped?

Yes, but there's more. I warned Fitzwilliam on several occasions about correct protocols and maintaining appropriate distance. Before you started in your role I had to warn him about sharing too many personal details with human staff—did he adhere to that?

Lydia's taken aback by the question, and can feel herself

growing tipsy. *Yes, he did. But listen—you know how it is, the nature of being a translator—*

If you're going to suggest it's impossible to maintain distance, I disagree—it's perfectly possible—

I've had training in this stuff and I never had an issue with his boundaries at all, and I don't see—

We also have concerns over the people you've spoken to about your work—

Lydia laughs out loud. *I don't speak to anyone! This job takes up all my time, my entire social life. I don't have any friends, I don't have anyone to tell!*

Security has been compromised somehow. Look at the lack of response from the drones—and, if indeed his murderer did break into this building—

What do you mean, "if"? You think I let them in? Or that I did it, even?

This is far too serious to rule out a suspect merely because she can claim a good working relationship with the victim. This isn't personal. We would be doing Fitzwilliam a disservice if we didn't consider you.

Nothing Lydia can say will change Madison's mind and she just wants all these people to leave.

"Good," says Marat awkwardly. "We've prepared a room for you in the language school, so if you want to pack whatever you need, we can send for the rest."

"At NYSTL?" That's way out in Queens. That's no good to her. "I'm not supposed to leave Manhattan."

Marat shakes his head. "We checked with the police and it's fine as long as you don't leave New York City."

"But I'd . . . rather stay here," she says.

The guy from HR leans in. "This really isn't the best place for you right now. It's not good to stay at the site of a trauma."

"I'm fine," says Lydia with a confidence she does not feel.

"You're not needed here," says Marat, "and it's much easier for us to reach you if you're at the school."

Much easier for them to keep an eye on her, essentially. They may be assessing her fitness to return to service: resisting might cause them to decide she's not. But what if this voice she's hearing is real? She has to stay and find out, and if it's real she has to stay and help. "I can . . . fill in for Fitz until his replacement gets here."

No you can't, says Madison. *That's not how any of this works, and it's rather insulting that you feel you can replace him after less than a year—*

I'm not talking about replacing him, Lydia says. *But just be here as a point of contact. I kept track of all his business, I know everyone he was talking to, I can take all his calls and deal with his mail and make sure everything's kept tidy. Please—I'll feel much better if I can be useful.*

"Lydia," says Marat patiently, "you understand that being under investigation means you're suspended?"

"But I didn't do anything."

"No one's saying you did anything, but we can't say either way until we've investigated."

Lydia sighs and stands up. There's no way out of this, literally none. "I'll go pack."

As Lydia distractedly throws her things in her case, wondering how many books she can fit in there and if she'll get in trouble for taking them, she speaks to Fitz: it might be her last chance.

I'm so sorry, she says. *I know what you said, and I tried—*

I know, I know, he replies. *I might be able to help you break back in? I can tell you how the security protocols work.*

Yeah, because that'll really help with the investigation into my conduct, won't it? Anyway they're bound to lock me out, plus there's a cop on the door at all times. But apart from that, brilliant.

I'll think of something.

I'm sorry.

There's nothing you could've done. This isn't your fault.

I don't know what's going on anymore. I feel so powerless. And they're going to fire me, I know it.

But you didn't do anything. Surely they'll want to clear your name to instill confidence in their selection and training procedures?

No, I think they'll want to distance themselves from me as much as possible. If I was management they'd try to save me but I'm replaceable. It's all very clear to her. They're going to do it all politely and in accordance with proper procedure—but this is where it ends.

Assuming the cops don't still decide to pin it on her.

Assuming she didn't kill him herself and doesn't remember.

I'll try to come back, she tells Fitz. *But I don't know if I'll be able to, and if I can't—*

I'm sure we'll speak again.

As Lydia returns downstairs, a lively discussion is taking place in the reception room. New voices have been added to the mix, and she recognizes one of them: Sturges, who handled her final interview at the station. Lydia puts her head around the door and everyone turns to look at her: Next to Sturges is a pale young woman with an impassive face and straight white hair, styled in a bob. She's not in uniform but wears a white shirt with a badge pinned to the pocket indicating she's a police translator.

"Quite a party," Lydia says. "I didn't offer anyone a drink, did I? I'm a terrible host."

Sturges offers a genial smile. "Ms. Southwell—I came straight over here as soon as I learned the agency was planning to move you. I'm real sorry for the confusion."

"That's OK," says Lydia reflexively even though nothing about this situation is OK. She wonders how he heard. Is the residence bugged? Was the cop on the doorstep listening in?

"The agency and embassy *were* both informed you weren't supposed to leave Manhattan—"

"I know, I tried to tell them—"

"I'm sure you did, and quite frankly we did *not* expect—"

"We were told it was fine as long as she didn't leave *New York*," says Marat testily.

"You realize what could've happened if you'd forced her to break those restrictions? Could've been very serious for her, *and* you. She'd've been classed as a flight risk. I suggest you people pay more attention to communications in future, OK?"

Marat wants to say more, but stops himself and turns to Lydia. "Could you take a seat please?"

All the seats are occupied now, so Lydia perches on the windowsill.

"So, we've taken on board your views—"

Lydia just about stops herself from laughing out loud at this, so tickled is she by the notion this might have been a significant factor in their decision. Marat sees her expression change, and it's enough to give him pause: Lydia puts on her serious face again, and he continues.

"And we accept it makes sense for you to stay here."

"I thought you didn't have a choice?"

"We discussed the possibility of moving you to a hotel, or to the embassy itself. But the NYPD's preference is for you to remain here, as this building is easier for them to guard, and we agree that, though we're suspending you from your normal duties, it makes sense for someone to be here as a point of contact and put matters in order for the next cultural attaché."

Lydia's stunned by this. It was just some bullshit she came up with off the top of her head, she didn't expect that one to land. Are they just trying to make it look more like their own choice, rather than something they're being forced into? Probably. Who cares. "Great," she says, dropping the snarky vibe. "I won't let you down, I really do know Fitz's affairs pretty well and—"

"But this can't all fall on your shoulders. I'm sure you can be useful to Madison—she'll be staying here so she can be across everything until further notice."

Oh fuck.

Madison brings her fingers to her temples in a gesture Lydia knows means *welcome,* but in a paternalistic, patronizing sort of way: it's not a gesture one should ever do to a superior, or even an equal, unless you actively want to insult them. Madison adds: *I look forward to working with you, Lydia.*

As Lydia drags her case back upstairs, she hears the embassy translator in the hallway making relaxed small talk with the one the cops brought over. Why's she never been able to do that? Before arriving in New York she'd assumed all the translators would share enough common ground that she'd make friends among them, but it's never happened. She finds it profoundly depressing that even a *cop* translator is part of the club while she remains on the outside. But then, this is just a part of her broader failure during her time in this city, which will all be over soon anyway.

THREE

BOOKMARK

As Lydia lies back on her bed, that passing remark from Sturges about the cops learning of the agency's intentions is playing on her mind. She has to assume she's under surveillance, and wonders where from and how she might stop it. The top floor of the house next door is a separate apartment and the guy who lives there is currently summering in Quebec, and it'd be all too easy for the cops to commandeer it as a base for spying on her: the more she thinks about it, the more certain she is that they have done this. Well, they won't be able to eavesdrop on her conversations with Fitz—but Madison might.

Will she know if I'm talking to you? she asks him.

Not from this distance, he replies.

Madison is downstairs right now, in Fitz's study. Lydia is expected to make herself available if needed.

I suppose if I can't sense her, thinks Lydia, *then she can't sense me.*

You seem on edge. Is it because they almost forced you to leave?

Partly that.

No need to worry about what might have been—thanks to the police, you're still here and you'll be staying here.

The cops didn't do it to be nice—they want to keep me here, specifically in this house, because they hope I might lead them to the murder weapon, and they want to keep me in Manhattan because it's harder for me to skip out, unless I've got a helicopter. None of this is going to endear me to the agency, or the embassy—and they already hate me.

It's a little strong to say they hate you.

I'm a problem for them. They can't wait to get rid of me. Lydia listens out for a moment, in case Madison is anywhere near. She hears nothing. *Have you tried speaking to Madison?*

No, and I don't intend to. I don't trust her, and I don't want her to suspect you've been talking to me. It's safer if she has no contact with me at all.

I told the police to question her about your murder. Is there any chance she was involved?

I doubt it. We had our differences, but she wouldn't go that far.

No. It was a stupid thought really.

But don't be too quick to rule her out. Nothing's impossible. Don't let her know you're trying to find out who killed me: she won't help, and may interfere.

Lydia sighs and unfurls her scroll to find hundreds of notes and pings from every possible direction.

@LMBFFFFFOOO / You are a sick and evil individual and I hope you get murdered in prison

@MonkeyMike456 / Do you even understand what you've done? The history books will remember you as the woman who started a war

@LostPride2058 / Finally someone is willing to TAKE ACTION, you are a great American hero

@dodohunter89 / I have started a crowdfund for your legal expenses and we have already raised over $3100!

@ClassicBoi00 / When I imagine what you did to him I find it very exciting and am willing to pay for a private session for you to tell me about it in detail

That's quite enough of that.

She's also been ceeceed on a public statement from that Illogic Alliance group, claiming she's being charged with the murder and this is a terrible injustice: they're less clear on whether she actually did it, and some of the replies assume she's falsely accused while others say she was right to kill him.

She switches to her news feed. She knows Fitz's death is bound to be a big story but can't quite get it into her head that a thing which happened to *her* is playing out in public like this. It's by far the biggest story in New York and has made headlines worldwide. Speculation on the killer keeps it in the news cycle. Despite the efforts of the agency Lydia's picture appears repeatedly in these stories, and of course lots of people assume she did it. Lydia is not in control of any of this. She already feels like there are other versions of her out there, constructed by the people following this story. She doesn't even feel like she's involved. But unfortunately she is.

What strikes her is how gripped everyone is by the mystery. The cops have had to release the fact they have no security data, in order to explain the uncertainty around the case. This situation isn't entirely unheard of—lots of murder victims are people who led shady existences and avoided having their actions recorded as much as possible—but for someone in an official position with extensive security arrangements to have died like this is astounding.

Everyone wants to know who killed you, she tells Fitz. *What makes you think I'll be able to work it out? The cops have got proper resources and do this for a living, plus there's loads of them. I'm just one woman who doesn't have anyone to help, doesn't really know the city that well, and is drunk a lot of the time.*

My concern is the police are under pressure and if they can't get a result soon, will try to fit this to the most convenient suspect.

Yeah, and I'm very aware that could be me, if it's not Hari.

Who's Hari?

Just someone I . . . met back home, who's turned up in New York for some reason, and if they decide it's him they're bound to connect it back to me.

This is what I mean—I think it's vital you investigate this, for your own sake as much as mine.

Investigate what though, specifically? I have no leads, no information—I was asleep at the time for fuck's sake—

Calm down, Lydia.

It's all very well for you to tell me to calm down, you're dead, what do you have to worry about—

I have you to worry about.

Lydia bites back tears. At least someone in this city is worried about her, even if he *is* dead.

OK, she says, *what do I do first?*

You could start by looking into some abusive correspondence that arrived for me while you were away.

Don't you get abusive correspondence all the time, though?

Yes. But this one was unusually well written.

If it's in the study I won't be able to get to it. Madison won't be OK with me digging around in your files.

It's not in the study. I can tell you where to find it.

Lydia enters Fitz's bedroom feeling like an alarm's about to go off. She's never been in here before. It wasn't explicitly forbidden because it didn't need to be. It never even occurred to her to go inside.

She hears a noise from downstairs, but it's just Madison moving around in the study: she waits a few moments but the noise doesn't recur. If she's discovered in here she'll say she's looking for a book—which is, conveniently, true.

The room is tastefully decorated, with deep red walls. There's little inside except Fitz's clothes, respiratory support equipment and his bed (a sort of low-ceilinged four-poster bed which creates an atmosphere bubble when slept in, enabling him to take off his face wrap at night). He always said he preferred to keep all his clutter in his study so he could escape it when he came up here, but he was using the inkout of the offending message as a bookmark, as he often did—and the book he was reading is still in his room.

Lydia hasn't told Fitz, but she intends to use this as a test of his reality and her sanity. Her logic goes like this: She has no prior knowledge of the existence of this message or its location. If the voice leads her to a message, that information can't possibly have come from inside her own head. So that'll prove Fitz is communicating with her. Won't it?

He told her it was in the drawer on the near side of the bed. She looks down and there is indeed a drawer there. She opens the drawer and there is indeed a book inside: an illustrated history of Pacific Island artistic traditions which he was given on their recent tour. She puts the book on the floor and takes a few seconds to prepare herself: after all, she's about to learn whether or not she's gone mad, and that's a big moment in anyone's life.

She closes her eyes.

She opens the book.

She opens her eyes.

A folded piece of paper is wedged in the pages.

This is a good start. But Fitz often used scrap paper for bookmarks: She needs to see if this one is what he said it was. She takes the paper out, unfolds it and sees the words—

make you regret ever coming to this planet before
you die

OK, it's what he said it was. She goes to close the book, but then it strikes her that a book with a bookmark inside implies someone has merely gone away, and will be back to finish it soon. Removing the bookmark takes on a horrible finality in the light of this, and suddenly Lydia doesn't want to close the book without the piece of paper in it.

Then she hears Madison moving around downstairs again. She closes the book, puts it back where she found it and, treading as lightly as she can, takes the paper upstairs.

In her room, with a cup of tea and a cookie brought by the domestic, Lydia unfolds the paper. It's an inkout of the original message, written in English: usually Fitz would get her to read such things out to him or ask the written translation service to do it, but he tells her he was practicing his reading skills the day he got this. The data at the top of the inkout indicates it's anonymous, sent via a trollbox.

Mr. Fitzwilliam, I am writing to you because your conspiracy to suppress and destroy human culture has gone on more than long enough. You presumably think you are being very subtle but to some of us it is very obvious what you are doing. It is no coincidence that some of our classic texts have all but vanished since you established yourselves on Earth, supplanted by new works which so clearly bear the telltale signs of your influence. Your seemingly benign role is quite the opposite. In some ways you are the worst of them.

I advise you quit your role and return home. This is a sincere and friendly warning for your safety. I of course would never seek to harm you but I should let you know the strength of feeling you have unleashed in the people whose culture and identity you have set yourself on destroying. Your security will not save you. They know how to get past it. I doubt they will kill you quickly. They will

From there the message descends into violent fantasies about how Fitz might die. Lydia flinches, then skims the rest. *Bloody hell,* she says. She's had some abuse in her time, but there's a weird calmness to the tone of this one that freaks her out.

It's interesting, isn't it.

Not sure that's the word I'd use. And it's not that well written, I think maybe you polished it up when you translated it for yourself.

It's quite lucid and direct though, wouldn't you say?

Yes, says Lydia, skimming the paper again. *That's a fair description.*

And there are those specific references to getting through my security, and with it arriving just a few days before . . .

So do I give it to the police? Maybe they could trace who sent it?

The police will already have it. They'll have access to all my accounts. But they'll see this as one troll among many. Maybe it is. But I think there could be something else to it.

There's not a lot I can do with this though, it's anonymous.

I know someone who could trace this for us. She's helped me with such things in the past.

"Such things"?

Threats I wanted to trace, that I preferred to handle privately.

Weirdly ominous, but OK. *She'll want paying though, right? And I don't have much money. I don't even know if I'm getting paid at the moment.*

You can sell some of my rare books.

Lydia almost spits out her tea. *What the fuck?*

I don't mind.

Yeah but how am I supposed to explain to people that you spoke to me from beyond the grave and said you didn't mind?

You can say I gave them to you before I died. They can't prove I didn't.

No, but it looks fucking suspicious and even if they believe me, it's pretty hard-hearted to start selling the presents someone gave you two days after they die.

I doubt anyone will even notice, Lydia. It's just a few books among thousands.

They might notice if my bank records show up a large payment from an antique bookseller.

Then cut out the middleman. Pay her in books.

TRACING PAPER

Ah, Lydia, says Madison as Lydia walks past the study door.

The problem with talking to Logi is you can't claim not to have heard them. When Lydia lived at home, if Mum asked where she was going and she didn't want to say—for instance, if she was on her way to go driving with Gil—she'd just pretend to be wearing her buds and walk out of the door. But Logi know when you've heard them. It's like a pingback, they feel the thought as it lands in your mind.

Lydia pauses, adjusts her messenger bag so it's more or less hidden behind her body and moves back into the doorway. *I was about to go out,* she replies.

Where? Madison says, looking up from a folder of Fitz's paperwork. She's sitting in the exact spot where he died. Lydia wonders whether or not to point this out.

To get something to eat.

You can't get something delivered?

I want a walk. I've been cooped up all day.

I need to know about this, says Madison, jabbing a finger at the folder. *There's some reference in this correspondence to a partnership with the Chicago Institute of Art, but it doesn't seem to have gone anywhere.*

Oh, it turned out it wasn't really them.

Madison flicks a finger across the top of one eye, a gesture analogous to a double take. *Someone was posing as the Chicago Institute of Art?*

Yeah. They were pretty convincing. Spoofed their contacts, intercepted all our comms, mocapped the director of exhibitions and wore her skin whenever we called them. But it was all a con.

Madison looks back down at the paperwork. *Good grief.* She's momentarily distracted so Lydia chooses to assume that's all, and she quietly moves away and out of the front door.

A cop is stationed on the porch along with a police drone: Arthur and Martha have been requisitioned as evidence, and in any case need to be given a full overhaul before they can be trusted in service again. The porch cop nods and makes no move to stop Lydia or check her messenger bag. Even if he did, would he think there was anything odd about her carrying a couple of dusty old books? He surely wouldn't realize that, being a first edition of Thackeray's two-volume novel *The Newcomes* liberated from the shelves in the dining room, they were actually worth stealing. But then that's the kind of assumption Lydia hates when other people make it about her.

Lydia assumes she's being watched everywhere. Her face is on the NYPD's reclist and their sweepers will be looking for suspicious activity, so she needs to act very normal, make sure the sweepers don't raise any flags and alert any actual humans to analyze what she's up to. She's got plenty of time, so she goes into a few stores before heading to the cathouse to make it look like she's not going anywhere in particular.

She was surprised how readily Fitz's associate agreed to be paid in rare books, but maybe she shouldn't have been. The authorities can trace money easily. Tracing an old book is much more effort. As currency goes, it's cleaner than the dark crypto the dealers in Halifax used to use.

Fitz allowed Lydia to contact her on an anonymous Chapp account she didn't know he had. As she logged in using the password he'd given her, she promised him she wouldn't look at any of the other messages. He said there was nothing to see: he always deleted everything.

Lydia feels like she's seeing another side of him, and is starting to wonder if he was, in fact, more than just a cultural attaché. But she spent so much time with him, and he couldn't lie to her—surely she, of all people, would've noticed if he was hiding anything?

Lydia arrives at the cathouse on Rockefeller Plaza and is greeted by a very clean-looking young host with very straight white teeth and unsettlingly realistic cat ears on his head (they twitch as he speaks, and the band that fixes them in place is very well hidden). "Welcome!" he says. "This your first time here?"

This immediately messes with Lydia's strategy, which is to act like she comes here all the time and this is totally normal behavior for her. "Er . . . ," she says.

There's a pause while the host reads something from his glasses. "Our records suggest you haven't—is that correct?"

It's no good, she's going to have to say yes, so she does.

"No problem at all," the host reassures her redundantly: What kind of problem might there be? Perhaps they search to make sure you're not on some kind of animal cruelty register? Imagine being blacklisted from every petting establishment in the tri-state area.

The host tells her the rules and regs should be flashing up on her glasses right now (they are) and he draws her attention to the rate card. Lydia pays for one hour with one cat—this is how long she was told to pay for, and one cat is the cheapest option—and the host beams, says "Great!" and guides her to her pen. There are dozens of pens on the cathouse floor, all of them circular with padded, quilted floors and walls. Lydia is shown into one of the smaller ones, which contains a low seat, a scratching post, some toys and feeding bowls. One of the bowls contains water, the other a sachet of food. The host leaves, closing the door behind himself, and a message flashes across Lydia's glasses instructing her to sit on the seat.

A hatch opens at the opposite end of the pen and a short-haired silver tabby cat pads in, looking around. It doesn't seem nervous of Lydia. She's instructed to open the sachet of food and tip it into the bowl, which she does. The cat gratefully hurries over to the bowl and guzzles the food. While it does this Lydia is informed the cat's name is Kaylee, she is six years old and is available to buy. Lydia pokes at the now-locked hatch, wondering where it leads and how they make the cats come inside on demand.

When Kaylee has finished eating, Lydia picks her up and places her on her lap. Kaylee makes no objection, but after less than a minute standing there without settling, she hops off and curls up inside a cardboard box on the floor by the scratching post. This is a less interactive experience than Lydia hoped for but at least it confirms they're not genetically engineering the cats to do whatever the patrons want. That would just be depressing.

A ping invites Lydia to connect to a local pri:net, hosted by someone called Alison. This is not the contact's real name but it's the one she said she'd use. Lydia is surprised she doesn't use a cooler alias, like Scorpio or Silverghost or something. But actually she finds this encouraging, that this woman doesn't feel the need to sound cool. Lydia connects to the pri:net. Its range is deliberately tiny, which means "Alison" must be very close by. Lydia is about to stand up and look around for her, then realizes the contact chose this place precisely so they wouldn't be looking at each other.

"Glad you could make it," says Alison over the chat. She has a low, cultured East Coast voice. Lydia wants to save a recording for her collection, but figures this would be a bad idea.

"Thanks for meeting me," Lydia replies. Another advantage of this place: if anyone sees you talking, it looks like you're talking to your cat(s).

"Sorry to hear about Fitzwilliam."

"Yeah. I mean, he was my boss, he wasn't like a friend or—"

"You were inside each other's heads all the time. It must be intense."

Lydia shrugs. "I guess." She doesn't know how to feel about it, doesn't know what's appropriate. It doesn't help that she's gone on talking to him after his death.

"Sorry, it's none of my business."

"No, it's fine, I just . . . ," Lydia wasn't expecting there to be small talk. She's not sure what she was expecting.

"So. What do you want me to look at?"

Lydia sends a scan of the inkout over to Alison.

"OK . . . ," says Alison, then there's a few minutes' silence while she reads it. Lydia shuffles across the floor on her knees until she reaches Kaylee, who seems to be happily dozing in her box. Lydia strokes the cat, who purrs.

"You realize it might just be a bot?" says Alison finally. For a moment Lydia thinks she's talking about the cat, but she means the sender of the message.

"Yeah, but our sweeper is good and catches most of those, so nearly all of what we see is real. And also, it's an explicit death threat that turned up days before he died, so—"

"Sure, yeah. Just wanted to warn you. OK, this won't be quick—I'm gonna have to reverse engineer it—but we'll be done within the hour."

Lydia supposes she may as well enjoy herself while she's here. She orders a pizza and a beer, reluctantly paying from her personal account: Fitz may have sent her on this errand, but he can't exactly sign off her expense claims anymore.

Lydia convinces Kaylee to emerge from her box and settle on her lap as she sits cross-legged on the floor, eating her pizza. She's practically forgotten why she's even here—in fact she's *almost* forgotten that everything connected to her life is presently a clusterfuck—when she hears Alison's voice again.

"It's not a bot."

"Oh," says Lydia, pulled unpleasantly out of her reverie. "Right."

She's expecting more, but after another minute or so realizes there isn't any, yet. So she goes back to stroking the cat and idly wonders whether she could afford to buy it. She checks the prices and immediately learns she could not.

"They're way overpriced here," says Alison.

"Excuse me?"

"Sorry—I can see all your activity via this connection. Nothing personal, just like to know if people are talking to anyone else while they're talking to me."

"Right. No, that makes sense. And I wasn't going to buy one, I was just curious."

"People get suckered into taking these cats home because they think they have a special bond or whatever. Also, Manhattanites always think any creature from outside the city will be feral or diseased so they won't get one from a shelter."

"I'm not a Manhattanite. Not really."

"Oh I didn't mean *you,* just, you know . . . people. Anyway I've found him. Your sender, I mean."

"You're sure?"

"Yeah. It was routed through a couple of CADs but I've got a definite idee. He's used an off-the-shelf kit. I got you the location reference, the device it was sent from and who that device is registered to. It's *possible* someone else sent it on their device, but I'll give you ten-to-one he doesn't even turn printrec off, so the device will remember if it was him or not, and anyway ninety-nine point nine percent of the time when someone says 'I didn't post that, someone else must've used my device,' it's bullshit. So yeah, basically this is your guy."

"Thanks," says Lydia. "So how do I—"

"Leave the books outside the door of your pen when you go."

"Sure. I think I've got another ten minutes or so—"

"That's OK. When you're ready."

Lydia strokes Kaylee, drains her beer and decides there's something else she'd like to know. "Um. You don't have to answer this—"

"All the best questions start like that."

"Sorry."

"No, go on."

"What sort of stuff did you do for Fitz?"

"Stuff like this. Tracing correspondence."

"Other threats?"

"Not all of them. A lot of the time he didn't give me the content, just headers and tags, so I don't know."

"That's weird."

"Not really. Most people I trace for don't want to share the content, or anything they don't have to—and I'd prefer not to know."

"It's weird though. Doesn't seem like Fitz at all. Why didn't he just pass it on to the embassy, or the police?"

"Some people just prefer to deal with their own shit."

And to be fair, that *does* seem like Fitz.

When the time's up, Lydia says good-bye to Kaylee, the hatch opens and the cat goes into it. (How do they make them *do* that?) The door clicks open and on her way out of the pen Lydia places the books on the floor, as instructed. She glances back as she heads for the exit, worried the wrong person might pick them up—and sees a middle-aged woman with light brown hair tied up in a bun and bright yellow lipstick, wearing a dark gray zip-up tracksuit, collect the books. Can that be her? She looks like a soccer mom. But she catches Lydia's eye, nods and smiles.

As Lydia walks out of the cathouse and onto the street she checks the data Alison has found, and is surprised that she not only knows who the sender is, she also remembers meeting him.

UNREAD BOOKSHELVES

There's no cop stationed on the front porch when Lydia returns to the residence, but her hopes of getting past the study door unnoticed are dashed when Madison's voice says, *Oh good, you're back, Lydia—you just walked out without saying anything. Please don't do that.*

Madison and the porch cop are standing in the study. The tension in their body language is immediately apparent. "You've got to talk to her," the cop says.

"I thought you were finished," Lydia says before realizing she's answered the wrong person's question and directs the same statement at Madison.

I need you to talk to him, says Madison.

That's more or less what he just said, says Lydia.

"Did you hear me?" says the cop.

"I'm just—What's the problem here?"

He came in and started picking up paperwork and messing up my system, says Madison, pointing at Fitz's paperwork, which has been laid out on the floor. The system is not immediately apparent.

At the same time, the cop is explaining himself. "There're documents here that have been requisitioned by the guys at the station, so I came in here to find them and—"

Lydia tells them both to shut up for a second, which doesn't go down well with either party, but allows them to begin the unnecessarily protracted negotiations which end with Lydia making copies of the relevant documents so the cop can take them to the station. It seems she's Madison's PA now.

———

It's easy for Lydia to get in touch with the man who sent the death threat, because that time they met he gave her his contact details. She keeps a work diary with details of where she's been and who she and Fitz talked to: she was taught to do this at LSTL because the Logi often have trouble telling humans apart, and it's helpful if translators can retain this information and prompt where necessary. So she immediately recognized the name Roman Shayne, and her diary confirms she and Fitz met him at a launch event for a collaborative book of travel writing back in February. He works in the acquisitions department of a midsize publisher called Yeet Books.

Lydia goes to the bookcase by the door of her room and looks through the lower three shelves, which hold nearly all the English-language books she and Fitz have been given, but which she has not yet got around to reading. As she expected, the collection includes several books from Yeet: Roman sent Fitz a package a few days after the launch and Fitz sent it straight up to Lydia. She sees one called *Dancers of the Sun* which she read the first three chapters of and then got stuck and put back on the shelf. She sits on the bed and skims the book, refreshing her memory until she feels able to bluff a short conversation.

Lydia pings Roman's workspace and his ayaie, a creamy-complexioned young woman with anime eyes and a cartoonish cleavage, replies. A few judiciously placed keywords from Lydia ensure the ping is put through to Roman himself: a tall, floppy-haired young man who sits a little too close to the camera.

"Lydia, hi!" he says, nodding. "Great to catch up!" Then he remembers to dial down his glee at her getting in touch; "So sorry to hear about Fitz. It's an awful thing."

"It's been a real shock."

"*Such* a shock. We're all very sad over here in the workspace."

Lydia shakes her head somberly, indicating the senselessness of it all. "I don't understand it. He was such a lovely guy."

Roman nods. Lydia's testing him to see how quickly he becomes impatient to get down to business, partly because she thinks it might tell her something useful, but mostly for her own amusement. She finds it unlikely this man killed Fitz: he was probably bitter about his failure to convince Fitz to translate any of his books, and that's why he sent the death threat, and it seems implausible he took it further. But maybe he knew something? Maybe he hangs out on darkrooms and heard someone bragging about what they were going to do? It cost a first edition of *The Newcomes* to find him, so she may as well follow it up.

"I mean," Roman says. "If there's anything I can do to help—"

"Actually, I think there's something *I* can do to help *you*."

"Oh?"

"Just before Fitz died, I was about to talk to him because I finally read this." She holds up *Dancers of the Sun*. "I'm so sorry I didn't get around to it sooner."

Roman's eyes light up. He tries to play it cool. "No no, no problem—so what did you think?"

"Loved it," she says, ostentatiously pressing the book to her chest.

He smiles. "I'm so glad. I think it's a really special book."

"It really is." She steers the conversation onward before he asks her about the book's content. "I was all set to recommend it to Fitz, until . . ." She doesn't want to over-egg it—she knows she's no actress—but allows her face to crumple a little as the sentence tails off.

And now she does get to have a little fun, as she sees Roman try to look sympathetic and solemn while he ponders the agonizing possibility that he's been robbed of a chance to launch this book into a new market: she's checked and Yeet have never published anything extraglobally before. "It's such a tragedy," Roman tells her.

Lydia nods, pretends to find it hard to go on. "So I didn't get a chance to talk to him about it. But he did give me access to the fund he used for translations, and if I recommended something he'd always give it a go."

"Right."

"And it'd be such a shame if this book missed out on wider exposure just because of these terrible events. I don't think that's what he'd have wanted at all."

"From what I know of him, I'm sure that's true."

"I was hoping you and I could meet in person to discuss it." Annoyingly she can think of no good reason they can't do all this over ping, but she has to meet him in person where he can't just disconnect.

"Of course," he says, and Lydia realizes he's the kind of guy who will *always* take the opportunity to get inappropriately close to a young woman. Which suits her purposes, but still, ugh.

I don't like him, says Fitz after the call is finished and Lydia is changing her outfit.

Judging from the message he sent you, Lydia replies, *the feeling's mutual.*

GHOSTED

Lydia enters Graziella's, which she chose as the venue for the meeting due to its mirrored panels all along the walls: if she sits facing one of these she'll be able to see everything that's going on in the coffeehouse from all angles, she can see if there's anyone watching her, she can make sure Roman doesn't pretend to head for the bathroom and then sneak out. Admittedly the panels are those tricked-out mirrors which process the reflection so it shows the café as it might have been in the 1950s, and if you look in the mirror you see yourself dressed in period attire. But it'll do the job, and she is quietly pleased with herself for having thought of it.

As she sits down and orders a tea and a slice of cheesecake, Lydia glances up at her reflection, which is wearing a polka-dot dress she wouldn't be seen dead in. This is the mirror's default selection for anyone above a size 12: fucking *polka dots*. It's given her a nice swept-across hairstyle, though, and she likes the lipstick. She remembers the cleanskin kids she went drinking with in Hidden Palace and how she told them it was different being here, and it is—so it seems strange how places like this try so hard to make it feel like you're in a sim of Manhattan as it was, which you could easily do at home.

Lydia is so caught up in these thoughts she's startled when Roman walks up to her table and greets her. She actually *watched* his reflection walk through the café, but didn't notice it was him because his reflection is wearing a beautifully cut three-piece suit and a hat. In reality Roman is wearing lemon-yellow shorts and a matching waistcoat with no shirt underneath it. As she glances in the mirror she notices she has cheesecake on her lower lip and she's about to wipe it off with a napkin, but Roman leans in to kiss her on the cheek and she has a sudden intrusive thought that he might lick the cheesecake off and she flinches away before his lips make contact.

"Sorry," says Roman, perturbed by her reaction.

"No, I'm sorry—I just remembered I've got a cold, and you shouldn't . . . do that."

"Oh. Well. That was a close one, huh," he replies, sitting down, unconvinced by her unconvincing lie.

"Thanks for meeting me so quickly."

"I was thrilled when you called."

I bloody bet you were, Lydia thinks, and while he orders a coffee she wonders how to play this. It might be helpful to let him settle in first, develop a false sense of security? So she asks him about his work: He'll be flattered and let his guard down. He talks about sales figures and campaigns for *Dancers of the Sun* but she doesn't take it in, instead rehearsing what she's going to say and judging when exactly to say it. She'll make her move after his coffee arrives: it will prompt a break in the conversation and he'll be wrong-footed.

The waitress comes to their table (looking the same in the mirror as she does in real life, the uniforms have that 1950s styling anyway) and puts a coffee in front of Roman. Lydia already has her hand on her bag, waiting for him to stop talking so she can flourish the inkout and demand he explain himself. But he doesn't pause for breath, even as he puts shuga in his coffee and stirs it, barely looking down at what he's doing, talking about how popular the novel's auxiliary fic has been and how he cut that particular deal. It just goes on.

Eventually, when Roman considers his coffee has cooled sufficiently, he pauses in the middle of a sentence to take a sip, and Lydia slaps the inkout on the table and blurts "Recognize this?" She'd hoped to pull this off in a much cooler, more controlled way, but it is what it is.

Roman is startled, but very clearly does recognize it. Lydia can practically see his stomach knotting. He looks up and says, "Should I?"

"I think so."

"I don't . . ." He tails off, rereading the inkout. "Who wrote this?"

"You did."

And look, right on cue, here comes the forced you-can't-be-serious laugh. He's going to ask her if this is a joke and actually she can't bear to listen, it's so predictable it's like talking to a really cheap ayaie, so she picks up the inkout, says "You won't mind if I send it to your boss then," stands and turns to leave—

And in a voice that starts loud and abruptly goes quiet, he says "NO, SIT down . . ."

Lydia has a glance around to see if anyone's noticed this exchange. A few people have. Good. She sits back down.

Seething, Roman looks up at her. "You're not going to commission a translation of *Dancers of the Sun,* are you?"

She laughs. "That's the first thing you want to know?"

He makes an exasperated grunt. "I already told the author I was meeting with you about it—we've always felt the book has real crossover potential, *literally* universal themes—and it'll be embarrassing if I have to go back to her and tell her it's not happening."

"More embarrassing than being outed as a bigot?"

"I'm not a—Look, can you just tell me if the translation's happening?"

"Of course it fucking isn't. I don't have the authority to commission one, and even if I did, I didn't like the book, I found it ponderous. I didn't actually finish it." It's unnecessary to tell him this, but she enjoys doing so. She's especially satisfied to have alighted on the word *ponderous.*

"So what's this about? Blackmail?"

"No." This hadn't occurred to her. But now that he's mentioned it, she fleetingly considers it: How rich is this guy? How important is it to him that nobody knows he sent this? But no, she has a job to do. "I want to know why you sent it."

He shrugs. "I don't really remember. I was pretty wasted, I was in a shitty mood, it seemed funny at the time. You know how it is with trollboxes, once you install it, it does all that intrusive shit, looks at your other activity and suggests who you might like to troll?"

Lydia shakes her head. "I've never used a trollbox."

Roman raises an eyebrow, which might be a gesture of skepticism, then continues: "It's impossible to turn off. I swear it pings you more when you're drunk or whatever. Anyway I do remember sending it but as for the exact thought process . . . I dunno." He waves a hand in the air.

"You do get how serious this all is, right? Less than a fortnight ago you threatened him, now he's *dead*."

He sits up straighter, glares at her. Genuine surprise this time? Interesting. "Hey, look—you can't possibly think I had anything to do with it?"

"What am I supposed to think?"

"I didn't threaten him—look at the message. I said *people meant him harm*. It's a warning, not a threat. And I was right, wasn't I?"

"So how'd you know?"

He laughs hollowly. "I don't have any special insight. *Obviously* people mean him harm because he's, like . . . one of *them*. I'm sure there are people who mean *you* harm, just by association."

"Oh charming."

"I'm just being honest. I don't think it's a good thing, or—"

"Then why send the message? You still haven't explained why someone in your position would send a message like that—"

"He was ghosting me," Roman snaps.

"Ghosting you?"

"I was chasing up that contact, trying to get a meeting with him, and he was ignoring me."

"He was always busy—"

"We're *all* busy, all the time." He's raising his voice. "People think it's all ayaied now and I sit in my workspace all day reading books and jerking off but it all just makes *more work*. Everything that was meant to lighten the load makes *more work,* it just makes *more shit* for you to deal with. Everything's squeezed and the margins are tiny and that bony motherfucker you used to work for—god rest his soul—could make *such* a difference to us, to *me,* and he fucking ghosted me." This outburst has not gone unnoticed by other patrons of the café, and Roman falls quiet, looking down at the tabletop.

"So you just wanted to scare him because you were pissed off with him?"

"I didn't really think about scaring him. I didn't think he'd even read it. I get ten times more notes than I can deal with. If something looks like it's bullshit I don't read past the second line."

"Why send it then?"

"Don't you ever just want to vent?"

"Yeah but I do it inside my head."

"See, I think that's unhealthy. You need an outlet."

"I could use *you* as a fucking outlet, mate."

He laughs, then composes himself. "I'm serious. You've been through some grim shit. You need to look after yourself."

"How d'you know what I've been through? You've not asked me a thing about myself since you sat down."

"It's all over the feeds. I saw a recon of the moment you found his body—*eeesh*."

"There's a *recon* of that?"

"Yeah but the girl in it doesn't look like you. They probably didn't want to get hammered over the image rights."

Lydia no longer wants to be having this conversation. "Look, if you know anything that might help us work out who might have killed him—"

"Isn't that kind of the cops' job?"

"Well yeah, but my boss is dead so what else am I going to do with my time?"

"Read the books I sent you? But no, I—" He pauses. "Actually when I was writing that message, I was sort of pastiching something someone sent me." He pulls open his scroll.

"So that wasn't how you normally write?"

He winces. "Please. I wanted it to look like a real one. And it's not like I edited it or anything, plus I was high . . ." He scrolls down, then nods. "OK, yep—tell no one I gave you this, this is *very* unprofessional." And he flicks a document across to her glasses.

EPIC VIPER SQUAD!

Lydia is grudgingly grateful to Roman for allowing her to return to Fitz with *something*. The document is a pitch for a book, *The Blanking of the Slate: The Erasure of Human Culture in the Era of the Logi and How We Can Stop It* by Jonas Sheppard. It includes the entire manuscript, which the data says is 633 pages long: Lydia has no reason to doubt this, as the style is that of someone who did not find it a chore to write 633 pages on the subject of the pernicious influence of the Logi on human culture, but was less keen on editing it afterwards. It also doesn't appear to have been read back at all—it's filled with repetition and incomplete sentences, and may even have been transcribed from speech. However hastily it was written, it was apparently researched in even less time, as its factual basis ranges from shaky to nonexistent.

Lydia's surprised Roman read past the first paragraph of this junk, but he said there can be a good market for extended polemics on "buzzy topics," and publishers have cleanup ayaies that can smooth out the prose considerably before an actual editor works on it. But he rejected this one as unsuitable, going beyond a "reasonable level" of paranoia. Unsurprisingly, given the focus on culture, Fitz is mentioned numerous times.

Have you heard of this guy? Lydia asks Fitz.

No. But then, I don't keep abreast of such things.

Neither would I, in your shoes.

Sheppard is easy enough to find online. He has a very active feed and most of the content in his book has already been put on it in one form or another.

@OneStopShep / NEW: How the Western was forced to change after First Contact / TR65

@OneStopShep / NEW: Settling for a virtual world while our real one is

stripped by the Logi? What's really behind contemporary gaming and social trends? / TR58

@OneStopShep / NEW: Four-hour conversation with leading Preserva-
tionist Daniel Bryant including some exciting VIPER discoveries! / TR59

There are images of Sheppard: he's twenty-nine and clearly
uses the kind of filters that balance out a sallow complexion. He
does appear to be a real person though; he's got verification seals
and when Lydia runs his account through Fleshpoint it gives him a
score of 89 percent, indicating "very likely to be real." His bio says
he lives in Utah, and who'd lie about that? In terms of the murder
though, it'd be difficult for someone to cross so many state lines
without being noticed, and with a profile like his, police ayaies
would make the connection immediately and flag him. In any case
he seems quite content to rant from Utah.

I'm interested to see what he said about me, says Fitz. *Could you
translate?*

What, the whole thing?

Good grief, no. Just the parts about me.

Lydia sings a snatch of "You're So Vain" to him in her head, and
even as she's doing it she realizes there's no chance of him under-
standing this reference—it doesn't even scan when translated into
Logisi. But he responds with a ripple of amusement. He's always
surprising her with the bits of Earth culture he knows. It's unlikely
anyone else in existence had the kind of knowledge he had, or his
particular perspective on it, and she feels depressed by the thought
it's been snuffed out.

Lydia searches the manuscript for Fitz's name, as well as references to cultural attachés in general, and translates for him. She
finds the process soothing. Right now she doesn't have to think for
herself or make daunting decisions, she just has to choose the most
appropriate words to express another person's sentiments, at her
own pace. In this case the sentiments are incoherent and unpleasant, but you can't have everything.

Fitz is just one player in the book's central conspiracy theory—a
Mandela Effect type thing about how the Logi have literally erased

bits of human culture, that there's stuff people remember from years ago that nobody can find any trace of now. No references online. Look for an old file or hardcopy, it'll have gone missing. All that's left are fragments—a reference in an old newspaper, a hardcopy visible in the background of an old photo—and memories. Sheppard asserts that this is Fitz's true purpose on Earth, to identify such texts and recommend them for removal—otherwise why put such extensive resources at the disposal of the *"cultural exchange"* program? (Sheppard always puts *"cultural exchange"* in inverted commas *and* italics.)

Whole chapters are taken up with descriptions of texts Sheppard claims have been lost, which he solemnly refers to as an act of preservation. If Lydia didn't know better she'd say this was just someone's collection of ideas for books and movies and TV shows which they hadn't fully worked through: sketchy premises and plots with a few memorable moments noted. The longest of these chapters deals with a children's animated series called *Epic Viper Squad!* which he claims ran for two seasons, was Canadian in origin and which he can find no trace of now, apart from chats where people try to find other people who remember it. It's about a crack special ops team who can transform into giant snakes and travel through time and space via wormholes. Most sources agree one of the team was called Ariadne and they fought an evil organization called G.O.O.N.Z. The chapter includes a crowdsourced episode guide for the show which goes on for forty pages, as well as a sound file of the author's (presumably) best attempt at playing the theme tune.

It's not clear to Lydia why the Logi might want to erase this cartoon, or indeed any of the other texts mentioned in the book, from existence—but Sheppard devotes another chapter to extensive speculation on the topic, trying to find connections between this seemingly random collection of material.

You don't need to read this part, says Fitz.

Because it's not about you? Lydia replies.

Well, yes.

I can see why Roman didn't just dismiss it out of hand. It's oddly fascinating.

You think?

I'm not believing any of it, don't worry—it's just so detailed. If it was fiction it'd be . . . well, not good, but sort of impressive.

Are there any more references to me?

Lydia checks her search. *Some in chapter seventeen apparently.* She's been translating for a couple of hours and her ability to focus on the screen is deteriorating and she's getting to the point where she won't even remember this stuff tomorrow. She jumps to chapter seventeen, the final chapter (apart from the appendices, which total about a hundred pages on their own), which discusses a belief among some groups that the Logi aren't as incapable of dealing with digital technology as they like to make out, and the reason for this is they're covertly manipulating us, including by the erasure of the aforementioned texts. Lydia finds this theory hard to take seriously, having spent several months dealing with the day-to-day needs of someone who couldn't use translation software and struggled with computers. It slowed so many things down and rendered him unable to communicate every time she clocked off. If it was an act, it had better be worth the hassle. Would they go through all that just so they could covertly erase (nearly) all traces of a cartoon from the internet?

Lydia keeps relating the content of the chapter to Fitz, but she's not really taking it in at this point—she's about to tell Fitz she needs to stop and rest when he says—

Read that part again.

What part?

The quoted part.

Lydia looks back up the page. There's a substantial block quote. She starts again from the top:

> *What's really notable about the Logi's refusal to engage with us in our own language and media is how they've forced us to communicate on their terms. Our dire economic need to forge*

a productive relationship with another species has made us accept them and their demands. This gives them a lot more control over how they're seen, meanwhile forcing us to put all the effort into communication, such as our network of translators. While human beings long ago lost control over how we're seen by one another—images of us and recordings of our words are easily captured, manipulated and circulated freely, and we can have no idea who has seen them, heard them, read them—the Logi avoid this process. Only if they elect to have their words relayed by a servant do those words reach the public sphere, so they never get caught out making idle chatter. Their words are not recorded in their original form. Translators are trained in diplomatic language and sentiment, and warn their masters if their words are likely to provoke a negative reaction: if all else fails, they can simply claim a translation error.

Above all the Logi operate in our world at their own speed, which is how they avoid making mistakes. The rest of us are helplessly caught up in the hellish pace of contemporary life, but the Logi are able to stand back from it and observe us. We can't underestimate the advantage this gives them.

Now Lydia looks at it, that bit is noticeably better written than the rest.

Who said that? asks Fitz.

The referencing system is a mess and it takes Lydia a moment to locate it in the endnotes: Professor Marcia Booth.

We've met her, Fitz says.

Have we? asks Lydia. *When?*

Just before I died.

Lydia tries but she has no memory of meeting Prof. Booth. Fitz thinks it was late on at the conference banquet and he says they had a substantial conversation. Indeed, it was this conversation that prompted him to ask Lydia to repeat the passage quoted in

Sheppard's book—Booth spoke of how the need for translation changed the pace of life.

The phrasing was extremely similar, Fitz says. *It must be a pet theory of hers.*

And I translated all this for you at the time? Lydia asks.

Of course.

Was it in any way comprehensible?

Absolutely. By that stage most of the attendees were a little drunk themselves, so I doubt they noticed anything amiss.

"A little drunk" is not the same as "Can't remember anything whatsoever" drunk. *Did anyone notice I'd lost my glasses?*

I don't recall. But nobody mentioned it, no.

Of course not, thinks Lydia to herself: Why would they? No one looks at me. *So if I'm going to meet this woman, will she remember me?*

Probably.

OK, what did we talk about?

The keynote, mainly. She teaches at NYNU. I don't really know the place.

Lydia doesn't either, so she starts by looking up what NYNU stands for. After getting distracted by a longread about a similar incident two decades ago (The first Logi to die on Earth—and the eerie parallels with today / TR89) she learns it's New York New University, founded four decades ago "to promote and protect independent thought and free speech." It's not a large institution but it's based in an expensive part of town, the Upper East Side, close to the park. Booth is part of the Literature and Culture Department and specializes in Culture War Studies.

D'you think she had anything to do with it? Lydia doesn't have to specify she means Fitz's death: one of the elegant things about Logisi is a shift in tone usually makes clear what you're referring to without having to refer to it directly.

I really didn't get any sense of hostility from her when we spoke—not the kind of hostility that comes across in this quote. Perhaps it's the context?

Or—and I realize this is a bit radical—it might just be that she was nice to your face and then shitty about you behind your back.

I'm familiar with the experience, thank you, Lydia. I'm just trying to give her the benefit of the doubt.

Why though?

It's getting late but Lydia's got nothing to get up for tomorrow, so she keeps digging and turns up an interview with Booth, conducted by Sheppard for his feed just under a year ago, which has over seven million views and a higher TR than most of his stuff (71). In the video they appear to be sitting in an old-fashioned TV news studio, facing each other in chairs with slim silver frames and black leather seats, a stylized skyline behind them—one of the default interview environments that comes with the casting app. Booth herself is probably in her fifties, with long blond hair and soft skin offset by hard blue eyes and a squareness to her jaw. She wears simple jewelry and a slim, unfussy, royal blue dress that draws the eye and ensures the ayaie director keeps focusing on her.

Sheppard is thrilled to be interviewing Booth but he's visibly struggling to keep up: the less certain he is of what she's talking about, the more he nods. Mostly he lets her talk about whatever she wants to talk about. And what she wants to talk about is Fitz.

BOOTH: Take New York City, where I live—the literary capital of this country, and also the theater capital, and arguably the intellectual capital too.

SHEPPARD: Of course.

BOOTH: Which is why the Logi have a cultural attaché based there and not in Portland, or Chicago, or somewhere in Canada, even. And the whole scene is in thrall to this guy. It's all about money and influence, and what he approves of has a huge effect on what you get to see and read. Not everyone knows this.

SHEPPARD: (*nodding*) People are so ignorant.

BOOTH: It's not people's fault.

SHEPPARD: No no, of course not.

BOOTH: We don't get an honest discussion of these issues in the messum.

SHEPPARD: You can't trust the messum.

BOOTH: They play down his influence.

SHEPPARD: It's why I do what I do, I want to provide balance.

BOOTH: Ultimately what this is really about is soft power.

SHEPPARD: (*nodding vigorously*) Absolutely. Soft power.

BOOTH: Because if you can control the stories a culture tells about itself, you can control who they are.

SHEPPARD: Wow.

BOOTH: And that's what the cultural attaché is really for.

NEW YORK
NEW UNIVERSITY

Lydia has had about five hours' sleep when Madison sends the domestic up to wake her because she wants help with some correspondence. Talking to Madison has made Lydia realize Fitz was a man of few words, or at least a man capable of restricting himself to a few words. Madison thinks aloud constantly, largely not expecting any replies, but whenever Lydia tunes out and goes on her scroll Madison will abruptly address a question to her and then get cross when she has to repeat herself. In these snatched moments Lydia does manage to go on Booth's homeroom on the NYNU site, where she finds a list of office hours. Any students can come and see her at these times. A perfect opportunity for Lydia to bluff her way in . . . and it's slipping away. Booth's only office hour this week starts at eleven o'clock, which is in eight minutes.

Lydia's attention is called back to Madison, who has questions about Fitz's role in the bid to bring the Winter Olympics to Vermont, and also questions about what the Winter Olympics is and what it's for. Lydia pretends to know less about this subject than she does because she needs to get out of here and get down to NYNU.

I could really use a break, she says after explaining what a biathlon is. And she *does* need a break, she's absorbed a lot of words in a short space of time and feels completely smashed.

Madison reluctantly accepts Lydia will be afunctional if this continues much longer.

Cheers, Lydia says as she clambers down from the chair and puts her feet on the floor.

Where are you going?

Fresh air? Lydia takes a step towards the door.

You're standing on the paperwork!

Sorry—

Lydia steps back, falling against the chair and knocking it over, before landing on her arse. *I'm alright,* she says as she picks herself up off the floor. *I'm fine.* She carefully makes her way to the door, keeping to the edges of the room and holding on to the bookshelves for balance.

NYNU is located in what used to be the Consulate General of France, along with a neighboring building that was probably an apartment block. Lydia hurries into the lobby shortly before midday, drinking a can of Wired she bought from a vending machine in the hope it might sober her up, and is confronted with security gates, which she should have anticipated. Yet looking to her right she sees a series of terminals which claim to offer instant access to the university in return for payment. Turns out it's possible to take classes on a pay-as-you-go basis, then cash in any credits you earn for a degree: They offer "fractional degrees" after as little as one class and a one-hour assessment. No previous qualifications are required. Lydia realizes these are aimed at tourists, allowing them to boast a "degree" from a New York university in exchange for the same time and money they'd spend going to a museum. Frame it and put it in your hallway. It's a pretty good grift.

Lydia selects a fractional degree in American literature and pays the fee. The terminal captures an image of her while processing her application, then a message flashes up saying YOU'VE BEEN ACCEPTED! and her student idee card is spat out into the tray at the bottom. The hologram of her looks dreadful, she's all sweaty and red-faced from rushing over here, but she tells herself nobody's going to look at it: her bioprint is on the university's records, the card is just another souvenir for tourists. Sure enough, when she approaches the security gates they open for her without any need to wave the card.

When Lydia reaches the English department on the fifth floor of the neighboring building, it's 11:49. The door of Prof. Booth's office is closed and she appears to be with a student: their muffled voices can be heard inside. One other student, a skinny, smartly dressed young man with an extremely weak jawline, is waiting his turn. This is promising. Lydia joins the end of the queue.

The minutes pass.

A loud wailing sound comes from within the office. It's not the voice of Prof. Booth, but the voice of the student she's talking to. The wailing settles into snotty, shuddering crying, the sort where someone wants to get it under control but can't.

The skinny student turns to Lydia and rolls his eyes. She makes a similar gesture in return as if she knows exactly what he means.

The student in the office cries on. The monotonous voice of Prof. Booth can be heard in the gaps between sobs. From what she's seen of the woman, Lydia can't imagine her being strong on emotional support, but eventually the crying ebbs away, replaced by sniffles and low muttering.

"This is bullshit," the skinny student says to no one. "Office hours are for *academic* issues." He makes a show of checking the time even though his only audience is Lydia.

Lydia also checks the time: it's 11:54. "It's fucking ridiculous," she agrees, speaking in an American accent though she's unsure why. Seems more . . . incognito or something? It's wank, she decides, but she's stuck with it now. She's still drunk from this morning's lengthy translation session and needs to interrogate her decisions more thoroughly. "Don't these guys realize we've got places to be?"

"Exactly," he replies, fidgeting. Then he checks the time again and storms away down the corridor with a stage whisper about how he pays his fees for *contact time,* not standing around in a fucking *corridor* time. . . .

A minute after he's gone the office door opens and the weepy student emerges, looking hollowed out. He seems surprised to find Lydia there, like it's only just occurred to him that anyone outside the door might be able to hear. Then he hurries away.

Lydia enters the office to find a tutting Prof. Booth directing her domestic to pick up the used tissues the weeping student has left scattered across the floor. The office is not at all like she expected a literary scholar's to be: slick, white with hints of gray, very little color at all except for Booth herself, who is today wearing a purple dress of a very similar cut to the one she wore for the interview with Sheppard. Against the monochrome backdrop of her office it has a similar effect: she seems bold, larger than life. Lydia is surprised the purple seems to suit her just as well as the blue, before realizing Booth must have tweaked her skin tone to complement the dress. Just three items sit on the glass-topped desk: a screen, a dark gray stone bust of some old guy, and a box of tissues. The only shelving in the office is a small, three-tiered corner unit that holds no more than thirty books, half of which are by Booth herself.

"Are you the last one?" Booth asks without really looking at Lydia.

"Yes," says Lydia, dropping the fake American accent and hoping Booth didn't hear when she spoke in the hallway.

"I can give you four minutes, max. Turn off your cam please."

Commercial models of glasses can easily be pinged to check if they're recording, so the person they're recording has the opportunity to withhold consent. Lydia wonders if it's worth trying to get hold of a sprung pair that can't be pinged.

"Sorry," says Lydia, turning it off and sitting down. "I didn't realize it was on."

"I encourage my students to cultivate something called a private life. People used to have them, many years ago. And I don't want anything I say in this room getting repurposed or decontextualized." Booth looks Lydia full in the face for the first time and frowns. "You're not a student here. But I know you. Where do I know you from?"

"I am a student here, actually." Lydia holds up her new idee for Booth to see. "Just registered. So no need to call security."

"I wasn't going to." She leans back in her high-backed chair and points at Lydia. "The cultural attaché's translator."

"That's right."

Booth nods. "It's a terrible shock, what's happened. It must have been only a few hours after we spoke."

"It was. And yeah, it was a shock."

"So you're . . . taking a course here?" says Booth, looking at her curiously.

"Yes, I'm just . . . trying to keep busy and, er—"

"Why here?"

"Well, it's a good university, isn't it?" Lydia has no idea if it's a good university but Booth is hardly likely to disagree. "Er, Professor—"

"Marcia, please."

"Thank you"—*Why are you thanking her? Shut up*—"I didn't know anything about you before we met, but last night I was thinking of signing up for this course and looked you up and found your view of my late boss was . . . not quite what you made it out to be when you spoke to him?"

Booth appears perfectly calm. "What did I make it out to be?"

Lydia can't answer this question so she answers a different one. "I saw an interview you gave—"

"With that Sheppard guy?"

"Yeah."

Booth shakes her head. "He misrepresented what I said, cut and smoothed it to hell. No real journalist would do that."

Lydia doesn't buy this: To her it felt like Booth was being given all the space she wanted to say her piece. But of course she'd say that's what Sheppard *wanted* the audience to think. These things just go round and round and who the fuck knows what's true. But: "Why didn't you challenge it?"

Booth snorts. "You ever tried invoking Good Faith?"

"I did once, yeah." Sometimes people generate fakes from her feed—sometimes not even people, ayaies churn out vids of her saying words culled from old movies or articles or chat archives—to support some stupid bait about the Logi. Usually they come and go and it doesn't bother her. But there was one where someone had her talking about books like she just hadn't understood them, like she thought *To Kill A Mockingbird* was about an actual mockingbird, stuff like that, making her look really thick, and it circulated quite a bit. That was when Fitz suggested she lodge a complaint under the Good Faith laws.

"Did it work?" asks Booth.

"Yeah. But it was a huge hassle, I had to give them loads of evidence."

Booth shrugs. "I don't have that kind of time."

Lydia's hackles rise at the implication her time is less valuable than Booth's, but she lets it slide. "I looked at some other things you wrote though—"

"Yes," Booth says, a tone creeping into her voice as one might use to a foolish child. "I've often taken a critical view of the Logi and how they operate, as is my right. Sorry but I don't see your point, and my office hour is now up, so—"

"OK," says Lydia, deciding to deploy a tactic she's not completely sure about, but she can't come out and accuse Booth of killing Fitz because she'll sound insane, and this is the best idea she's got. "The real reason I came is the police suspect me of killing Fitz—"

"You mean Fitzwilliam?"

"Yes, I always called him Fitz—and the thing is, I *was* in the building when he died, and there's no record of what happened and who else was there, and I can't remember *anything*."

Booth raises her eyebrows. "Can't remember?"

"Yes, the translation process—"

"Ah, the intoxication thing." She leans back in her chair. "Wow. That's inconvenient. What does it have to do with me?"

"I don't actually remember speaking to you at the banquet either."

Booth laughs. "Oh."

"But we did speak?"

"Yes. How did you know, if you can't remember?"

Shit. "Er, someone else who was there said they'd seen Fitz talking to you. And I just, er . . . like, how did he seem to you? Like, did he seem worried about anything?" She's fishing here—doesn't know what she's looking for.

"I'm afraid I find his people very hard to read. May I say, you didn't strike me as excessively intoxicated, I thought you were very professional."

"Thank you, but unfortunately I need people to believe I *was* intoxicated and really don't remember anything, and I'm not just making it up because I don't have an alibi."

Booth gives her a sympathetic look. "You're in a heap of trouble, aren't you?"

Lydia nods. She has slightly exaggerated how much trouble she's in, but she *is* in trouble. She's hoping Booth might inadvertently reveal something, like maybe let slip she knows Lydia didn't kill Fitz because she has some idea who did.

"I can think of someone the police might want to talk to, in regard to all this," Booth says.

"Really?" Fucking hell. Lydia hadn't expected a *name*—but she runs with it.

"I had a student a couple years back," Booth continues. "Quite a good student. Used to come to me in sessions like this, wanted to talk about my work on the cultural interface. I encouraged her to become a postgrad, but she had a breakdown in her final year and never completed. I kept in touch, telling her we were keeping her place open and her credits on record. Told her she could get a B point nine two if she just went through the formal exit process. But she never replied—*until* I did that interview with Sheppard."

"Ah."

"She assumed I was into all his dumb conspiracy theories, and she started sending me more of them."

"Like the one about them erasing all those texts?"

"*Much* more far-out than that. Sheppard's thing is an overblown and very simplistic version of a thing that's really happening. But the stuff I was getting from this student was like, nanobots controlling our brains, First Contact happened in the 1980s and it's been covered up, the Logi caused climate change . . ."

"And you don't agree with that stuff?"

Booth laughs shortly. "I'm a critic, not a crackpot."

"So you'd let me know who this student is?"

"On two conditions," says Booth, tapping the desk so the interface for her screen appears.

"Right."

"First, don't tell anyone I gave you this, it's against data laws.

Second, she's troubled and may not be in a great state of mind, and if the police approach her they have to do so carefully, right?"

"Sure, of course, yeah."

Booth flicks the contact card across to Lydia and it appears in the corner of her glasses. It includes a name—Jene Connor—and a last known address.

"I hope she's OK," Booth says. "I feel like I should have done more for her. I told myself I had enough responsibilities already, and if she was no longer a student, she wasn't my problem. But if she's gotten into anything bad, I'll feel partly to blame."

LIBERTY VIEW

Lydia catches the subway directly downtown from NYNU and on the way she checks her notes, which have piled up during the morning.

@HYPERTRUTH / FITZWILLIAM LATEST: Fugitive suspect is Brit "Logi serial killer" with SEVEN previous victims / TR18
@ EVERYTHING_YAAAS / Murdered Logi's BODY stolen from NYPD morgue for use in SATANIC ritual! Exclusive images / TR09

Jesus. She's lowered her standards so Chime will send her anything related to the case because she feels she should know what people are saying: Even if it's bullshit, it might be useful to know. But it really is bullshit.

She looks for more info on Jene. Her name and the fact she attended NYNU within the last few years is enough to locate her, but her profile is remarkably unremarkable. She looks like any number of relatively well-off girls Lydia knew at LSTL—blond, tanned, manicured eyebrows, eerily straight teeth. Her stream is a mix of socials and urban landscapes and she expresses herself mostly via seeji animals, with foxes and penguins being particular favorites. There's no substantial writing from her: she tags her images with fragmentary sentences, she doesn't monolog. Her most recent post on main is a couple of weeks old.

Lydia wonders if she's definitely got the right person. Jene doesn't look the type to send reams of conspiracy theories to her old literature tutor. But perhaps that's deliberate. People who advance conspiracy theories are paranoiacs. Maybe she was careful not to attract attention.

———

The south tip of Manhattan is by far the cheapest part to live on because it's the most vulnerable to freak high tides. It's been six years since an overflow event but property values have never recovered from the last one, after which an extra tier was built onto the seawall, which does its job but blocks even more natural light. The lower stories of the buildings near the wall are in gloom for most of the day, and while the upper ones have a good view there are concerns over water damage and accessibility, and in the springtime they get absolutely lashed with rain. It occurs to Lydia that if Jene had to live here while studying at NYNU (which is quite some distance away), perhaps she wasn't as well off as her stream suggested, and that impression of moneyed blandness was something she affected to fit in? If so, Lydia sympathizes. It's not how she dealt with it, but it's a valid strategy.

Before proceeding to the apartment where Jene lives (or lived), Lydia walks through what used to be the port where you could take a ferry to the Statue of Liberty. Instead of the port there's now a line of periscopes, and for five dollars you can look through one and see the statue. In theory you can still get to it over the water, but since the land was submerged and seawater started lapping around Lady Liberty's base, people don't like to any more. Something about it makes them uneasy, and so it's no longer viable to run ferries. You can still get there via helicopter, if you can afford it. Lydia's neighbor Mrs. Kloves insists the statue stands higher than it used to, and the government covertly built up the plinth because the submerged Statue of Liberty was always such a staple image of apocalypse fiction, and the government was determined it shouldn't become a barometer of how fucked everything was. (Lydia finds it unlikely this could be achieved unnoticed, but Mrs. Kloves is adamant.)

Lydia doesn't look through any of the periscopes. Instead she lets the Mappoint in her glasses guide her over to Jene's apartment on the second floor of a four-story block called Liberty View. You can tell the block postdates the seawall because it's been built in a U-shape with the ends of the U facing the wall, and there are no windows on that end. This means there are very few apartments offering a view of the statue and the building's name seems like a bleak joke but, to be fair, if you stand on the rooftop you probably *can* see the statue. The apartments are small, probably inhabited by the young, the old and people without children or the means to get anything better. In fact you *could* get something better out in Queens or the Bronx without having to live on the floodplains, but for some people that's their line in the sand: she remembers Anders at the reception saying how he never left Manhattan.

Lydia walks up to apartment 16 and rings the doorbell. A tallish young man with curly, coppery hair and freckles, wearing loose trousers and a basketball vest, answers the door. "Yes?" he says.

"Hi, I'm looking for Jene Connor?" Lydia has rehearsed her little piece for this on the way over here, and has prompts on her glasses to help her stay on script. Thankfully she feels a good deal more sober now.

"Why?" the young man replies, which strikes Lydia as an interesting reaction.

"I'm from NYNU; I'm chasing up students who didn't complete, offering them the chance either to return or cash in their credits for a fractional degree."

"I doubt she's interested." His expression has already turned from neutral to sour.

"I'd really like to speak to her. Her record says she could get a B point nine two," she adds, reading from her glasses. "All she has to do is confirm her exit, it's very easy—or come back and finish."

"She's not here."

"Will she be back later, or—"

"She doesn't live here, OK?" The young man seems like he's about to close the door, and Lydia sticks her foot in the gap, despite the fact she's wearing canvas open-toed sneakers. She should have worn sturdier ones with thick soles, that can block a door *and* protect her foot, and she resolves to do this from now on.

"But she used to?" she asks. "You know her?"

"Yes."

"Do you know where I can find her now?"

"I really don't think she'd be interested."

"I need to confirm that with her personally rather than take your word for it."

"Can't you just ping her?"

"She hasn't replied."

"That should tell you something." An aggressive edge enters his voice.

"I'm just trying to help—"

"She doesn't need a degree—shit like that doesn't interest her anymore, OK?"

Aha. "What d'you mean?"

"She's not gonna get a job, she's not gonna do anything—you say you want to help her, you're wasting your time. I tried to help her, she doesn't want it, she doesn't listen."

"How do you know her, if you don't mind me—"

"She was my girlfriend."

Lydia assumed as much: this strength of feeling doesn't come from being passing acquaintances. "I see."

"I told her everything you're saying. At first I thought it was just, like, option paralysis—she didn't want to go back and she didn't want to end it—"

"Your relationship?"

"What? No—her college degree."

"Oh, I see."

"Like, it seemed like she didn't want the finality of quitting, so wanted to leave the option open, but she also couldn't face going back once she left, you see what I mean?"

"Absolutely," says Lydia, because she does, but also she seems to have hit on something and wants him to know she understands and is listening.

"So I was like, you need to move past this, you can't live in this limbo where you can potentially do both things because you're not doing either thing. That makes sense, right?"

"That sounds very astute to me."

"Right? I thought I'd nailed it, but she was like, No, no, that's not it, and I was trying to make her see she was in denial and this was stopping her getting on with her life, and we had this conversation several times and she'd just drop it or change the subject or walk out, even. Then one time she *screamed* at me that *she* wasn't the one stopping her getting on with her life, it was *them*—"

"Who's them?"

"That's what I said, and she said, Who do you think? It's the fucking aliens, Todd."

Lydia points at him. "Are you Todd?"

"What? Oh—yes, Todd, that's me. And I was like, this is just another dumb excuse, right? Like, it's got to the point where she'll blame *anyone* but herself for her situation. But she went into this whole thing about how they were manipulating everything and we no longer had free will, that all our decisions were basically being made for us. I'm not exaggerating, she literally said that."

"And what did you say?"

"I told her she was crazy."

"And how did that go down?"

"She packed a bag and walked out. Half her stuff is still here. If you see her, tell her I'm gonna cycle it all if she doesn't come by to pick it up soon."

"You know where she is, then?"

"I know where she *went,* I don't know if she's still there."

"Could you tell me where that is please?"

Todd's brow crinkles. "You still want to try and talk her round? After everything I just told you?"

"Yeah, I . . . See, it's my job to get these off the records as positive outcomes. If they come back or we make a fractional award, that's a positive. But if the record lies dormant for two years it gets purged, and that looks bad on our statistics, you see, because it goes down as a fail." Lydia's pleased with this bit, and tries not to smile—she's supposed to look deeply concerned. "And if we get too many fails, people will think I'm crap at my job. But I can sit with her and take her through the process. If I can find her."

This appeals to Todd, she can see. It would vindicate him. Jene is a loose end in his life he would like to tie off. He asks a few more questions first, but she knows he's going to tell her where she is.

Before Lydia leaves Liberty View she decides to find out if you can see the statue from the roof. She fully expects to get kicked out of this country soon and it could be her last chance, so she steps into an elevator and takes it to the top.

She emerges into the afternoon heat haze, walks across the smooth dark solar panels that make up the roof and yes, she can see the statue—just about. She walks around to one end of the U, adjusting her glasses to use the binocular setting. She leans on the railing and stands there awhile, taking in the view, the calm up here—it feels like she doesn't have to deal with anything that's going on below while she—

"Lydia!"

WHAT THE FUCK.

Lydia spins around to see where the voice came from, the thought already occurring to her that the accent is not American, in fact it's quite like her own—

Three men stand on the rooftop behind her, emerging from the doorway at the base of the U, the one that leads back down into the building. One of them is Hari.

"I've been looking for you," he says, and the three of them march across the rooftop in Lydia's direction.

FOUR

FOUR

FREEDOM OF
THE CITY

Lydia edges back as Hari and the other two approach: she glances behind herself and finds the railing that runs around the edge of the rooftop. There's no fire exit she can see. She's trapped at one end of the U: there's nowhere to go.

The two men with Hari are muttering to each other while eyeing her and grinning and Lydia senses something malevolent about them. They're nothing like the people Hari was hanging out with back in Halifax: heavily tattooed and overdressed for the heat in garish, shiny jackets, worn open over metallic shirts. They half swagger, half stagger, clearly inebriated, and in fact Hari looks wasted too—tired and grimy, his face slack. All three of them look like they're on kettin.

One of the shiny-jacket guys trips on a vent and stumbles and his shiny jacket gapes open, allowing Lydia a glimpse of the gun stuffed in his pocket. She looks at his mate and sees how one side of his jacket hangs lower than the other: he's got a gun too. Her glasses take account of her heart rate and register she's alone with three men and has nowhere to run, and a note pops up telling her to double-blink if she wants to call the police, and Lydia does so. She doesn't even need to speak: her location and images of the situation are automatically attached.

She assumed she was being watched by the cops already, and maybe she still is—but surely they'd react pretty quick when they saw this? Wouldn't they swoop the moment they saw Hari heading her way? She never thought she'd be wishing for *more* police surveillance.

"So this is the girl you fucked back in England?" asks one of the shiny-jacket guys.

"Oi," says Hari, looking embarrassed.

"She's venny," says the other, taking another step towards her. He could reach out and touch her from here and she feels acutely afraid that he'll do so: something in his eyes suggests that's his intention. A notification pops up in her glasses saying the police will arrive in approximately six minutes, and hopefully that's accurate but six minutes is a long time to stand here and not get thrown off a roof.

"Hey, Cale," says Hari, seeming to belatedly realize how close his companion is to touching Lydia. "Don't do that, mate."

The guy called Cale doesn't move back, and instead his mate takes a step towards Lydia too, looking her up and down in that way guys do when they're saving the image for later and don't care that you know it.

"Oi—guys," says Hari. "Come on, I said be cool."

Cale shoots him a venomous glance. "You're fucking telling *us* we're not being cool?" He turns back to Lydia and, as if it's a private joke between her and him, says: "Prick."

Lydia looks past the two strangers to address Hari: "Have you been following me?"

"We followed you up here, yeah," Hari says, "but—"

"And how long have you been following me?"

"You're stalking this girl?" says the other guy to Hari.

"No," says Hari. "Fucksake, Miro, don't say that—" He implores Lydia. "He's joking, he's been with me since yesterday, he knows I haven't been stalking you."

"How the fuck did you find me?" says Lydia.

"I . . . saw you down by the periscopes, like, fifteen minutes ago."

"You're saying it's just a coincidence you found me here?"

"Yeah, it is. I came over to talk to you, but you were already heading inside the building so we waited for you on the steps, then Cale saw you on the roof just now so we came up."

"OK but . . . what the fuck are you *doing* in New York?"

An explosion of laughter from Cale and Miro. "You said she was a friend, man," says Miro.

"Shut the fuck up," replies Hari.

Miro turns sharply and fronts up to Hari. "Don't fucking talk to me like that." He feigns a punch and Hari shrinks back. Miro laughs hard, and is joined by Cale and eventually by Hari himself. They seem to be having those surges of mood and energy you get on kettin, and they might do anything at any moment. The cops' ETA is now four and a half minutes. Lydia still wants to know what's going on here, but for the moment the guys' attention is off her so she's not going to rock the boat.

Abruptly Cale turns back to her and says, giggling, "He came here because of you."

Lydia lets her eyes slide to Hari. "All this way? Just to see me?"

"Not to *see* you," says Hari, exasperated, "*because* of you. Talking to you made me realize I've never *seen* anywhere, and I kept thinking about it, and I had some money from when my dad died—"

"Why didn't you tell me you were coming?"

"You didn't give me a contact."

Actually yes, she remembers very deliberately not doing this. "It was just a one-off—"

"I got that," he says, keen to cut her off, "and that was fine. I came here to see the *city,* I just . . . couldn't stop thinking about it."

"I hope I didn't build it up too much."

He gives her a fried, exhausted, euphoric grin. "It's incredible."

"Glad you're not disappointed. So it's my fault for painting such vivid pictures with words, is that it?"

"I didn't say that—"

"I was joking. So the police haven't talked to you?"

Lydia didn't fully consider these words before speaking them: If she had, she would have anticipated Cale and Miro's reaction. They glance at each other anxiously, then Miro says: "Hari? You talked to the cops?"

"No!" says Hari. "No, no—why would—"

"They've been looking for you for days," says Lydia. "How've you avoided them all this time?"

"Why are they looking for *me*?"

"Because they think you murdered my boss."

Hari laughs. "What?" Then his expression changes as he realizes this time she's not joking.

"Fuck!" says Cale. "That's core as fuck, man."

"Why do they think I murdered your boss?"

"Because you arrived into New York a few hours before he was killed," says Lydia. "Haven't you heard about this? It's all over the feeds."

"My feed's out, it's a roaming problem—why do they think I killed him just because I got here the day he died?"

"Because the cops think I passed on information about him and how to get round our security when I was back in Halifax, maybe—which I didn't, obviously but—"

"Do *you* think I did it?"

Lydia is distracted: Cale and Miro have retreated slightly, and she's wondering if they're conferring over chat and if so what they're saying.

"You *do* think I did it!" Hari says.

"No," Lydia replies, snapping back to the conversation. "If you'd done it you wouldn't hang around waiting to be arrested, would you? And you wouldn't come up to me, the only person in the city who knows . . ." She trails off. The only person in the city who knows him. And he's approached her on a high roof, accompanied by two armed men. She glances nervously behind herself, then blurts: "I've called the police, by the way."

Cale and Miro hear this and dart towards the bottom of the U, to the doorway that leads back down. Hari sees them go, halfheartedly shouts at them to stop—then turns back to Lydia. "What'd you call the police for?"

"Because you fucking scared me!"

"I just came over to say hello—"

"On a high roof, completely wasted, with Tweedletwat and Tweedlecunt in tow—who *were* those guys?"

"I met them in the bar at the hostel, and I didn't know anyone, and they seemed like guys who'd give me, like, an authentic experience of the city."

"I'm assuming they got you to pay for all that authenticity?"

"Yeah . . ." Hari looks down at the rooftop, the grubby solar panels offering a dim reflection. "To be honest they were scaring me but I couldn't get them to piss off."

Lydia smiles, gestures to the door they just disappeared through. "Five minutes with me and they're gone. You're welcome."

Hari's not amused. "Man, I can't fucking *believe* you called the cops on me."

"How have they not found you already? How've you avoided them all this time?"

"I didn't even know they were after me."

"But they can facerec *anyone,* especially if you've been wandering all round the tourist spots; but you've managed to not get picked up for two whole days without even *trying*? It doesn't make sense."

There's a momentary silence between them, and in the midst of this they both notice the sirens approaching. A note pops up to tell Lydia it's taken the cops five minutes and fifty-three seconds to get here, and it invites her to rate this service.

The cops are anticipating a tense standoff, but Hari doesn't give them one: he doesn't resist arrest or threaten to hurl Lydia from the roof if they don't back off, but kneels down with his hands raised as instructed. Every device in the block is flooded with a message telling everyone to stay where they are.

"I'm sorry," Lydia tells Hari while they're waiting for the cops to emerge onto the roof. "They'd have got you eventually anyway, when you went to catch the hopper back."

Hari doesn't answer.

"When were you planning to go back home? To Halifax?" Lydia adds.

"I thought maybe I wouldn't have to. I thought maybe I could stay here."

"Do you know how hard it is to—"

"*Yeah,* I know how hard it is to get leave to remain, thanks. But it happens, doesn't it? People stay here—*you* did." There's a note of pleading in his voice, as if she might help him. But she's not sure she can, or should, or wants to.

ABSOLUTE NEUTRAL

After the cops have taken Hari away, they want to speak to Lydia—which is fine because she wants to speak to them too. She waits for them in the lobby of Liberty View and checks the local feeds.

@GeezLoueeze17 / Cops telling everyone in Liberty View to stay inside—wanted criminal on the roof! Should I go up there and check it out?? / TR83
@happynesta1010 / Guys just checked my sillcam and saw the suspect in the Fitzwilliam murder walking into Liberty View fifteen minutes ago . . . coincidence?? / TR90

The latter post has been picked up and spread, and although the cops haven't announced Hari is in police custody it's common knowledge. He *is* the story now.

A small, stout officer arrives and asks Lydia to take her through what happened on the roof.

"First," Lydia says, "can I just say at no point did he threaten me, and I felt much more intimidated by the other two guys who were with him."

"Other guys?" says the officer.

Lydia explains about the shiny-jacket guys, and how they ran off when they knew the police were coming. "They were right shady little bastards."

The officer raises an eyebrow and highlights this last sentence in the live transcript on her scroll. "So Mr. Dessai approached you."

"Yes, and of course I knew you were looking for him, so I called you straightaway," Lydia says. She's at a loss for how she should play this. Her fear is that the cops will pin Fitz's murder on Hari regardless of whether he did it, and this will look bad for her. So she doesn't want to push them towards that conclusion, or help them build a case against him, by making him out to be dangerous.

However, if he goes down for it—and she reminds herself it's still possible he's guilty—it will look even worse for her if she's been lobbying on his behalf. She knows this seems cold, but she tells herself it's not her fault if the cops pin it on him.

Ultimately she wants to neither drop him in it nor help him out of it, so she relates the sequence of events as neutrally as possible, omitting any mention of his inebriation. (They'll find that out for themselves soon enough.) When she reaches the bit about him finding her entirely by accident, the officer pulls her up on it.

"Wait wait wait—he told you he didn't track you here?"

"Yeah, he saw me over by the periscopes, totally randomly."

"That's a hell of a coincidence."

"That's what I said."

"So he finds you in a city of ten million people when *we* couldn't find *him* in two days."

This is interesting: it really does seem like they don't have her under close surveillance, and she wonders why not. "He also didn't know you were looking for him."

This earns her an odd look from the officer. "I find that *extremely* hard to believe."

"I'm just telling you what he told me." It *is* hard to believe—but that's what makes it such a weird thing to lie about, especially to her. "He said he was just . . . seeing the sights."

"We had *everyone* looking for him, alerts on every account he's got, algos plotting likely patterns of behavior from what we knew about him; we hunted down every image we could and fed it into rec—we even had people on the *street* using their *eyes*. Only way he could've avoided us all that time is if he holed up somewhere indoors, didn't plug in, didn't log on and didn't spend any money. He expects us to believe he was just *walking around*?"

Lydia shrugs.

The officer shakes her head. "Doesn't add up."

She's right, it doesn't. So it must add up to something else. But Lydia's fucked if she knows what it is.

"One last thing, ma'am—why were you here?"

"Sorry?" says Lydia, unprepared for this question and unsure what she should say.

"What brought you here, now?"

"Ms. Southwell," says another voice from behind Lydia. She turns to see Sturges walking up to her, the sleeves of his dress shirt rolled up to reveal spiraling tattoos down his arms. He removes his aviators before speaking to her and jabs the air with them for emphasis as he speaks. "I wanted to come down here in person to thank you for finding that guy. You've done us a considerable service."

"Oh," replies Lydia, "I was just telling your colleague here he came up to me, I didn't really *find* him as such."

"I've seen the footage and you handled it like a pro."

Lydia feels this does not say reassuring things about professionals, but she knows he doesn't literally mean it: He's just trying to flatter her to keep her onside, ready for the next time he needs her to cooperate. The ulterior motive behind his genial attitude is pretty blatant—but still, she appreciates someone being nice to her for a change. "Yeah cheers," she says.

"Let's hope you don't have to deal with any more shit over all this. You've been through more than enough."

Lydia nods as if she agrees.

Sturges offers her a ride back to the residence, which she declines, then he leads the other officer away, saying they need to put together a media statement. For a moment Lydia wonders if she ought to tell them about Jene Connor—but it still seems flimsy, tenuous. She doesn't trust them to follow it up. And she doesn't want to tell them she's making her own inquiries, not yet, because they might tell her to stop.

ABOVE THE SHOE PLACE

The address Todd gave Lydia is over in the Village, in one of the pedestrianized streets where the buildings have crept forward in recent years, pop-up establishments having opened on the sidewalks and never popped down, eventually becoming incorporated into the architecture. The structures are untidy and feel like they're just going to grow unchecked and become entangled like ivy.

Lydia has to pass through a shoe shop to reach the apartment block beyond: she fends off an assistant who insists she has the perfect pair for her, then goes through the doorway at the back and into the lobby. The block no longer has elevators—they've been removed and the elevator shaft knocked through to create more apartments—so Lydia must climb the stairs to the fifth floor. As she does so she passes a lot of people hanging around in clusters: it's not clear to her whether they live in the apartments, or in some other place, or on the stairs. Through a haze of cannavape Lydia glances at their faces, trying not to attract their attention, and calls up Jene's student idee picture, looking for a match.

There's this one girl slumped in the corner of the hallway on the third floor, eyes closed but not asleep, trying to participate in a conversation between two dudes who are ignoring her. Her hair is longer and messier than in the idee, but there's something around the shape of her mouth and nose. It *could* be . . .

Lydia stops as she passes the girl and leans down. "Jene?"

The girl's eyes open and immediately Lydia sees they're more closely set than Jene's. It's not her. The girl looks up at Lydia, puzzled. "You talking to me?"

The dudes stop talking and stare at Lydia.

Lydia straightens up. "Yeah sorry, I thought you were someone else." Before the sentence is finished she's walking quickly on. As she ascends she can hear them laughing and mocking her accent and asking who the fuck Jene is. Lydia arrives at apartment 23 and knocks on the door, really hoping someone lets her inside so she doesn't have to walk back past those people: if she can stay awhile they might be gone when she goes down.

The person who answers the door is not Jene either, so that's not a great start. She's a young woman about the same age as Jene, a little shorter than Lydia: she has dark bobbed hair and porcelain skin that's kind of doughy. She wears a flimsy printed-lace cardigan over a minidress and holds a glass of red wine.

"Yeah?" she says.

"I'm looking for Jene Connor—a friend of hers said she might be here."

"Todd?"

"Yes."

"You're a friend of Todd's?"

"No no," Lydia says, "I just went to her old apartment at Liberty View and he was there."

Lydia suspected this was the answer the young woman wanted to hear, and she's correct. The young woman smirks. "He still lives in that dump?" She speaks with a haughty East Coast drawl. Lydia suspects she might be quite posh, but she's never quite sure with Americans—posh is different here. (She decides she will record this one for her collection.)

"He seems very unhappy, if it pleases you to hear that."

The young woman nods. "It does, it does. But I haven't seen Jene for a few days, I'm sorry."

"Then she *has* been here?"

"She's been crashing here, yeah, more than anywhere else. How come you're looking for her?"

Lydia considers deploying her story about being from the university again, but something tells her to play this one straighter. This woman isn't going to be comparing notes with Todd, so Lydia's free to invent something new. "I'm worried about her. I haven't seen her for a while and she's been sending me weird messages."

A weary look crosses the young woman's face. "That figures. How d'you know her?"

"From NYNU." Lydia's guess is this woman will have gone to a classier institution than NYNU, somewhere they don't give out degrees to tourists and the professors don't give interviews to conspiracy theorists. "My name's Lydia."

"I'm Ondine. Would you like to come in?"

Lydia accepts the invitation and steps inside. Ondine's apartment is wood-paneled and the rooms are small and filled with thrift-store junk. Ondine moves a pile of vintage magazines from the '90s and '00s off a chair and invites Lydia to sit.

"Can I get you a drink?" Ondine asks, putting her glass on the table.

Lydia accepts, feeling this will make her seem more congenial, but resolves to stop at one. Trying to do stuff while drunk is what got her into this mess.

While Ondine turns to the apartment's galley kitchen and searches for another glass, Lydia takes a moment to look around. There's a workspace at the opposite end of the room: a large industrial printer, surrounded by semirecognizable common objects, all of them old-fashioned to some degree and altered in some way. An old laptop computer with a creature bursting from its screen. A chair with human feet. A lamp whose bulb is choked with flowers. When Ondine returns with the glass, she sees Lydia looking and asks, "You like them?"

Lydia's not a hundred percent sure what they are, but Ondine obviously wants the answer to be yes, so that's the answer Lydia gives.

"I look for old printplans in archives," says Ondine, handing Lydia her drink and sitting opposite, "stuff that's like out of copyright or made by dead companies, and I go into the code and manipulate it, and then print it. And these are the results."

"Cool," says Lydia, but now she's worrying that if Ondine moves in art circles, it's possible she'll recognize Lydia: perhaps not straightaway, but it might click for her. Lydia doesn't remember having met this woman at any openings or art school exhibitions, and certainly hasn't made a note of her. While Ondine explains about her process and how she destroys all her modded printplans after printing the final copy so each work is unique, Lydia runs a facerec to see if Ondine is in any of her stored images. She's not there but people can block themselves on those things. Hopefully Ondine is either a complete dilettante or a fierce outsider, entirely uninvolved in the scene.

"So," says Ondine, "what sort of things did Jene message you about?"

Lydia has no quick answer for this, so she covers by sipping her wine, which is the strong stuff they make over in Jersey: they'd never serve anything like this at the receptions Lydia goes to. She's missed cheap booze. "Oh, they were pretty incoherent really," she says, which seems a plausible catchall reply.

Ondine nods. "Sounds about right."

But Lydia sees she's missed a trick, and adds: "But she often mentioned the Logi, actually. Like, weird rambling messages about them."

Ondine nods more vigorously. "She talks about them *a lot.* There was a stretch a few months ago where she wouldn't go out, she was convinced they'd hired someone to, I dunno . . . eliminate her or whatever?"

"Wow."

"I tried telling her it seemed *highly* unlikely. Like, she's not that important? I mean, I didn't say *that* but I said it in a, you know, more sensitive way, I forget exactly how I said it."

"I didn't realize she'd got so bad."

"It was hard for me to do my work, y'know, in such a small space, because she was here *all the time,* just reading and downloading stuff and *inking* it and leaving piles of it everywhere. I sort of hinted I needed her out of my way for a while. I feel bad, but she needs help. Like, *real* help."

"Todd said something similar."

Ondine rolls her eyes. "Todd doesn't give a fuck about anything except being right."

"Where is she now?"

"She said if I needed some space it was cool and she could crash with other friends. Thing is," Ondine says, rubbing her right eye, "usually I'd expect her to message to ask when she can come back to stay. Seems like she feels safer here, for some reason. . . ." She throws up the hand that was rubbing her eye, making a gesture of resignation, and Lydia notices how graceful and fluid it is: she moves like a dancer. "Last thing she sent was just a picture of a duck she saw in the park on Saturday morning, and I replied to her like, *nice duck!,* and I was expecting her to ask if she could come back, but nothing. . . ."

Saturday morning: the day of the conference. Lydia tells herself this is not, in itself, meaningful. Just because she wants it all to fit together doesn't mean it does.

"Have you tried to get in touch with her since then?" Lydia asks.

Ondine looks at the floor. "No and I know that's bad. I've been worried but I didn't want to reach out because if she's OK I don't want to bring her back too soon because I need a break. So I told myself she'd be fine, she's not my problem, she can look after herself." She taps her glasses. "I'll ping her now."

"Yeah, of course."

"If she responds we can go find her right away. I mean, if you want to."

"That'd be great. What do you think might have happened?"

Ondine shrugs, picks up her scroll, idly unfurls it and lets it snap closed again. Its back skin is like a black lace handkerchief, the kind of thing a Victorian widow would cry into at a funeral; when she unfurls it a puff of holographic glitter rises from the screen. She opens and closes it over and over for a minute or so before she speaks again, and in that time Lydia learns the value of being silent instead of asking another question, because sometimes people will fill that silence of their own accord. "I don't know," Ondine says eventually. "Something stupid. To herself, or to someone else . . . I mean, she never hurt anyone before," she adds hurriedly. "I don't wanna make out she was a *psycho* or anything. But if she stopped caring about what happened to her, y'know . . ." She looks down at her open scroll and summons an image from it, then holds up the scroll for Lydia to see.

The image is a loop, showing Ondine with her arm around a young woman with hooded eyes and sharp features: her dark, springy, curly hair half obscures Ondine's face. The woman is Jene, of course, but Lydia has to look closely to recognize her as the person from the student idee. In that picture she looked plainer and more withdrawn, her hair more wavy and lank, but maybe that was just down to bad lighting or different filters or a hangover on the day the idees were being done, because here Lydia sees an image of someone livelier and more confident. Jene and Ondine are in the park on a winter's day, the air just about cold enough for their breath to fog, and they're enjoying the novelty of it. The loop is almost seamless but you can see the join where one breath dissipates and another (in truth, the same breath repeated) begins. They both look utterly untroubled: but then, this is just a moment. Anyone can forget their troubles in a moment.

Lydia doesn't ask for a copy of the loop—it seems too personal—but she makes sure to remember Jene can also look like this. And Lydia feels she ought to remember it anyway: this is the first thing that's made her see Jene as a *person,* rather than an absence, or a puzzle, or a solution.

Lydia hands the scroll back and asks Ondine if she can use the bathroom.

Lydia doesn't particularly need to use the bathroom, but she wants to have a look around. She's not sure what she's looking for: if nothing else it's fascinating to see an ordinary New Yorker's apartment, as she never usually gets to go in any. She wonders if Ondine owns this place—if not she's certainly bedded herself in. Every scrap of wall space seems to be used for storage or decoration.

Lydia enters the bathroom and sits on the toilet. A pile of fruit boxes filled with untidy stacks of white paper has been left in the opposite corner. She recalls what Ondine said about Jene inking things off, and she reaches for the top sheet and reads it.

It's the press release for a strategy game, like the ones her mum plays: it's called *Take Back the Night* and is set in a dystopian future where an entire city has been seized by a criminal gang. You play a member of a civilian defense group sworn to succeed where the authorities failed (it says here) and interact with real players and/ or ayaies in a co-op to defeat the gang. The document runs to several pages, and after opening with a breathless description of its scenario and accolades for other games by the same developer, it settles into a dry list of facts and figures about downloads and engagements, game-hours clocked up by players, recognition factor, in-game sales made, etc. The press release is dated six months ago, but Lydia makes a quick search and can find no reference to the game, only a song of the same title by someone called Justin Timberlake.

Lydia peels more sheets off the pile. There's a lot of this. It can't have been cheap, inking it all off. Under the press release she finds reams of chat which seems to be between the game's programmers—far too much to read but lots of it self-evidently mundane, lists of bugs and suggestions for fixes, comments on design and feedback on narrative, discussion of market research . . .

Lydia stays in the bathroom long after she's finished using the toilet, lifting each box aside so she can examine the one underneath. The lower ones seem entirely filled with inkouts of raw code. Lydia knows very little about coding—she dropped it after Year 11 and what they taught her is probably out of date (the school's computers certainly were)—but could this be the code for *Take Back the Night,* or part of it at least? The complete data for a game like this would be impossible to ink off, with all the art, sound and animation files, but what's on this inkout could be all the actual *code*—maybe. She's not sure.

Why ink it off, though? Why ink *any* of this off?

There's a knock on the door.

"You OK in there?" asks Ondine.

"Oh—yes," says Lydia. "I was just . . ." She wonders whether to claim she's suffering from some digestive or medical malady. But it's reasonable to have some curiosity about this stack of paper, she decides, and opens the door. "I got distracted by looking at all this."

"Oh god," says Ondine. "I keep meaning to throw it away. I told her if she wanted to keep it she needed to find somewhere else to put it. It's not safe, having all this paper around—what if it caught fire? You know buildings used to catch fire *all the time*?"

"Wasn't that because of cigarettes?"

"Yeah, but the cigarettes needed something to burn, didn't they? That's why I keep all this paper in the bathroom, I figure it's not gonna catch fire in here and if it does, there's plenty of water to put it out with."

"So Jene inked all this?"

"Uh-huh." Ondine picks up some of the papers and leafs through them.

"Did she ever say why?"

"She just said it was important to keep it all in case it got deleted. But it's just some junk about a game. I didn't even know my inker *worked,* I got it from a junk shop because I thought I could mod it into a shoe rack or something. . . ."

"I've . . . got plenty of space in my apartment. Sorry, I know you've only just met me but—"

"I would be *overjoyed* if you took it away—I sort of can't bring myself to do anything with it." Ondine flips through more of the pages but she's not reading them. "I don't think this stuff did her any good. It can't really be important—can it?"

TEMPORAL CONCERTINA

There's no way Lydia can casually walk into the residence while carrying this much paper, not least because she has to do it in three trips. She briefly considers asking for help from the porch cop, but decides not to push it. She walks past him, just a normal modern young woman carrying two boxes of paper, it's what all the cool kids are doing these days—

"Heard you caught him!" the cop says.

She looks up and sees it's a different cop than the one from this morning—she's started noting their numbers. She's not sure what she might do with this information but it feels like the kind of thing she ought to pay attention to.

"Sorry, what?" she replies, because she wasn't really paying attention to what he said.

"The suspect."

"Oh! Yeah, he approached me when I was—out."

"You OK, though?" Porch cop seems genuinely concerned for her welfare.

"Fine, yeah. Absolutely fine." These boxes are heavy and the cab's waiting—

"Dumb mistake on his part to talk to you, the only one in the city who knows him."

"I think that's exactly why he talked to me."

"Because he figured you'd help him out?"

"No no, he didn't even know he was in trouble. He just wanted to say hello."

The cop shrugs. "Some people are good at acting innocent. Some even convince themselves they are. Let's hope he's our guy."

"Well, we'll see," says Lydia meaninglessly to bring the conversation to an end, and she enters the residence. Madison isn't here, *thank fuck,* so Lydia puts her boxes down and heads back to the cab for the rest—only to find the cop has brought them in for her. She thanks him, he nods and returns to the porch, where no doubt he'll report her box-related activity to his superiors.

You've been gone a long time, says Fitz as Lydia carries the last of the boxes into her room.

Yeah, it's been quite a day, says Lydia, trying to remember which of the things buzzing around her head happened today and which of them happened yesterday: to her surprise she realizes they *all* happened today. Fitz perceives time very differently than she does because he doesn't have access to the constant updates humans take for granted: he absorbs events in larger packages, not the data plankton she's used to. Time isn't a constant, and for some reason humans have worked hard to make it feel like it's passing faster—but to Lydia, today seems to have lasted an eternity.

It takes awhile to put events in order for Fitz because Lydia keeps remembering more details and having to go back and fill them in, but it's helping her get it straight in her own head.

What makes you think all this paper is important? asks Fitz.

I don't know, but Jene thought it was important. Anyway it's all I've got to go on at the moment. Lydia feels increasingly alarmed as she feels the truth of this: It is all she has to go on. She hasn't found Jene, she's just found this. *I don't know if any of it adds up to much,* she admits. *I mean that death threat wasn't really anything, and nor was that professor woman, and now I'm looking for some girl who went mad and started inking out game code. I don't know what I'm doing really.*

Don't underrate yourself, Lydia. You have good instincts.

Lydia needs to take advantage of Madison not being here, so she takes a box of the inked-out code down to the study and feeds it into Fitz's scanner. He used the scanner constantly, and it's a top-of-the-range model—he wrote a lot of his correspondence longhand, fed it in here and sent it over to the embassy's typing pool. It scans in under 1.2 seconds with crystal clarity (in fact, drawing the next page into place takes far more time than the actual scanning) and can pull text with high precision. So it's the best tool for the job she could ask for, but even so, one missing page or a blurred spot might make the entire thing fail. She doesn't even know how much of the game is on these pages, or even if it will produce something functional without the elements—she may be able to draft in some generic art and sound, but she's not sure how she'll tell the game where to find it.

Do you mind if I sit on your sofa? Lydia asks. It's strange speaking to Fitz down here: she hasn't done so since he died, in case Madison overheard.

Why would I mind?

I dunno. It's just . . . that was your place.

By all means sit there.

She sits on the sofa and starts looking through the other inkouts she brought down: the chat logs. When Madison comes back Lydia will sense her approaching and can grab the paper out of the scanner and pretend she came in here to read one of Fitz's books—in fact, she gets one of the books down so she can have it on hand for this purpose. She places the box the code came in behind the arm of the sofa, out of sight: it would be easier to bring all the boxes down here, but a pile of boxes would be far more conspicuous, so she'll have to bring them down one at a time. She doesn't want to answer any questions about why she's doing this.

The thing about this, she tells Fitz, *is I get why Jene wanted to ink off the press release, because that explains what the game is.*

Yes.

And presumably she wanted to ink off the code because she was looking for something in the game?

Or, says Fitz, *because she was trying to preserve it?*

It's not really preserving it though, because this isn't all of it. If she wanted to preserve it she could've just burned a copy onto an imager, that would work.

The curious thing is, inking it off is exactly what I would do. Maybe she just didn't trust digital media?

But why keep all this chat? says Lydia, running her thumb across the edges of the pages. *There's loads of it. Maybe if I knew anything about coding I might get why it's important.*

I'm afraid I won't be much help, Fitz replies. *It's all a mystery to me.*

Lydia starts reading the pages—not every word obviously, or even most of the words, but glancing down each page and taking in what they're about. The deeper she goes into them the more baffling in-jokes and office politics she finds: it's like being a temp at the edge of a workspace, not really part of the team, hearing everything but unsure if she's allowed to join in. It's clear they all work remotely and rely on this chat to connect them—and accordingly this can't be the complete chat log, there'll be far more than this. Someone—Jene? or someone else?—has curated it. So what were they trying to keep?

Lydia's about a third of the way in, explaining the contents to Fitz as she goes, when she starts to grasp the story underlying it. She becomes so absorbed in it, she barely wonders why Madison hasn't yet returned. She pauses only to feed more paper into the scanner, or occasionally to fetch another box from upstairs.

The team's boss is a French guy called Jules who takes the ironic xenophobic jokes of his team with good humor—but suddenly one day Jules is gone. No one knows why he's quit. There's talk he might have been forced out, or resigned on a point of principle. What no one can believe is he appears to have handed over the ayaies that do a lot of the rote work of the operation, which he personally holds the patents on. The project will continue without him. A newly installed manager passes down decisions without getting involved in less formal group chat.

The tone of the chat is far more businesslike from this point on. Some of the team note their queries up the chain have gone unanswered. Some have been given whole chunks of code to insert without being told what it's for. They're puzzled playtesting is happening without their consultation. They're all being required to work punishingly long hours.

But this story lacks an ending. It's half a story, or maybe two-thirds. As the pages dwindle, Lydia fights to hold the picture of it all in her head. Several of the team have left under a cloud and the game, though it's coming together, no longer generates the excitement it did. Everyone just wants it to be over.

On the last page, Lydia finds a message from one of the senior designers, a woman called Paz:

> So I was playtesting the Shopping Mall Siege side-quest and used the jerry-rigged pay phone you find there, because you know that's been buggy, and I heard these overlapping voices and I thought great, now it's gone buggy in a whole different way. One of the voices was meant to be there but the other one was like narration and didn't seem to connect to anything in the game, so I figured a sound file had been copied in by mistake or something and I logged it, though whether they take action on bugs or not seems totally random now. Kept playing, finished the quest, mostly everything looked solid.
>
> Then I logged out of the game and went to make myself some soup and, like, I don't know if you ever get intrusive thoughts? I used to get them a lot but my medication dampens them down these days. But they just started up, random stuff, I couldn't focus on anything. It took me an hour to think straight again afterwards. I can't explain how disturbing it was. Thing is, the thoughts didn't seem like they were in my voice, if you see what I mean? They were in the voice I'd heard in the game, the buggy voice on the phone. I was gonna report it but then I thought: What if this is exactly what the game's meant to do?
>
> Fuck it, I'm out of here. I can't keep working on this thing. And I strongly advise all of you not to play it.

Lydia reads this page again, dizzy from absorbing it all while explaining it to Fitz, and lays her head on the arm of the sofa, thinking: Maybe this story lacks an ending because it hasn't happened yet?

YESTERDAY'S CLOTHES

Lydia awakens to find she's still on Fitz's sofa, wearing her clothes from yesterday, and the final pages of inkout are stuck to her face. She has drooled on them. They slowly come detached from her face and fall on the floor. This, she feels, is not how real detectives handle important evidence. What time is it? Where are her glasses? She wonders if she's alone in the house or—

There's a noise in the kitchen. Someone's moving around.

Then she hears: *Are you awake yet?* Inevitably, it's Madison.

Er, yes, Lydia replies. Her eyes dart to the scanner—a pile of inked-out code still lies on its out-tray. A larger pile of already-scanned paper is on the floor. She can't remember how much was left to scan when she fell asleep last night. She has a not inconsiderable hangover from talking to Fitz.

Madison steps into the doorway. Lydia feels the waves of disapproval and anger coming off her before she speaks. *Where did you go yesterday?*

I had things to do.

You said you were stepping out for some fresh air and never came back.

Oh god. She did say that. She felt quite drunk at the time, and then loads of stuff happened and it all went hazy. *Yes—sorry. I had to meet someone very urgently.*

And you couldn't have informed me of this?

There wasn't time. Sorry.

I messaged you repeatedly.

Lydia now recalls blocking Madison's messages yesterday morning. *Really? I didn't get them. I don't know what happened there.*

You were gone all day. I needed you.

Lydia can feel her future employment prospects, already very low, vanishing to a dot on the horizon. *I really am sorry,* she says because she doesn't know what else to say. The worst part is, it's not true: She is not, in fact, sorry. She just wishes it hadn't happened, which is a different thing.

Why were you sleeping in here?

Although Lydia can't lie about this, it may be possible for her to pick her way around the truth. The danger is if she hits a point where she can't, it'll be obvious she was being less than honest with her previous answers. *I didn't mean to,* she tells Madison. *I was up late reading.* Her best hope is Madison simply doesn't care enough about Lydia and her life to inquire further, or ask about the pile of paper on the floor.

What's that pile of paper on the floor? Madison asks.

Someone gave it to me yesterday. Lydia tries to make this as offhand as possible: she's not being evasive, it's just not worth going into. *They wanted it out of their way.* It's hitting her now that not only is she hungover, she's also incredibly, *incredibly* tired—not just from the physical exertion of walking around the city all day but also the multiple deceptions, the encounter with Hari, talking to the police, and on top of all that the constant whirring of her mind. She needs a day off from this and she's not going to get one. Maybe she can deflect the conversation on to Madison instead. *Where were you last night?*

Madison considers whether to reject this as none of Lydia's business. *At the embassy,* she says. *To discuss the latest developments.*

Right—Hari. Of course.

I hear it was you who found him. Well done.

He found me, really. It's not like I was out there combing the streets for him.

No, you were dealing with this emergency of yours, weren't you.

I didn't know anything about him being in New York, you know. Not until the police told me.

So I understand. Madison steps over to the paper on the floor and points at it. *Could you move all this out of the way?* The word *this* resonates with strong hints of *junk.*

Of course, Lydia says, lurching forward to pick up the paper—

and her head throbs from the sudden movement. She pushes through the pain and gathers the inkout before Madison can get a good look at it, though Madison won't be able to *read* them, will she? Or even recognize what the documents are? But she can't be sure of this. She searches for the box the inkout came in: it's not where she expects it to be. *So you were at the embassy all night?* she asks, a fairly empty question employed to distract Madison from thinking about the paper.

It went on late. I used one of the rooms there.

So what are they saying about the arrest?

I can't talk about that.

Of course not, sorry. Lydia dumps the paper back in the box, and to her alarm realizes she has no idea if it's still in order. *Er, I think that's all of it,* she says.

Thank you, says Madison. She steps onto the sofa, kneels against the back and starts running a flat-ended tool around the edge of the broken canvas.

What are you doing?

Fixing this. I don't need your help right now.

Lydia wasn't offering her help. She is surprised to see Madison doing manual work though: She doesn't seem the type. Maybe she couldn't get a technician from the embassy to come and fix it. Maybe she's got a reason for wanting it fixed quickly.

Anyway Lydia shouldn't hang around here, she should take full advantage of the distraction. *I'll get out of your way,* she says and walks quickly towards the study door, wondering if Madison can tell she's hiding anything. She has little experience of this: she never had cause to mislead Fitz.

I may need you later, says Madison.

Fine, replies Lydia. It isn't, but whatever.

When Lydia reaches the relative safety of her room she looks in her niche: The scanner has copied its output there in the form of a text-file, which she checks against the inkout. There were four boxes of code, of which she's done two and most of a third, and she's worried now that the third box isn't in sequence anymore. She might be able to scan the rest with her glasses, but it'd take ages and be far less reliable—if the light bounces off one page in a weird way the whole thing might be fucked. But who knows when she'll get another chance to use the scanner?

She peels off yesterday's clothes and mulls it over in the shower. She's not sure whether Fitz can see her in there: he seems to be able to see things. She drifts off into wondering how you can see if you have no form, since the optic nerve is a physical thing that reacts to light. Maybe he doesn't "see" as such, but senses what's going on via ripples in whatever state he's in, or something? To be fair she doesn't exactly know how her own eyes work, so arguably it's unreasonable for her to expect a dead alien to know how his ghost eyes work.

She uses the tilepad next to the shower controls to check the feeds, but since the reports of Hari's arrest there's been no actual news about the murder.

@THE_LAST_SLICE / OPINION: Why the Fitzwilliam murder has been a long time coming—and should have been foreseen / TR77

@FACTS4FRIENDS / Leaked CIA comms reveal new arrest in Fitzwilliam case is "agent of foreign power" / TR49

@ WHAT_ARE_YA? / Wake up! "Fitzwilliam" "murder case" is pure distraction—he never existed and his usefulness was at an end / TR23

There are people who think you never existed in the first place, Lydia remarks.

It's a shame my murderer wasn't one of them, he replies.

The deadpan joke takes Lydia by surprise and she laughs, accidentally breathing in water from the shower in the process and suffering a coughing fit.

It doesn't surprise me, Fitz adds. *There are plenty of humans who think my entire civilization is a hoax.*

Lydia is more than familiar with this notion. In fact, when she messaged her dad to say she'd got into LSTL, he replied with a ted that went into the theory in detail. She wasn't sure if he believed it or if he was just negging her like always. Anyway she never bothered getting in touch with him again, so that's the last she heard from him.

Did anyone ever try telling you that to your face? she asks Fitz.

Yes—someone once asserted I was a puppet.

A literal puppet?

Or some kind of mechanically engineered thing, or a hologram. I'm not clear why they believe your governments would collude on this—it would involve enormous effort, and for what benefit?

Lydia has spent quite some time thinking on this, and never got around to talking to Fitz about it while he was still alive. *I guess they think it's like how people in power used to use gods or, like, the idea of gods, to back up their decisions. It's a way of passing on responsibility. You know what I mean?*

No.

That's because I'm not explaining it very well. She steps out of the shower. *People in power often find it useful to have a higher authority, or some outside element they can blame for anything that's unpopular or goes badly, right? Once they'd have blamed the gods. Then they moved on to other countries, so the Americans would say it was the Russians' fault and the Russians would blame the Americans. Or the economy, like we have to cut this and get rid of that for the good of the economy.*

So people think we were invented by your authorities as an all-purpose scapegoat.

It sort of makes sense.

Does it?

Well, not really, but I can see why people think it. Things were really falling apart before your lot turned up, y'know. Major countries descending into chaos, wars breaking out like forest fires. And also, actual forest fires. Then you got here and it was all about pulling together to take the opportunities on offer, and that dictated a lot of what we could and couldn't do, and politicians do kind of use that as a way of passing the buck.

Ah, I think I see. So people believe it was a ploy to deflect criticism and create unity.

Yeah, some people believe that. But some people just don't want the world to be bigger than it is. Freaks them out. It's easier to believe it's an elaborate conspiracy.

Is it?

For some people it is, yeah.

She puts her glasses back on and finds a note from Ondine.

CHESS PLAYERS

At midday Lydia sits in Madison Square Park watching people play chess. The old pros who pitch up here play the tourists and students and hipsters for money, and you can't use an ayaie to advise your moves, they're strict about that and have an enforcer to kick the crap out of anyone caught cheating. The crowds love it when that happens, it's all part of the fun. Lydia sometimes comes down here when she has an afternoon off, and one time she saw some little smartarse getting caught cold. The enforcer threw him in a dumpster. It was quite satisfying to watch.

Ondine said she'd meet Lydia here, and together they'd meet this guy who knows something about where Jene is—but there's no sign of her yet. Lydia pings her to check. The reply from Ondine comes moments later:

Yeah sorry, I really did mean to turn up, honestly, but ultimately I realized I really don't like this guy and don't want to see him again

How reassuring. Lydia pings back: Who is he???

Just some sketchy loser who was always hanging around my friends, Ondine replies. He's bad news but that doesn't mean he hasn't seen Jene

Lydia bites her lip and sends: WHAT IS HIS NAME AND HOW DO I RECOGNISE HIM

A minute later Ondine gets back to her with: Oh yeah he's called Marius here's a pic

This last message is written on an image of a scruffy man with a blotchy complexion, a little older than she is, maybe thirty? His hair is shoulder-length and dirty orange. Lydia sweeps the words aside to get a clearer look at him, then she looks up. . . .

There he is, in the crowd watching the chess, drinking a coffee. He sees her and makes eye contact, then heads in her direction. "Sketchy loser" is fair. He's twitchy, wears thick boots and a long brown coat that's really unnecessary in this weather, and she can't help wondering if he's hiding a gun under it. Lydia assesses her surroundings: there're lots of witnesses, he won't be able to try anything. She is certainly not going anywhere with him.

Marius stops about three meters away, looks Lydia up and down and asks if her name is Lydia.

"Who wants to know?" she replies.

"Ondine said you'd be here." His voice is hoarse and a little shaky. "She said you're looking for Jene?"

Lydia nods and Marius sits by her.

"So how do you know her?" he asks.

"NYNU," replies Lydia.

"And you haven't heard from her since Saturday either?"

"No."

He nods. "I'm pretty sure she's dead." He says this with little emotion, as if it's just one of those things, and sips his coffee.

"Why?"

"Because she's crazy. I mean like *scary* crazy. She's up and then she's down, she's scared and then she's, like, euphoric. I've known a lot of people who killed themselves," he adds as if expecting Lydia to contradict this. "I know the signs."

Lydia's unsure what he expects her to say. "Sorry about your friends."

He shrugs. "I stopped feeling sorry for them awhile ago. I carry them around with me, that's enough. Someone else can feel sorry for them. That probably sounds kind of harsh to you."

He's posturing, and Lydia finds it tiresome. "It's important I find out what happened to Jene."

"She's dead, trust me. People come to me when they're ready to die, I don't know why."

Or you seek them out, you creep. "So she came to you . . . when?"

"Last week, Wednesday, she turned up at my apartment after Ondine kicked her out. She seemed upset, shaken—*broken,* really. We got high and fucked. That's another sign someone's on the way out, when they start fucking like each time could be the last."

Christ this guy's really dull and unpleasant. Lydia can see why Ondine didn't want to come. "And then what?"

"She just hung out at mine, we talked. Sometimes I'd read books and she'd just stare into space. Didn't use her scroll or glasses, like she was offgrid—in fact one night I woke up and found her messing with my apartment's data box, trying to wipe any trace of her being there."

"Did she manage it?"

He nods. "Cloud and all. I asked her where she learned to do that, she said you can teach yourself anything if you have enough time on your hands."

"And when did she leave?"

"On Saturday she seemed more chill, much happier. That evening she went out to get some Cokes, or at least that's what she said, and I didn't see her again."

"But if she's dead, surely someone will have found her and the police will know?"

He shrugs again. "Depends how she did it. But maybe. I don't get involved with cops."

Lydia pings Ondine: Sorry but someone needs to check with cops if she's been found dead. Can you?

"So," she says to Marius, "would you prefer if I kept your name out of it?"

He shrugs. That's getting really annoying now.

Ondine pings back: Sure, I'll do it

"What it is," Lydia tells Marius, "is she might have been in some kind of trouble before she came to you."

"Probably, but she didn't talk to me about it."

"No hints? No kind of sense she was carrying around any secrets, or I don't know, anything?"

Marius stares at her for a few moments, unblinking, unspeaking. Then he reaches into his inside coat pocket and brings out a scroll. He unfurls it—the back is skinned to look like an old Chinese take-out menu—then draws a pattern on it with his finger. Four small images of women rise to stand on its surface, all of them younger than Marius. They vary in appearance—two look like teenagers but one is heavily modded and wildly dressed, the other looks very clean and preppy. A third is a bright, cheerful art-teacher type with hair piled up on her head. The fourth is Jene.

"I told you I carry them around with me," says Marius.

Lydia stares at them. "These are all your friends who killed themselves?" She's seen these kind of representations at funerals and so on, ones you can talk to and they'll parrot the kind of stuff that person used to say. But it was always seen as a comforting thing: They wouldn't say anything that surprised you because it was all stuff you'd heard them say before. They weren't going to spill the family secrets or anything like that.

"I pull together everything they left about themselves online," says Marius, "everything they did and liked and didn't like—"

"But people aren't honest about themselves online. They say things they don't do and do things they don't say—"

"So it's how they wanted to be instead of who they were. I'm cool with that."

"OK, you've got a pocketful of sad, dead women—how does this help me?"

"I let them add anything they like, anything they were maybe afraid to talk about, anything they wanted to get off their chest."

"You do this *before* they're dead?"

Marius nods. "Jene talked to hers after I went to sleep one night. I dunno what she said—but if you want to ask her anything, go for it."

Lydia looks down at the figure on the scroll. This looks more like the first picture she saw, the one on her student record: withdrawn, eyes cast slightly down and into the middle distance. If she asks this mini-Jene, this Jene genie, how will she know she can trust the answer? How will she know the real Jene was being truthful when she said it? How will she know Marius hasn't fed this information in himself?

Well, all she can do is ask.

She looks around the park and sees towering buildings on all sides, the sun directly overhead, casting no shadows to speak of.

She wonders if she should do this somewhere more secluded, in case someone's watching or listening in. But she doesn't want to go somewhere more secluded with Marius. So she'll have to take the risk.

She addresses the figure and says hello.

"Hi," says Jene, snapping into life. The other three women fade back into the scroll.

"I'm sorry you died." This is a ridiculous thing to say and when Lydia looks up she expects to see Marius smirking at her, but he's still looking at Jene and listening.

"Thanks," says Jene without much feeling. This could be a shortcoming of the ayaie that drives her, but Lydia suspects it's authentic to the real Jene.

"Jene," Marius says suddenly, "did you know Lydia when you were alive?"

"I don't think so," says Jene.

Lydia's eyes travel up to Marius, who looks back at her coolly.

"I thought I'd seen you somewhere before," he says. "I ran a facerec. You were the translator for that Logi who got murdered. You can't have gone to NYNU, you'd have been at language school."

Fuck. She knows her picture has been in the news but not with her hair this color, and people are so bombarded with images every day, she hadn't expected anyone to actually recognize her. He's a better detective than she is. "Yes," she says.

He smiles. "I didn't need you to confirm it."

"So . . ."

He points at the chess players. "I'm gonna walk back over there and watch those guys for a bit. Just come give me my scroll back after you ask what you need to ask." He stands and is about to walk away before he says: "You should be careful. If I can figure you out, other people can." And then he walks back to the crowd, which has grown, with a hubbub of excitement coming from it: maybe someone's been caught cheating.

The most annoying thing, of course, is that Marius is right. She needs to get a shift on if she's got any chance of getting to the bottom of all this.

Lydia addresses Jene again. "Were you in some kind of trouble before you died?"

"I knew about the voice in the game," Jene replies. "I tried to tell people. No one believed me."

"What voice?" says Lydia.

"The voice in the game."

Obviously Jene didn't supply this avatar with more information than that. Lydia asks what she was going to do about it.

"It wouldn't make any difference to tell anyone," says Jene. "So I'm going to kill the voice."

FIVE

DEPRESSING PASTORAL SCENE

You're just in time, says Madison when Lydia returns to the residence to find her completing the repairs on the canvas. *Press your hand there.* She indicates a spot near where the bullet hit: she seems to have laid a new layer over the top of the entire canvas. Lydia has never touched the canvas before. She splays her hand on the surface: it looks like glass but feels like very stiff paper, the kind you'd use for painting watercolors. *Press down harder,* says Madison. *Use both hands.* Lydia obeys. Then Madison runs that blunt tool all around the edge of the canvas again, and steps back.

Can I stop pressing down now? Lydia asks.

Slowly. Take one hand away at a time.

Lydia takes her left hand away, then her right hand—and the canvas returns to life, colors springing to its surface.

Good, says Madison.

Lydia steps back to stand next to her and they watch the image on the canvas take shape. It's a pastoral scene: a field with a barn on the horizon, rendered in an almost naive style. But in the foreground is a secluded ditch, muddy at the bottom, and Lydia's eye is drawn to it even though it's the darkest part of the image. It's like a bog that sucks in your gaze.

I've never seen it look like that before, says Lydia.

It'll take awhile to pick up on the mood of the room. This will be whatever image it was showing when it was broken.

Lydia is startled by this casual remark. *You mean when Fitz was killed?*

Well, yes.

But it might be important, surely?

You mean it might tell us who killed him?

Maybe.

It doesn't work like that, Lydia, says Madison with a gently patronizing air. *It reacts to emotions, he won't have left a message in it during his dying moments. Anyway look at it—I can't see any clues in there, can you?*

Lydia peers at the canvas, searching for something to prove Madison wrong. But the scene is empty of anything significant, as far as she can tell, and all it's giving her is a sense of unease. She tells her glasses to save the image, then goes to leave the study.

Where are you going? asks Madison.

Upstairs.

I told you I needed your help.

I thought you just meant with that, says Lydia, pointing at the canvas.

No, there's much more I need you for.

While Lydia was out, Madison has amassed fresh questions about Fitz's calendar, about funding allocations, about projects to which he'd given tentative support but hadn't yet committed. Lydia has to muster the patience from somewhere to deal with all this, hoping that the faster they get through it, the faster she can go upstairs and talk to Fitz. But each matter they resolve seems to give rise to several more, and it's extremely hard to pay attention what with everything else that's going on and how drunk she feels right now.

Please could you stop spinning on that chair? says Madison irritably.

Y'what? says Lydia.

The chair. You keep spinning on it.

Yes.

Could you stop it please?

Why?

I find it distracting.

Sorry. It's just, I'm a bit . . .

Yes, I can see—Look, what's this devised theater event about? Why are we sponsoring this? Madison holds out an inkout that's written in Logisi and Lydia lets her glasses scan the code in the corner, so her scroll pulls up the relevant English version from Fitz's files.

Oh, says Lydia when she sees what it is. *That's the thing Anders Lewton is doing.*

The man you assaulted?

That's the guy, yes.

I see. Madison looks down at the document, then puts it to one side. *I think we'll review that.*

Lydia starts with alarm. *But you—*

Madison looks up. *But what?*

It's just, sponsoring his event was part of the agreement that he wouldn't press charges over the, er, incident. The main part, really. So if you pull out—

I realize that, Lydia, and I sympathize—but I'm afraid Fitz and I differed on this issue. I don't think this is how we ought to conduct business.

I'm so sorry, says Fitz.

It's my own fault, Lydia replies, lying facedown on her bed. *You didn't punch that guy. You didn't even tell me to.*

She's being very harsh. Not just on you, but on me and the event. I didn't support it only because of what happened with you. I rather resent the suggestion I'd put my name to an unworthy project.

I could go to prison because of this, Lydia responds testily, appealing for perspective.

Sorry, yes—of course. Maybe if you find out who killed me, that might earn you a little credit, and they might reconsider? Did you learn anything useful from this person you went to meet?

Oh . . . possibly. I didn't like him. I need to look into some other stuff first.

She has a note from Ondine. The police don't have any record of Jene's body being found—but Ondine has reported her missing, which should speed matters along.

Lydia wakes to find it's dark. She checks her fitstats and discovers she fell asleep at 19:28. It's now 02:14. She turns over and prepares to go back to sleep, but then it strikes her—is the study free?

Fitz? she says, because maybe he knows. But there's no reply. Maybe alien ghosts need sleep too.

Lydia heads downstairs, treading as lightly as she can, with a box of inkout under her arm. If Madison, or anyone else, sees her, she was just going downstairs to get herself a drink. With . . . a box full of paper. She passes the guest bedroom and thinks she detects Madison's presence behind it, but can't be sure. She continues down the stairs—

And the study door is open and the lights are off. As Lydia slips inside the study, she sees a cop is still stationed on the porch. She wonders what would happen if she told the cop there was an intruder and led him to the room where Madison is. Get him all hyped up and jumpy first. Make sure she can play it as an honest mistake on her part, and they'd write it off as an accident. That cop's probably itching for an excuse to take a pop at a Logi. They hate having to be deferential to anyone, you can tell. Maybe she could engineer it. Wouldn't make *all* her problems go away but it'd sort some of them out.

This train of thought clatters through her head at great speed and is gone. She can't do that. Not just for moral reasons, though there is that. She doesn't think she could carry it off even if she wanted to. She dismisses it as a tangent of a tired mind in the middle of the night, and enters the study.

START NEW GAME

Lydia manages to sleep past 10:00 A.M. before the domestic wakes her up at Madison's behest. She was up until four, waiting while the scanner processed every last page, and then she cleared up the study before going to bed, anxious she'd left something out of place, some telltale sign of her presence. She's become paranoid about Madison finding out what she's up to: by this point she feels Madison would block her efforts out of sheer spite, and would probably find it laughable that Lydia even considered herself capable of finding the killer, which she doesn't, really.

Lydia is still lying in bed feeling useless and thwarted and above all tired when the domestic returns with a reminder to get up. She does so and, without bothering to change out of her pajamas, goes downstairs.

Lydia? comes Madison's voice from the study as Lydia descends the last flight of steps.

Yes? Lydia replies.

I need to make some calls later.

OK.

Local calls. So I'll need you to translate for me.

Lydia really wants to tell Madison to go fuck herself. She's suspended. She does not work for Madison. Technically she's not meant to be working at all. And Madison has more or less told her she's got no future in the service, so what's she got to lose at this point? But she still holds out some vain hope that if she doesn't burn her bridges she might just be able to salvage something from all this.

OK, Lydia says: She goes to the kitchen, makes tea, unfurls her scroll and looks at the program the scanner produced for her. She runs it through an app that checks for code errors and gaps and makes a best guess at how they're supposed to function, and if it can't fix them it tries to remove them. The results are rarely perfect but the aim is to prevent these errors causing a complete failure.

Once the check has finished, she tries to run the program, just in case it's compatible with her scroll (she's not expecting it to be).

The program immediately starts downloading more files. Lydia panics for a moment—this could be anything. It could be malicious, it could be illegal. It's probably both of those things. Any moment now her scroll will explode and she'll be arrested—

But then she looks at some of the new files. Images, animations, sounds and other sensory data, all being gathered together in a folder. She can't see where these are being drawn from, the address isn't visible to her—probably she could find out if she knew what she was doing—but it looks to her like these are the components needed to run the game. Someone—possibly Jene, possibly someone else—stashed them somewhere online, but without the game code they wouldn't work, in fact they'd be meaningless.

Lydia stops feeling worried and starts feeling excited. It really seems like this thing will work—but not on her scroll. It needs a veearr system, and she doesn't have one, and Fitz didn't have one either. She'll have to go and play it at a veebar—there's one a couple of blocks away—but she doesn't know the first thing about these games.

But she knows someone who does.

"Now, Mum—you absolutely *cannot* stream this to anyone else, right? Just help me play it."

"Yes, love, I get it," says Mum testily.

It's not that Lydia doesn't trust Mum, it's just default behavior with her—something interesting happens and she flicks her stream on, especially when she's gaming. And if she ever manages to get early access to anything she always posts a firstlook, which is the easiest and most lucrative type of content there is, if you get on it before the streams get flooded. But Lydia can see the stream they're on now is padlocked, and Mum assures her she's not going to set up another. Lydia hasn't told Mum why this secrecy is necessary, because it would just worry her and they wouldn't be able to get down to what needs to be done, but Lydia is concerned this means Mum won't appreciate the importance of it.

It's late afternoon in Halifax and Lydia has interrupted Mum in the middle of an interminable customer services chat with the tram company over an unpaid fare. She hasn't taken a tram in months and insists her idee must have been spoofed. She doesn't want to break off from the call because she'll lose her place: she went on for a bit about how the "place in the queue" was a ridiculous fiction designed to get you to give up, since the whole thing is run by ayaies anyway and they can deal with thousands of queries at once with no noticeable slowdown. While this was going on, Lydia used the time to transfer the folder containing all the game elements across an encrypted connection. She doesn't want to install it on the veebar's own servers—she's going to play it remotely from Mum's home system, which should be slightly more secure. The veebar is pretty dead at this time of the morning, its grimy booths being cleaned while monitors show highlights of last night's action: Lydia has deselected that option on her own session, but suspects there's still some loophole she hasn't spotted.

"Has the game installed yet?" Lydia asks.

"This is going in a bloody loop," mutters Mum.

Lydia is alarmed. "Why, what's happening?"

"He's giving me the same answers he was half an hour ago."

"You mean the ayaie and your tram thing?"

"Yeah. He's asking me for details of the incident. I don't bloody know the details of the incident because I wasn't there, you stupid bloody thing."

"I thought you were talking about the game."

"No, that's nearly done. What am I supposed to do, lodge a complaint with the customer services bots to tell them the customer services bots aren't working?"

"Mum, I'll help you with it but can you help me with this game first?"

"Alright, but I don't see why you urgently need to play it when you never usually touch these things."

"It's . . . someone I know is on a deadline and needs this beta tested and he thinks it might be OK for people with my condition to play."

"Can't we both play it?"

No, because it might be dangerous, Mum. "My friend said not to let anyone else play it. Please, Mum, I don't know how to play these games and I need your help."

"Right, fine. Starting now."

Lydia pulls on the hood and it fits snugly around her eye sockets and molds itself to her ears, and the outside world completely vanishes. The smell of the cleaners' antiseptic is gone. She can't even feel the warm, stuffy air of the veebar, an aspect she always finds worrying—if your brain thinks you're cold when you're actually warm, won't it regulate your body wrongly? But presumably they've thought of that. Anyway she's not going to be using it for long. She just has to remember not to eat anything, because taste is the one that really goes haywire for her, like static on her tongue.

The scene around her fades up and Lydia finds herself standing in a deserted museum. The opening credits seem to be absent, so with a jerk the game goes into a cutscene: a young man with gang tattoos is hauled through the door of a vandalized exhibition room. There's obviously some holes in the code—the sound doesn't stay in sync, half the enpeecees don't have faces and one wall of the classroom is entirely blank. It's hard to say whether this is down to errors in scanning the code or if the code was unfinished.

"This is rough as dogs' arses," says Mum, whose voice is audible to Lydia but not to the other characters. It's weirdly like talking to the Logi, she realizes.

"I know, Mum—I need to listen."

The scene unfolds, with Lydia able to contribute to the characters' discussion but Mum explains these things last longer only if you start interacting with them, and it's better to just get them out of the way. It's not especially well written but explains how the gang came to seize the city, and then outlines which people are still living here in spite of the grim situation and what resources they have. This is where the citizens make a decision to start fighting back, and in the process everyone turns to the player(s), appealing to them to take charge. At this point the game proper begins.

It's weird playing a veearr. Lydia was always so jealous of the other kids at school who banged on about playing them *all the time*. It had more effect on her than she ever admitted: she made out she liked being different, because that was better than everyone knowing you hated being different. She was expecting this game to be nothing like the ones she played back then, back before she discovered she couldn't—but actually it seems very similar. She remembers that uncanny quality in the movements and body language of the enpeecees: how it seems so realistic at first you'd believe you were speaking to a real person, but before long you start to see repetitions and patterns. Bugs and unfinished areas aside, though, it feels very like a real place—it's a fictional city but seems partly based on New York, for instance the building they're in looks like the Museum Of Natural & Anthropological History. She's always wondered why games set in realistic locations are so popular when you can play games that let you be a Valkyrie and slay dragons, or an interdimensional wizard rewriting reality itself. But maybe people don't want fantasy, they want to feel they're in control, that they're playing by rules they understand and that it's possible to win.

"I really don't think much of this," says Mum. "Is it supposed to be retro?"

"No. I don't know. What do I do now?"

Mum directs Lydia to a wood-paneled room upstairs in the museum that's been kitted out as a command hub, with a big (paper) map of the city pinned to a wall. During the cutscene someone mentioned the phone networks are all down, which is why there's an antique corded phone on the desk: a makeshift modification has spliced what looks like a fibo cable into it. Mum tells Lydia there should be a paper notebook in her pocket: Lydia checks it and she's right, and when she opens it there are telephone numbers scribbled inside. Mum tells her to make some calls, deploy her resources. Lydia's impressed by how quickly Mum's got the hang of this.

Lydia listens closely to the people on the other end of the

phone as she gives her instructions, listening out for the voice Jene mentioned. But she's starting to get a headache, and her gums are tingling unpleasantly, and she knows the sickness is going to hit very soon. She looks up and sees a young man standing by the map.

"We just heard from the fire station over in Haverbrook," he says, pointing at an area of the map. "The citizens there have managed to get inside and they think the engines can be fixed. But we don't have anyone who can fix them."

"That gang kid we just picked up is a mechanic," says Lydia, a detail Mum picked up on from the cutscene. "He's in the basement."

"Will he help us?" says the young man skeptically.

"I'll have a try," says Lydia, and heads down to the basement. She speaks to the kid, and it takes her about ten minutes but she talks him round and he's on their side. Mum says this kind of exercise is all about hitting certain keywords and phrases—you find the ones they respond to and then work them in until the character cooperates, it's like cracking a code. It all seems quite mechanical to Lydia, not as absorbing as she expected, but that might just be because she feels appalling—a travel-sickness feeling in her guts, a sharp pain behind each eye. She feels like her nose is bleeding but each time she reaches up to her face, she finds nothing, and she can't shake the suspicion her nose *is* bleeding, just not in the game. The quicker she can get out of here, the better.

Lydia returns to the upstairs office—and the moment she walks in, the telephone rings: a high, loud, resonant trill, full of urgency, a remnant of a more organized world. Lydia feels compelled to act, as if the bell has set her a standard to live up to. This must be something in how the game's designed—she feels it's very important she answer the phone. How can they create that kind of reaction just with a sound?

Lydia picks up the receiver and says, "Hello?"

"Thank god," says a middle-aged man's voice from the other end. White noise in the background. "I've been trying to reach someone for hours . . ." And he talks about a siege situation in another part of town, clearly explaining where it is and who's involved. But alongside this Lydia hears another voice, cutting through the first one, speaking to her in Logisi.

"You can hear me."

The voice is Fitz's. But it's in her ear, not her mind. She's never heard his voice like this before.

"Don't worry," the voice continues. "It's normal to be able to hear me. It's not important right now that you hear me, but it will be. When you hear me again, be sure to listen."

It's like a test message, a placeholder. The kind of thing you say to check if a microphone's working. Lydia puts the phone down.

"Why did you put the phone down?" says Mum.

"What?"

"You didn't speak to that man. You just hung up on him."

"Didn't you hear the other voice?"

"What other voice?"

"He said 'It's normal to be able to hear me.' You didn't hear it?"

"No."

Lydia thinks for a moment. "I need to go, Mum. Thanks for your help."

"But we've hardly even started—you haven't even gone outside, you can't know if the atmospherics and lighting are right if you've not—"

"I have to go—just delete the game. Promise me you'll delete it, right?"

"Why?"

"Just promise, it's important."

"Alright, but—"

"I'll talk to you soon." And Lydia leaves the game and ends the call.

STRAWBERRY FIELDS

Lydia sits on a bench in Strawberry Fields in Central Park. Sitting on the other end of the bench is John Lennon.

"Alright, love," says Lennon, flashing her a grin.

"Hi, John," says Lydia.

"By 'eckers like, is that a Yorkshire accent?"

"Yeah."

"Ee bah gum," Lennon says loudly in broad imitation of Lydia. "Don't say that in America, they'll go 'Who buys gum? And why are you telling me this?'" No one else can hear him, because he's an ayaie that interacts with your glasses when you're in Strawberry Fields, and everyone has their own private Lennon—unless you turn him off. If you turn your head to the front and look out of the corner of your eye, around the edge of your glasses, he isn't there. Turn back and there he is, dressed in double denim and a NEW YORK CITY T-shirt.

Lydia is here because she's putting off a decision and, depending on the outcome of that decision, also a confrontation. She has a notion of what's going on but she has to get it all clear in her mind, because she's going to get only one chance to say it to Fitz and hear his immediate reaction: she won't even get to record it, she'll have to pay full attention in the moment. She looks for avenues she hasn't explored, possible ways she's misinterpreted things, potential evidence that Jene was just a sad, unstable fantasist—and the word is *was,* because on the way here she received a note from Ondine saying the police let her know Jene turned up in the sewers early this morning, dead from a self-inflicted gunshot wound, and she'd been there since Sunday. She wonders if the bullets will match those used to kill Fitz.

"You've got a face like a slapped arse," says Lennon.

"Yeah, cheers John."

"What's up with you?"

"Got a dilemma, mate. Someone I know might've done something shady, and I dunno whether to confront him with it or go to the police."

"That's not a dilemma," scoffs Lennon. "You don't dob a mate in to the bizzies."

"He's not exactly a mate. He's my boss."

"That is different." Lennon seems to consider this. "Do you like him?"

"Yeah. So I sort of don't believe he did this, or that if he did he must have had good reason."

"But if you grass him up—"

"Thing is, he can't get in trouble now. He's dead."

"Right."

"But I'm still talking to him."

Lennon shrugs. "I'm dead and you're still talking to me, love."

"Yeah, it's becoming a habit. I just . . . if there's nothing in this, I don't want to drag his reputation through the shite. I've got to be sure."

"You've got your answer then, haven't you?"

Lydia nods. She has. She knew it all along. But sometimes it takes an artificially intelligent simulation of a long dead Beatle to put things in perspective.

THE CONFRONTATION

Lydia returns to the residence, passing the cop on the porch. She remembers him—he's the one who had the dispute with Madison the other day. He nods as she enters and Lydia nods back. Now the next part is going to be awkward because before she left for the veebar, Madison told her she'd need her for those calls very soon and Lydia told her *Just a second* and then walked out of the front door, so—

Lydia? Madison's voice is like a firework going off inside Lydia's head. At school they said the Logi can make one another pass out if an argument is forceful enough, though she's never seen it happen. Can they do it to humans? No one's sure but there's no record of it happening. Some of the other pupils told stories about how the ambassador to Brazil once made a kid's head explode—that sort of shit. Lydia didn't believe them of course, but it's funny how those stories suddenly come back to her as she turns and sees Madison standing in the doorway of the study.

Yes, says Lydia, *it's me. Hello.*

What happened to you?

I went out for a walk.

But I told you I needed you.

Yes, I heard you. But I wanted to go out for a walk.

You didn't tell me.

Why do I have to tell you? I don't work for you. I'm suspended from service. You can't have it both ways.

But while you're living here—

I'm living here because the police said I had to! And it's clear you want me out when all this is over, so what's the point in my helping you? What am I going to get from it?

That's a very selfish attitude.

You're the one who expects me to drop everything to deal with your crap and never even says thank you. And Lydia heads up the stairs.

Why would it make a difference if I said thank you?

You're right, it wouldn't, says Lydia without turning around, *because I'd know you didn't mean it.* She expects Madison to demand she come back, but she doesn't.

This is not the frame of mind Lydia wanted to be in when she confronted Fitz, but unfortunately it's the frame of mind she's stuck with. She closes the door behind herself and ponders where to sit and then decides to stand.

Fitz? she says. She no longer cares if Madison overhears any of this. If she wants to disapprove or report her or whatever, fuck it.

Where did you go? he replies.

Fitz, I played the game that was on the inkouts Jene had.

Right. Anything useful?

You said you'd never heard of this game when I found those inkouts. But you're in it.

How do you mean?

I mean I played it and I heard your voice. And Jene wouldn't have been obsessed with it if it had nothing to do with the Logi and she said she was going to kill the voice in the game, and now she's dead. And so are you and your voice is in that game. Tell me this is all a coincidence.

He doesn't reply for a while.

I didn't have close involvement with it, he says.

Lydia was expecting this but that doesn't make it easier to hear. *Why did Jene think it was dangerous? What was going on with all those developers who got fired or quit? What did they know?*

I had nothing to do with that side of things.

Then why were you the voice? And why didn't Mum hear it?

It wasn't dangerous. Jene was wrong about that. It's all about communication. It could have been revolutionary—it still could be. The process just needs more work, that's why the game was delayed.

What was it for? To send us messages, like posthypnotic suggestion?

No—nothing like that. Humans are still suspicious of us, Lydia—you know that, and it's because most of you don't hear us. So we asked the programmers to insert something into the game that would start training your brains so everyone would be able to communicate with us. We're very inter-ested in the potential of games to reshape thought patterns. This was just a first step.

Towards what?

Opening your minds. Not yours obviously, you don't need it, but—

But this was being done secretly. You're talking about rewiring people's brains without their consent.

Sometimes you need to just do things before people really appreciate the benefits.

Oh god, says Lydia, the benefit of the doubt evaporating. *But why you?*

The embassy instructed me to study human culture and find a route to do this. I concluded a game would be best, and as we lacked the ability to make such a thing ourselves, we found a suitable project in development and took it over via a proxy company.

But you must have realized, when I turned up the stuff about the game, that I was getting close—why let me keep looking?

I wanted to know how much had got out there about the project, how much Jene knew, who she told. Fortunately it seems most of it died with her.

But you didn't tell me the truth, that you were involved in it—because you knew I wouldn't like it.

No, I just didn't want you to be implicated—you could get into trouble too.

Does Madison know about this? Is this why she's so hostile towards you?

She wants to take over the project. She disagreed with my direction for it. I expect that's why she's here—she's probably on to you already. You must get rid of all the evidence.

Lydia glances at the boxes of inkouts in the corner of her room. *All that paper, you mean?*

Yes, and delete the game. I'm glad it was you who found it—someone I can trust.

But it won't be over, says Lydia. *They'll start again, without you—there must be other copies—*

This is for your own safety. Just destroy everything, please.

Don't fucking tell me what to do, says Lydia. She needs to leave and she can't take all the inkout with her but she still has the game in

her niche and she can take the box containing the press release and
the chat, so she grabs that.

Where are you taking it? says Fitz.

I don't have to tell you anything.

To the police?

Maybe.

You won't make it. Madison will stop you.

*You're just bullshitting to manipulate me—why hasn't she done some-
thing sooner, if she already knows?*

*She's been waiting for you to find the evidence, like I did. What she'll do
with it is another question.*

*So you're saying I've got a choice between destroying this stuff and letting
her take it from me?*

*She'll destroy you too, discredit you—she may go further than that.
She's always seen you as a risk factor.*

Lydia nods. *I've got one other option,* she says, unfurling her scroll
and putting it on her desk. She sits down and angles it towards her
face. *I can do what Jene should've done. She didn't think it'd do any good to
tell the world—maybe she was right. But it's the only option I've got.*

This is a bad idea, Lydia.

Covertly altering people's brains without their consent was a bad idea,
says Lydia, gathering the inkouts and setting up a stream. *I'm going
to expose it. Way I see it, I've not got much to lose at this point.* She tries to
work out what she's going to say—usually when she does a stream
she writes out some key points first, and she edits before uploading
instead of going live, but this one really has to go out immediately.

Don't do this—please. You've got this all wrong.

Shut up, I'm concentrating—

Lydia? Madison's voice comes to her distantly. *Are you talking to
someone up there?*

Shit. Lydia listens out: she can hear Madison's footsteps on the
stairs.

Don't let her find you doing this, says Fitz.

I won't. Lydia rises from the desk and locks her door. Madison is
still approaching. How long will this stream take to get all the necessary information in? Well, if there's someone in the background

trying to batter the door down, that can only add weight to it. She returns to the desk, starts a twenty-second countdown for the stream and writes down a set of bullet points she needs to hit.

There's a knock at the door. Lydia ignores it.

Lydia, says Madison from the other side of the door, *who were you talking to?*

No one, says Lydia.

I can tell you're lying. I need to speak to you.

I'm not feeling well. I'll talk to you later.

Lydia—what's going on? If you've gone behind my back—

I haven't. Go away. Lydia glances at the screen: the stream is about to start.

Who's in there with you?

No one. Honestly. Please, just leave—

The lock clicks, the door opens and Madison enters.

How did you do that? says Lydia, now casting.

Madison looks around, expecting to see another Logi. *I can override any lock in this house—didn't you know that?*

Lydia did not, though she feels she should have guessed.

Where are they? says Madison, looking in the bathroom.

There's no one else here—could you leave me alone please?

Madison walks over to Lydia. *I came up here to discuss your position after your remarks downstairs—*

I bet you did.

But now I'm rather more interested in who you were talking to and why you're lying to me about it.

Lydia stares Madison full in the face. *I was talking to Fitz.*

Madison stares back. Knows Lydia isn't lying. *What on earth are you talking about?*

He talks to me. I know you think it's sacrilege or whatever for someone who isn't Logi to talk to the dead but he told me everything about the game and about what you want to do with it—

I have no idea what you mean—how can you talk to him?

I know you talk to the dead.

I assure you I don't.

I didn't just mean you, *I mean your people, you*—But as Lydia listens, she realizes Madison isn't lying either. She genuinely has no clue what Lydia means. *I've been talking to him for days, he's still here in the house.*

I can see you believe it, says Madison, her voice taking on a patronizing tone. *Lydia, are you sure you're quite sane?*

Yes, Lydia replies as if this isn't exactly what she's feared all along, *I'm perfectly*—

Because this sort of thing is not unknown. We often hear the voices of the dead for a while after they're gone. But it's not real, you know.

I know all that but this is—

I expect you've meshed what's happening to you with your own culture's mythology around death, ghosts and so on—*it's a normal reaction to something you don't understand.*

Lydia laughs. *Fuck off. I don't believe in ghosts*—*or at least I never used to before all this kicked off.*

This is so interesting, says Madison, *I've never come across this phenomenon before in human translators*—

He speaks to me! And don't tell me I'm imagining it—

But you must realize that's the rational explanation.

Lydia sways, holds on to the desk for support. *Of course I realize that! Don't you think my first thought was "Bloody hell, I'm going mad here"? But then he started telling me stuff I couldn't possibly know, that couldn't possibly have come from inside my own head.*

What makes you say that?

Because he told me where to find things—*things I didn't know about, like a document that was in his room, and he led me to this guy who'd been sending him threats, and then this academic who we apparently met the night he died and who I didn't remember, but she remembered me*—

But if you were there, and you forgot, perhaps these things you think Fitzwilliam is telling you are just your own memories resurfacing?

Lydia hesitates. That sounds annoyingly plausible. But she *hasn't* just made all this up. Ondine is real, Marius is real. This pile of paper is real, so's the game—this isn't her fantasy, not unless she's having some very, *very* lucid and fairly coherent hallucinations.

And then there's the drunkenness she's been feeling when talking to him. *Fitz asked me to track down who killed him and I found her. Or rather I found out who it was, she's dead.*

Who?

This woman called Jene Connor killed him because he's the one behind this game and I know you know about it and don't try to stop me exposing it, by the way, because we're casting right now. It strikes her that she should say something out loud very soon, or anyone who's watching will just swipe on.

Madison glances at Lydia's scroll. *I've no idea what this game is, but why haven't you told the police, if you know who killed Fitzwilliam?*

I only just worked it out now, and first I had to . . . Lydia also looks at her scroll, then back at Madison. *Tell me honestly—do you know anything about a veearr game developed with Logi involvement aimed at reshaping the brains of humans?*

It sounds absurd.

Please just give me a direct answer.

Of course I don't know anything—no such project exists.

That you know of.

No such project exists, Madison repeats.

Fitz? Lydia says. *She says she doesn't know anything about it. Maybe you should talk to her?*

There's no reply.

Fitz, says Lydia, *please—tell her you've been talking to me. I know I was angry but you can't just abandon me—*

Lydia, says Madison calmly, *if you genuinely have been hearing from him, there's only one explanation. He's still alive, and he's talking to you from . . .* Madison looks around. *Somewhere very close, but not inside the residence, otherwise we'd have seen him . . .*

Lydia's infuriated by Madison's refusal to accept what she says—but then she looks at the wall that adjoins the house next door. The one with the apartment at the top that's empty over the summer. The one she assumed the police had bugged.

Before she can even process the thought, her feet are racing down the stairs while her mind flails around, looking for possible explanations of how Fitz can be alive after she saw him dead. Madison's following and talking to her but Lydia's not listening, she's thinking about how she *saw* Fitz's body and the Logi don't all look alike to her, or at least Fitz certainly doesn't, and it was definitely him lying dead on the sofa in the study, and the police ideed him too. But has he somehow fooled everyone, including her? How, and why? As she steps out of the front door she vaguely registers there's no cop on the porch now (When did that happen?) but her mind is far too occupied to process this information.

She's walking out into the street, giving no thought as to how she's going to get into the apartment next door: her need to know is so powerful now she assumes it will punch through any obstacles. There's a gate that leads to a passage through to the back of the building where the steps are, but it's locked and too high to climb. Lydia rattles it fruitlessly, then walks up the house's front steps, waves her hand in front of the bell and hears it ring through the door, decides it doesn't convey her urgency and hammers her fist on the door instead. If no one answers she has no doubt she will try to kick it down, and she's vaguely aware there'll be consequences to this but can't bring herself to care anymore—

The door is opened by Mrs. Kloves, entirely bewildered by the appearance of her neighbor in such an agitated state. "Can I help you?" she asks.

"How do I get to the apartment upstairs? Can I get there through your house?"

"Yes, but—"

Lydia doesn't wait for a response, just marches in, ignoring Mrs. Kloves' protests. She can see straight down the hall to the back door, which is open—

There's a clatter coming from the metal steps at the back. Someone's coming down from the apartment—

And they *jump* the last two meters, land on the tiny lawn, stumble and run on. Lydia catches a glimpse of someone—a man?—in a tracksuit and what looks like a veearr hood as he pelts across the lawn. Whoever it is, it's certainly not Fitz. By now Lydia has also reached the garden—but her quarry is already scrambling up the fence.

"Stop!" shouts Lydia—but the guy is very keen *not* to stop, it seems. She reaches the fence herself and makes a vain grab for his foot as he disappears over the fence. Lydia knows there's no way she can scale the fence so she doesn't even try, and as she hears the guy dashing down the alley on the other side she puts in a call to the police—saying what, though? What's he done? Suspected burglar? That'll do.

She turns back to the house and finds Madison and Mrs. Kloves facing her.

Lydia, what are you doing? says Madison.

Lydia ignores her for now and addresses Mrs. Kloves. "Did you know that guy was up there?"

A bewildered Mrs. Kloves looks up at the apartment, then back to Lydia. "Who . . . who was he?"

"I don't bloody know—you mean don't know either?"

"It's been empty for weeks—I *thought* it was empty . . ."

Lydia looks up to the top of the metal steps, where the door to the apartment swings open. Lydia marches over there and ascends. She can hear the police arriving and wonders if she might get into trouble for going into the apartment, but if Fitz is there she *has* to talk to him—and if she waits for permission from the police they might not give it to her.

Fitz? she calls. A theory is brewing—perhaps that guy she saw running away was holding Fitz hostage, and making Fitz say those things? She doesn't know how he could be sure Fitz was doing as he was told, but maybe that'll become clear?

Then she arrives at the door to the apartment and it becomes clear and she wishes it hadn't.

The apartment is very tastefully decorated in a minimalist style, and the door opens directly onto the living room. On a glass-topped coffee table stands a fish tank with no fish inside. Instead it's filled with a sickly yellow liquid; various pipes and tubes feed into it, and bits of makeshift-looking electrical equipment are hooked to the side.

In the center of the tank is the severed head of a Logi.

The distorting effect of the liquid means Lydia can't immediately tell whose head it is, but she doesn't have to work hard to guess. Part of its cranium has been removed and cables have been patched into it, and over all this it's wearing a messy sort of framework helmet. She recognizes the helmet: Back when she was at LSTL she watched a video about this object multiple times, the thing she thought was going to end her career before it even began. It's the translation device, the one the Logi ordered all development on to be stopped.

Lydia walks to the wall that adjoins her bedroom and raps on it with her fist. The wall isn't that thick. An inch or so of board and plaster were all that separated her from this absolute horror while she slept.

Lydia finds she can't turn around, can't tear herself away from the wall and face what's inside the fish tank. She stays there, leaning against the wall, until the police come up and remove her.

A MATTER OF INTERPRETATION

The police have a lot of questions and Lydia has very few of the answers. All she can tell them is she's been hearing Fitz's voice, and based on the few bits of information he managed to give her, she investigated his murder and worked out who did it. Or at least, she thought she had.

"Why didn't you bring this to us as soon as you found out?" asks Rollo, who's interviewing her again, but this time on her turf, such as it is—the reception room of the residence.

"At first it didn't really seem like anything," Lydia says. "I was just trying to keep busy, I didn't expect you'd take it seriously—I didn't really take it seriously myself. But Fitz asked me to, or I thought he had, and it was the least I could do for him."

"And you really believed his . . . spirit, or whatever . . . was speaking to you?"

"I didn't know *what* was happening. I'd seen his body, I knew he was dead, but he was speaking to me, and yes it *did* occur to me I might be going mad but—"

"But you went to the apartment next door because you thought he might be there—that's what you said, wasn't it?"

"It was the only answer I could think of, that I'd been mistaken somehow—but I wasn't, was I? He *was* dead, and I *was* hearing his voice."

"But what I don't understand is—"

"Excuse me," says the cop translator, the same one who came with Sturges when he told everyone Lydia had to stay here, the white-haired one who was so slick and professional and who Lydia wished she could be friends with. Lydia has learned her name is

Dion. She's been relating the discussion for Madison's benefit in case she has anything to contribute.

"Yes?" asks Rollo.

"There's absolutely no way," says Dion, speaking on Madison's behalf, "that Lydia could reasonably have understood where the voice was coming from. None of us knew this was possible, and in her place I would've been just as confused."

Lydia's surprised by Madison's intervention, but gratefully accepts it. The police had been reluctant to share any further details about what was in the fish tank in the apartment above Mrs. Kloves' house, but Madison argued the embassy had the right to know what had happened to the body of one of its citizens, and eventually they told her. Fitz's head had been preserved in a chemical cocktail, and the equipment wired into his brain was indeed adapted from the rejected translation technology. Someone—presumably the man who'd run from the apartment—had been using it to communicate with Lydia *via* Fitz, accessing his speech centers and bypassing his cognitive functions, so to Lydia it seemed to be his voice. The grimy, invasive device even boosted it so she could hear him from the other end of the house.

"I'm far more concerned," Dion continues for Madison, "that someone stole Fitzwilliam's head from your morgue."

"We're conducting a full investigation," says Rollo.

"I should hope so. Have you checked the rest of his body is still there?"

"Yes."

"And?"

"Yes, it's there."

"Maybe the guy who had the head was the guy who killed Fitz?" says Lydia.

"We don't want to jump to conclusions. Yes, he's a suspect but we don't have anything connecting him with the actual murder."

"Nothing except *he had the murder victim's head in a fish tank.*"

"Which doesn't mean he was the murderer—the head was taken long after the murder."

"But doesn't it seem obvious he was using me to fit someone else up for the murder? He sent me off on that investigation and manipulated the whole thing—"

"Ah yes," says Rollo, "we checked out your suspect—Jene Connor, who we also have in the morgue, who did *indeed* kill herself. The ballistics don't match, but you say you found a motive?"

"I . . . think so? She'd uncovered something . . . or maybe just thought she had, I don't know. I don't know." For a brief moment a few hours ago Lydia thought it all fitted together, and what she'd learned was horrible but at least it made some kind of sense. Now she's more confused than ever.

Rollo tells Lydia and Madison that's all the questions they have for now. Dion excuses herself and leaves swiftly: she doesn't seem even slightly drunk. If that was Lydia she'd have swayed a bit at the very least.

The cops discuss stuff but all Lydia hears is the silence in her mind. She'll never walk into this house and hear Fitz's voice again, because he's really gone this time—in fact he always was. She takes a moment on her own, telling herself how daft this is. He was just her boss. They weren't friends or anything.

The police eventually leave—all of them. Lydia has got so used to there being a cop stationed on the doorstep, it's weird to look out and not see one. Like when you walk into your living room the day after you take the Christmas tree down.

So they've decided they no longer need to watch the house, says Madison, joining Lydia at the window.

They were never watching the house, Lydia replies. *They were watching me.* She recalls how there was no cop when she went to investigate the apartment next door.

The feeds don't have anything about Fitz's head being stolen.

@Back2life111 / Police activity outside the murder house and next door, new evidence? / TR93

@NOWPUNCHER / BREAKING: ATTACHÉ MURDER WEAPON FOUND IN APARTMENT NEXT DOOR / TR62

And so on and so on. None of them have got it right—though didn't she see something about his body being stolen from the morgue a couple of days ago? She tries in vain to find it again. She stops looking—if she searches for it too many times, one of the con-tengines will confect a story about it and get her to click.

At least we've explained your ghost situation, says Madison. *I thought there had to be a rational explanation.*

I thought you might want to apologize.

Madison airily looks out of the window as she says, *Apologize? What for?*

You basically said I was mad, or lying, or trying to wrap my primitive brain around what was happening to me and came up with some childish explanation.

I didn't say any of that.

Maybe not in those exact words, but—

You must see how strange your claims seemed to me.

I never said they weren't *strange, I knew they were strange.*

If I did cause any offense, I apologize—now come on, I need you to explain this business about a veearr game.

What about it?

I'd like to know what you think you know.

You're being patronizing again—

I'm not trying to be.

I've found things. I have. I don't know what they all mean but—

You found them through false information. That wasn't Fitzwilliam telling you those things.

But most of it didn't come from him. It was just, like, a loose thread I pulled on, and all this stuff came out of it.

Explain it to me, please. All of it.

Lydia's dubious about this. Madison could well be involved in whatever's going on, and so telling her what she knows might be a terrible idea. But on the other hand Madison might be able to help Lydia find the truth, and this business is so maddening Lydia is willing to take a few risks if it means getting to the bottom of it. So she tells Madison everything, and to her credit Madison listens, even though it's clear how badly she wants to pass comment.

Lydia has almost finished when the doorbell rings. *Whoever it is, get rid of them,* Madison says.

Lydia opens the front door.

"Hi," says Hari a little weakly. "There aren't any police still in there, are there?"

OUTSIDE ASSISTANCE

Who's this? asks Madison, coming to the door and standing beside Lydia. Hari's visibly intimidated by the sight of her, taking a step back: Lydia guesses he hasn't seen a Logi up close before. She tries to remember how she felt the first time she met one, at her interview for LSTL. She can't remember his name now. They didn't actually need a Logi to be there but they wanted to see how you reacted. Of course it was an advantage if you'd met them before, which lots of the other applicants had. But Lydia was excited—perhaps a bit too excited, she worried she'd blown the interview by talking too much while not answering the questions properly. Strange how commonplace it is to her now.

Maybe it's not so surprising lots of people think they don't exist, if they see them only via media.

This is Hari, Lydia tells Madison, then turns back to him. "You'd better come inside." Probably someone has already spotted Hari on the doorstep and posted an image, but the less time she spends talking to him in public view, the better. Hari enters the residence and nods to Madison respectfully as he walks past, a gesture she won't really get.

"When did the cops let you go?" Lydia asks him as she closes the door.

"A few hours ago," Hari replies. "I came down here but the place was swarming so I waited for them to go away—what happened? Why were they all here?"

"It's complicated and . . . weird—did they treat you OK?"

"Not really."

"Sorry. I didn't tell them it was you—I *never* thought it was you."

"You *did* call the cops on me though."

"I'm sorry. I panicked. Those guys you were with—"

He holds up a hand and nods. "I know, I can see how it must've looked. Also, those guys *were* arseholes."

Why is he here? asks Madison impatiently: Lydia hadn't quite finished explaining things to her.

I don't know, says Lydia. She'd like to know this too, so she asks Hari but frames it as Madison's question.

"Oh," he replies, "the capsule hostel I was staying at recycled all my stuff when I didn't come back and they charged a *big* non-payment fee to my account, so I don't have any clothes and I'm almost out of money, so . . ."

"You were hoping I could help you out?"

"I wouldn't have come to you because I know you're dealing with stuff but I don't know anyone else in this entire country, and I can't leave the city until the police tell me I can."

"So what do they expect you to do?"

"They said if I didn't have anywhere else to go I could spend another night in the cells."

Lydia rolls her eyes and tells Madison: *He needs somewhere to stay.*
You're only allowed visitors with permission.

You're not going to tell me I have to throw him out?

"Is everything all right?" says Hari, lingering in the hallway, unsure of his status.

"It's fine—you want to go through and help yourself to a tea or coffee?"

He looks from Lydia to Madison uncertainly. "Yeah thanks," he says and heads for the kitchen.

This is really not a time for houseguests, says Madison.

I'll give him some money and tell him to move on—let him sit down and have a cup of tea first while I finish telling you about this game.

Madison sweeps her arm up and in a curling motion, a gesture that means *Go ahead.*

When I confronted Fitz about the game he said it was designed to covertly rewire the human brain to make it receptive to communication with you.

Madison makes a light clicking noise that Lydia knows indicates skepticism, it's like when people do a short mirthless laugh. *But that wasn't really him. So I don't see how that's relevant.*

But the game exists though, I've played it and it has Fitz's voice in it, and I think we've established I've not been imagining things.

I want to see this game. Show it to me.

You can't play it, it's veearr.

There must be some way you can display it.

Lydia thinks for a moment. *Hang on,* she says, and goes to the kitchen, where Hari is asking the domestic to show him where the mugs are. He turns when he hears Lydia behind him.

"Is everything OK?" he asks.

Lydia holds up a finger. "I'm going to ask you something and it'd be really helpful for both of us if the answer is yes."

Is that safe, what he's doing? Madison asks as Hari instructs the desktop in the study to download various bits of shadeware.

Of course, says Lydia, even though she has no idea. "Is that safe?" she asks Hari.

"It's fine—I know what all this stuff is. I did have to suspend all the desktop's defenses because it's from unregistered publishers—"

Lydia sighs.

"But they're only unregistered because the licensing fees are a pisstake—"

"OK, just do it and don't tell me what you're doing and as far as *she* knows"—she jerks her head at Madison—"you told me it'd be fine."

Hari keeps working while Lydia stares at the canvas above the sofa. Weirdly it's showing what looks like an impressionistic rendition of Piece Hall in Halifax, which it must have got from her.

"They totally thought we were in it together, you know," Hari says.

"The cops?"

"They kept asking me if you gave me a plan of the house, or turned off the security system for me and told me when to come, or if you drugged him for me—"

"*Drugged* him?"

"Yeah, man. They had all manner of genius ideas."

Lydia suppresses a wave of anxiety at the thought of being fitted up for this. "Cops make up their own narratives if they need
to, don't they."

"Right," says Hari, pulling the desktop up into a vertical position so it can be used as a monitor, "that's good to go, I reckon."
Veearrs aren't designed to run on a flatscreen like this, partly because
they're optimized for veearr, but mostly because the sensory data
veearr systems collect during play is harvested by the manufacturers
so they can sell it on, and this is a very significant revenue stream
for them. But Hari has used this hooky software to trick the game
into thinking it's running on a veearr set. A sort of ovoid window
appears in the middle of the desktop. The touch, taste and smell out-
puts are approximated as text that runs down the side of the screen.

It's ready, says Lydia.

Finally, says Madison, who has drifted into reading one of Fitz's
books, about Japanese shopping mall design. She puts it aside and
comes to stand behind Lydia.

"It won't be perfect," Hari warns as the game loads.

"That's OK, the program isn't perfect—I had to scan it off an
inkout."

He looks up at her, surprised. "And it works?"

"Yeah, I ran it through a patcher, but—"

"Do you still have the inkout? Can I look at it?"

"If you like," says Lydia and tells him where to find it. Then
she turns back to Madison, who's staring blankly at the screen.
The cutscene in the museum is running. The image is weirdly flat-
tened, like a fish-eye view, but it's comprehensible.

What do I do? Madison asks.

Well, you play it, says Lydia.

How?

Hari has rigged up a stylus to act as an input, a bit like an Old
Skool controller—you can swish it at the screen to move and turn,
and double-point to pick something up, though Hari was unwilling
to promise you'd be able to interact with it. It feels like using a magic
wand. Lydia explains all this to Madison.

So . . . says Madison, *I treat it as if I was actually in the situation on the screen?*

Yes.

And as if the people were actual people.

Exactly.

Madison stares at the screen for a few moments and Lydia picks up a low-level murmur from her brain. She's trying to get her head around the whole notion of people doing this for enjoyment, or for any reason really. And she shouldn't judge all the Logi from Madison, of course, but at this moment it seems very unlikely any of them came up with any plan involving a veearr. It is literally alien to them.

Lydia has summarized the cutscene for Madison and is haltingly guiding her around the game area when Hari returns carrying a sheaf of inkout. "This is what you fed into the scanner?"

"Well, that's not *all* of it," Lydia replies.

"Yeah, no, I saw the rest—this code *might* be the code for that game, it might not, but I can tell you for sure it's not complete or in sequence."

What's he saying? says Madison.

Hang on— Lydia turns back to Hari. "But the code came from that inkout. I sat here and put the pages into the scanner myself, and then it downloaded the elements."

"Maybe it's what the scanner gave you—but the scanner didn't get it from that inkout, this wouldn't have been functional."

"I suppose it could have been part of the download? Maybe it overwrote the file—but then what was the point of all this bloody paper?"

"To trigger the download?"

"Then I sat here *all that time* feeding paper in for nothing?" Then Lydia's brain catches up. "Someone wanted me to think Jene found this game, because that's her motive for killing Fitz." It's like someone's knocking down a row of dominoes and she's trying to see what's on each one before they fall. Fitz admitted to making the game, but now she knows that wasn't Fitz. This paper Jene found wasn't the game—but there *was* all that chat from the people who made it . . . and that was probably fabricated too, and planted for her to find, to make it seem like there was something suspicious about the game. But Jene's definitely real, the police confirmed it, they found her body, and Lydia knows Jene had something against the Logi, because of what her friends said, and Prof. Booth—

Who she found because of a lead Fitz gave her. . . .

Except that wasn't Fitz.

"Oh fuck," says Lydia.

I think I'm getting the hang of this, says Madison, her attention still fixed on the screen. *What do I do next?*

THE CIRCUS HAS LEFT TOWN

The street in the Village looks much the same as it did when Lydia visited before, yet this time she feels like she's in a game where everything's been designed to have a specific effect on her, so she's seeing it all differently. In fact no, it feels more artificial than that—it's like she's on a stage, like when she saw *Hedda Gabler* with Fitz, and if she turns around she'll see the audience watching for what she does next. The diplomatic car has parked around the corner from Ondine's apartment: Madison gets out and tells Lydia to lead the way.

Neither she nor Madison even discussed contacting the NYPD. This was something they would investigate themselves, immediately, before the trail went cold. They couldn't bring Hari with them or leave him alone at the residence: Lydia was about to swish him some money for a hotel when Madison surprised her by swishing him money first, and telling Lydia to take his contact details in case they needed him again. Minutes later Lydia and Madison were being driven downtown.

They walk through the shoe vendor and head up to Ondine's floor. Is it just Lydia's imagination or are there fewer people lurking in the stairwell than last time? There're two in that corner there, but she can't see any others. They arrive at Ondine's door and Lydia rings the bell.

The door is opened by a stout man of about forty, wearing a green shirt with only two of the buttons done up and loose gray trousers. He holds a cutting tool and there's an acrid smell of scorched printstuff coming from the apartment. From what Lydia can see, the apartment is unchanged from her previous visit except for the

person in it. The man sees Lydia first, then Madison, and the sight of
the Logi causes him to do a double take. "Can I help you?" he says,
clearly unsure whether to direct the question at Lydia or Madison.

"Who are you?"

The man recoils slightly. "Who are *you*?"

What's he saying? Madison asks.

He's asking us who we are.

Why don't you tell him?

I was about to. This is all much easier when she's just translating
rather than trying to lead the conversation. "My name's Lydia and
this is Madison. You live here?"

He nods. "Kyle." He swaps his sculpting tool into his left
hand, then shakes Lydia's hand. His own hand is rough and cal-
loused.

"I was here a couple of days ago—"

"I wasn't here then."

"Yes, I know. I'm—*we're* looking for Ondine?"

He looks blank. "How d'you spell that?"

Lydia spells it for him.

He shakes his head. "Sorry, don't know anyone of that name."

"Whether you know her or not, she was here."

Kyle's brow creases in annoyance. "Was there a party going on?
Because the rental agreement says—"

"No, it was just her on her own—she said she lived here."

"There *was* a woman staying here," says Kyle, "but that wasn't
her name."

"OK, what was her name?"

"I don't give out details about my guests—what's this about?"

"I'm trying to find her—it's very important I speak to her
again. You say she was a guest?"

"Yeah, I let this place out sometimes and go stay with my
boyfriend for a few days. Means I can take bookings at short
notice."

Lydia peers inside. "This doesn't *look* like a holiday let."

Kyle laughs. "That's how they like it. Rich kids from Dakota
and Seattle go nuts for the Village vibe."

Lydia relates this to Madison as she gets her scroll from her pocket. While searching for something on the scroll she continues: "And this woman who stayed, she was a short-notice booking?"

"Uh-huh. Booked on Sunday, arrived Monday morning. Open-ended stay, she messaged me today to say she was leaving, gave me a five-star review."

Lydia holds up her scroll, which has a picture of Ondine on it. "Is this her?"

Kyle nods. "Yeah. But she wasn't called . . . Odine, you said?"

"Ondine—that's what she told me she was called."

He looks at her sympathetically. "Sometimes people want to be someone else when they come to the city, and they don't want you finding them afterwards."

"No, it's not like that—are you sure she gave *you* the right name?"

"Oh yeah. You need a verified idee and it's three-stepped at every stage. But like I say, I can't give out that info—I've already told you more than I should—"

"Don't worry," says Lydia, turning away and heading for the stairs, Madison following. "The police might turn up to ask you the same question, though."

A visit to Todd's apartment yields a similar result—nobody's there, and while he could just be out, Lydia speaks to two other people who live on his floor and neither of them recognize the name or the picture. Which means they need to trace the chain back another stage: Prof. Booth.

She was the first one to mention Jene, says Lydia as their car heads uptown. *At the time it seemed an unlikely lead, but then . . .*

Then you found evidence of a motive, says Madison. *From people who've since disappeared.*

It's like they're trying to cover up Fitz's murder—but why feed me with all this information? Why not send the police after the wrong suspect instead of getting me to do it?

Because they were able to manipulate you through Fitzwilliam's voice. It means they keep the police at a remove.

Yeah, but say I'd delivered my evidence to the police . . . it doesn't stand up. It hung together the way it was presented to me, but now I look a bit deeper, it's all falling apart. It'd never stand up in court. Perhaps it wasn't supposed to? Perhaps it was only meant to deflect attention away from the real killer long enough for the trail to go cold?

Hopefully this woman can give us some answers, Madison says, and Lydia can sense her displeasure at all these complications and loose ends. *Assuming there is such a person as Prof. Booth.*

There must be. She couldn't just hire an office at a university for the morning. Even as Lydia says this she realizes it might not be true. Probably if you offered NYNU enough money, they would let you hire an office and list you on their site as a member of staff for as long as you needed.

Lydia and Madison walk into NYNU to find Lydia's student idee has expired—it was good only for the day she obtained it.

I can sign up for another, she tells Madison, *but I'm a bit low on funds right now—*

The embassy will cover it, Madison replies. They're attracting stares from others in the lobby and Madison would probably prefer to get out of here.

Lydia tells the registration terminal she wants to re-enroll. The terminal tells her she's barred from entry and should leave the premises immediately. She tries again, hoping it's a case of mistaken identity, but two security guards come over to disabuse her of that notion.

"OK, let's go," says one of the guards, pointing a finger from Lydia to Madison and then to the door.

"I need to see Professor Booth," Lydia tells the guard.

"You're not permitted on the premises, miss," the guard replies.

Tell him it's diplomatic business, says Madison, and Lydia does so.

"That's irrelevant. Neither of you are permitted on the premises."

I'm allowed everywhere, Madison retorts. She persists with the argument for a few minutes, threatening to escalate this to the embassy, before the police turn up and arrest them both. Lydia can't help but notice the cops got here quicker than they did when she called them from the roof of Liberty View.

SIX

PATTERNS OF BEHAVIOR

Is this the first time you've been arrested? Lydia asks Madison as they wait on a bench in the police station.

Yes, replies Madison icily. Lydia briefly thought (hoped?) she might kick off in the lobby of NYNU, but she submitted to police custody with simmering resentment instead.

Me too, actually. But I'm sure they'll let us go. Those security guys just wanted us out of there.

This will not stand. The ambassador has been informed. At the absolute minimum I want an apology and the arrest to be stricken from the record.

Apology from who?

The police of course, who else?

I thought you might want an apology from the university.

Madison thinks for a moment. *Yes, that too. And I'll be pressing charges against those security guards, and demanding changes—* Then she looks up, because someone else is talking to her. Lydia turns to see Dion standing a few meters away, wearing a weird, timid expression—she must know how angry Madison will be.

They want to talk to me, Madison tells Lydia.

"Me too?" Lydia asks.

"Oh," says Dion. "No, I don't think so. Just her."

Madison stands slowly, taking her time, letting Dion know this is happening on her terms, then follows her down the corridor. Lydia's left waiting, tapping her foot.

"Back so soon?"

Lydia turns and sees the speaker is Rollo, approaching her with a quizzical grimace.

"Yeah, sorry," says Lydia, "couldn't resist going back for one last big score."

Rollo stops as he reaches the bench she's sitting on. He peers down at her. "I heard they picked up a Logi and her translator after an altercation at NYNU, I didn't expect it to be you."

"Yeah and I suppose arresting me's a better use of police time than, you know, trying to solve my boss's murder or finding that guy who stole his head?"

Rollo holds up his hands as if defending himself from attack. "Hey, I get that you're angry but we're doing our best—"

"They stole his fucking *head* out of this building and you didn't see it; you couldn't find Hari and now you can't find this guy! I thought this was a total surveillance culture? Like proper Orwellian shit?"

"It's not as simple as that. We can only work with the information we have."

"You must have something showing him going in and out—"

"I haven't been on that," snaps Rollo, "because *I've* been busy looking into Jene Connor's background."

Lydia straightens up on her seat. "Oh?"

"Spoke to her parents. Had to tread lightly, they weren't in the frame of mind to hear their daughter might've been a murderer."

"Obviously, but what did they say?"

"I asked about your boss, and the Logi, and she never showed *any* interest in the subject at all. Had a history of mental health problems, but they thought she had it under control. Didn't really have any friends, and—"

"Yeah but just because she never spoke to her parents about it, doesn't mean—"

"And she never went to NYNU."

Lydia looks at the floor and mutters, "Oh fuckery."

"She moved to the city about eighteen months ago; we've got patterns of behavior that don't match what you told us—she had a job as a PA at MJN, her last day at work was Friday, she killed herself Sunday morning. There's nothing to suggest she had the skills to get past your security or wipe the records. It just doesn't check out. *Any* of it."

Lydia sighs. "That's what I was afraid of. Look—a few days

ago a professor at NYNU told me Jene was one of her students. I looked up Jene's profile and there she was, ex-NYNU, and I tracked down some of her friends and talked to them and one of them had pictures of herself with Jene. But now her friends have vanished and the professor won't see me and none of it was true and why is someone doing this to me?"

Rollo weighs up whether this is something he ought to take seriously. "Doing what to you?"

"Leading me up the garden path. Her friends—who weren't even her real friends, fuck knows who they were—lied to me, and you should be looking for them, I've got images—"

"Why should we be looking for them?"

"Because they lied to me."

"That isn't illegal."

"I think they were trying to stop me finding the real killer."

"That's only illegal if they do it to *us*—" A note *pings* in his glasses and he apologizes, saying there's somewhere he needs to be, and Lydia is left alone to turn it over in her mind until Madison returns.

Well, they've apologized, she says. *Apparently they ought to have given us the opportunity to leave the scene peacefully.*

This has got to be about more than just setting Jene up as a plausible suspect for the murder, doesn't it? says Lydia.

What?

It's so much bigger than it needs to be. With the fake game and her fake friends and all the fake information about her online. Why not just paint her as a basic racist? Stick a load of stuff online of her saying she was going to kill an alien and backdate it? That would've been easier, no need for her to have uncovered this nefarious plot. . . . Lydia feels things clicking into place. *Because that was the point.*

What was the point?

This was all about leading me to the game, not Jene. They wanted me to find the game and think it was real.

Who's "they"?

I don't know yet, whoever set all this up—but they wanted me to go public with it, and I was just about to when you stopped me. And that's why they made me think I was talking to Fitz's ghost—it wasn't just to feed me clues and get me to investigate, they wanted me to confront him about it so I'd think he'd admitted everything and it was definitely true.

But people tell lies about us every day. Why go to so much effort to convince you of this one? They could've fed this story to someone who'd believe it in a moment and wouldn't question any of it.

Madison's right about this. The infowar and paranoia feeds spread this stuff around like diarrhea in a Jacuzzi.

Then it hits her.

But all those lies, she tells Madison, get marked up as lies. Their truthiness rating is complete junk, like sub-forty. Only people who already want to believe it ever see it. But what if they could make someone with no connections to anti-Logi groups, who in fact would be one of the least likely people to take against you, came out with a story she absolutely believed about you guys rewiring our brains?

Madison takes a moment to consider this.

If I'd gone public with that, Lydia continues, stuck it on my stream, the truthiness rating would've been way higher. I've got a really credible background and a clean history and I'd have believed what I was saying, because I followed the breadcrumbs and felt like I'd worked it out for myself. Would've broken big. Got around everyone's filters. People who usually never see stuff like that would've seen it.

Madison stares at Lydia for a moment. At the very least Madison must know that, whether she is right or wrong or deluded or whatever, she is sincere.

But you couldn't prove it, says Madison. You said yourself, the story didn't stand up to scrutiny.

But in the moment I said it, I'd believe it. By the time we found the holes in the story, even if I changed my mind about it later and retracted it all, it'd have already gone round the bloody world. A billion people would see the post, a thousand would see the correction. This is all about bypassing truth filters.

Lydia feels elated at having put this together, but the ramifications are crashing into her head. She wants it to be true because she needs to find answers, but on the other hand she doesn't want it to be true because maybe this is much bigger than she can deal with.

OK, says Madison. *What would happen next? In your opinion.*

I suppose people would demand action be taken.

Against who?

Anyone who was involved.

But no one was involved. There wouldn't be any evidence, so no action would be taken.

Which would only have made people angrier, Lydia goes on. *They'd think there'd been a cover-up or a whitewash or whatever. Fitz wouldn't be alive to defend himself. Everyone becomes more receptive to negative stories about you. What if this was just the start?*

A gunshot sounds across the room, shattering a window and ruining Lydia's concentration.

What in the world—says Madison, turning in the direction of the shot. It came from an interview room—the glass that shattered was the window in its door. A twitchy, middle-aged man in filthy clothes emerges from the room and brandishes the gun at everyone in sight. Some of them look at one another, considering how to address the situation; some of them duck down behind desks. Lydia, who has nothing to duck behind, envies them. Briefly she considers ducking behind Madison, who is a good deal larger than she is, but it becomes moot when the gunman marches over to her, grabs her by the arm and pulls her towards himself, pressing the gun into her neck.

"OK, listen up!" the gunman shouts. He smells rank. As his fingers dig into Lydia's flesh she can feel them jittering, the kind of jitter she gets when she relies too hard on &amp. There's a strong possibility this guy can't be reasoned with. He's loudly demanding the cops release his brother.

"Your brother's . . . dead," one of the cops tells him hesitantly, justifiably anxious he might literally shoot the messenger.

"Don't buy it," says the gunman, and underlines the point by pressing the gun harder into Lydia's neck. The jitter is traveling through the gun. He may well shoot her whether he chooses to or not.

Help me, Lydia says to Madison. She can't turn her head to see Madison but can sense she's still nearby, on her left.

How? Madison replies.

I was hoping you might have some ideas.

The gunman is still loudly refusing to believe his brother is dead and is demanding someone fetch him, whether it's from the cells or the morgue.

If I pretend to faint, says Lydia, *can you take him out?*

Is this wise?

I don't bloody know but I don't have time to workshop something better—look, he's not going to get his brother back and I don't think he's going to let me go, so can you do it?

Yes.

OK, so I'm going to faint on the count of three, right?

Right.

One . . . two . . . three—

Lydia tries to collapse in the least alarming way she can—no loud noises, just a sigh and then she goes slack, leaning into the gunman rather than away from him. The gunman's still gripping her arm tightly and she feels like he's going to rip it off, but as she slumps to the floor and resists putting out a hand to steady herself, she focuses on the fact the gun hasn't gone off yet which is *something* at least—

The gunman bends down to tell Lydia to get up, but gets only halfway through this instruction before he cries out in pain. Lydia's eyes are half-closed and she can't see what's happening but hears a dull *clunk* as the gun hits the floor next to her, then a loud *smack* and another agonized exclamation from the gunman before he too hits the floor.

Lydia rolls over and opens her eyes to see the dazed gunman being seized by cops. Madison helps Lydia to her feet and everyone in the station applauds Madison for her actions.

What are they doing? Madison asks.

Lydia remembers Fitz telling her he never quite got used to hearing applause, despite all the live events he attended where it happened as a matter of course. He simply couldn't comprehend why this banging together of limbs signified approval. Right now Lydia feels much the same, because although she can read this scene of relief and adulation, she does not trust a single person in this building—except, she's startled to realize, Madison.

They're saying thank you, she replies.

Acknowledge it for me, would you?

"She says it's no trouble," Lydia tells the room, who aren't listening to her anyway, then she says to Madison: *We need to leave.*

Yes—but first there's something we need to do. Madison heads in the opposite direction to the door.

We're not safe here, says Lydia, even as she follows Madison deeper into the police station.

I'm conscious of that but there's still something we need to do.

One of the cops dealing with the gunman sees them walking away and says, "Excuse me, miss—where are you—"

"*Don't* fucking talk to me," spits Lydia, unsure where this came from, aware it's unwise to take this tone with an officer of the law. But she feels it deeply; it's rooted in her fury at being dragged down here and put in this situation and her suspicions about what's behind it, and above all it works. The cop hesitates, is distracted by the gunman's shouts as he's dragged away, and Lydia hurries to catch up with Madison.

EVIDENCE OF A STRUGGLE

They're in on it, Lydia tells Madison as they stride through the corridors of the police station. *The cops, I mean.*

What leads you to that conclusion? Madison asks. There's nothing skeptical or mocking about this: she simply wants Lydia to show her work.

Lydia looks around, wondering where they're going. *I don't know how widespread it is—might just be a few of them, might be more—*

Yes, go on.

They've now let two major suspects in this case slip through their fingers. Like, I found Hari quicker than they did. I think someone's sabotaging the investigation from the inside.

But Hari was an ideal suspect—why conspire to stop him being caught?

To keep the case alive? Make sure I kept going with my investigation. Remember how the cops kept me in the residence when you and the agency wanted to move me out? And now I step inside a police station and instantly some random nutcase tries to kill me.

And then there's theft of Fitzwilliam's head from the morgue, of course—speaking of which, we're almost there.

The morgue?

No, the evidence store. That's where his head is and we're going to take it back. This way, adds Madison as she turns a corner and glides down a set of steps.

Can you just . . . take it?

I demanded it back at the same time I demanded an apology. They agreed but said they couldn't give it to me straightaway. I don't trust them with it and I'm not leaving this building without it. When we reach this counter, say hello.

Lydia and Madison arrive at a hatch where a desk sergeant sits, a windowless basement room behind her. The desk sergeant wears a badge that says HANDELL. She's been looking increasingly anxious as Lydia and Madison have approached.

"Hello," says Lydia pleasantly, then introduces herself and Madison.

"Can I help you?" says Sergeant Handell.

"We've come to take the head that came in earlier."

"The . . . head of the ambassador?" says Handell uncertainly.

"Cultural attaché, not ambassador."

"That's evidence."

"I think you'll find," says Lydia, trying to remember exactly how Madison phrased it, "the body of any member of diplomatic staff or parts thereof remain subject to diplomatic immunity and cannot be held by police or any other human authority without the express permission of the embassy, which is being withdrawn as of now."

"But you can't do that," says Handell, who plainly has no idea whether they can do it or not.

"She can, and you're lucky she hasn't already." Lydia is starting to feel light-headed, and there's a boldness creeping into her manner which she's not sure she can back up. "Your failure to properly safeguard that body is on the verge of causing a major diplomatic incident."

"The *morgue* had the body when the head was stolen."

"I don't mean you *personally*, I mean the whole department— and you're making things an awful lot worse right now by standing in her way."

"I do need to clear this—hold on." Handell taps her glasses and tries to find something to look at that isn't Madison or Lydia as she waits for her call to be answered. Momentarily she glances at a large box on the floor next to her, decorated with blue and orange diagonal stripes and the NYPD badge. Then she glances at it again, nervously. Lydia takes in the size of the box.

I think it's that box down there, she says to Madison.

You're sure?

No, but she keeps looking at it.

Madison also looks at the box and Lydia can sense her weighing up a decision. Then Madison reaches her long arms across and angles them down towards the box.

"Hey!" says Handell, looking up.

"It's all been agreed and I'm afraid I'm in a hurry," says Lydia as if translating. (Madison did not, in fact, say this but Lydia's sure she won't mind.) Lydia notes from Handell's reaction that Fitz's head is indeed in the box—if it wasn't she'd have said so. The desk sergeant tries to pull Madison's arm away and entirely fails.

"Don't touch me, please," says Lydia. (Madison did say this.)

Then Madison lifts the box off the picker, pulls it through the gap above the counter and clutches it to her chest. Lydia is only able to comprehend this movement while she's actually watching it: the box moves so smoothly it may as well be gliding on rails. Lydia recalls the tank inside the box is full of fluid, and therefore incredibly heavy. Handell looks in awe of this too.

Communicate my thanks to Sergeant Handell for her kind assistance, says Madison as she turns away. Lydia does so and then follows, ignoring Handell's warnings about how they won't get out of the building, about how the fire doors they're walking towards are locked and if they return the box now, she won't raise the alarm and they'll say no more about it. Foolishly, instead of raising the alarm straightaway, she's trying to save face over her failure to stop them taking the box.

Do you think she's telling the truth about those doors being locked? Madison asks. The doors in question are flat, gray and featureless, with an EXIT sign above them.

No, says Lydia. *It's illegal to lock a fire door in a public building to stop people getting out.*

You're full of useful information, aren't you? Open the door for me, please.

Lydia pushes open the door—and sees Madison has already summoned a diplomatic car around to this exit, and it's waiting for them. Slick.

Behind them an alarm sears the air.

HANDBRAKE TURN

The diplomatic car is driving them down Broadway, and Madison has the box on her lap, and Lydia can't believe they've got out of the station and feels something must have gone wrong.

A siren sounds from a couple of streets away. This was inevitable: the cops were never going to shrug and leave them to it. They got a good head start on the ones from the station, but the cops must be mobilizing other units.

They can't stop a diplomatic car, says Madison.

But they can stop us when we get out of it, can't they?

After the business at NYNU I'd like to see them try.

But all they need to do is take the box back. They could stop you long enough to do that.

If we're on embassy property they won't be able to get near us.

Is that where we're going?

Of course.

Lydia looks in the rearview mirror. A police car is following them a few cars behind, but its lights and siren are off. As Madison said, there's nothing they can legally do to make them stop, and they must have guessed where they're heading, so Lydia wonders what they're planning to—

A shock of lights and sirens surges into the road in front of them as another police car pulls out of a junction, making an illegal maneuver and forcing other cars to stop and swerve.

"Fucking hell!" Lydia blurts out loud.

What did you just say? asks Madison.

Lydia explains what she said.

Fair comment. They're trying to block us off.

Indeed, the other cars on the road automatically slow and move to the side, as they're programmed to do when an emergency vehicle is coming up behind. The diplomatic car has no such programming and follows in the wake of the police car: meanwhile its interface politely suggests they slow down and move to the side, though they are not obliged to do so.

What do we do? asks Lydia, who assumes Madison has anticipated this.

I don't know.

The police car in front of them begins to slow, forcing them to slow too. The one following behind is now tailgating them. A thick line of cars has stopped on either side, almost bumper-to-bumper. In moments they'll be boxed in.

Right, says Madison as their car slows to a halt. *When they tell us to get out, here's what we do.*

But Lydia has just seen a movement out of the corner of her eye: the car to their right has reached a junction and is taking the opportunity to turn and escape the traffic. The occupant isn't even looking at what's happening—he's on his scroll—and the car will have simply calculated a quicker route to his destination. The cars behind it will do the same when they process the movement of this car—but right now a gap is opening up and will not stay open for long. Lydia makes this calculation in a couple of seconds, and a couple of seconds is all she has.

Lydia pulls open the hatch in the dashboard and the emergency steering wheel pops out, a skinny thing made of metal and coated with rubber: it's less satisfying to hold than a proper one, in fact she immediately hates it. She releases the safety catch, overriding the Smartsteer and allowing the wheel to turn. Her feet search the floor of the car and find the pedals—they're not proper pedals, just pressure studs on the floor, and she doesn't like those either, you lose a lot of fine control. On top of all this she's out of practice and has never driven a left-hander. But apart from that this is a terrific plan.

What are you doing? asks Madison, her puzzlement so marked that Lydia feels sure she has never seen anyone physically drive a car before.

It's very important you don't talk to me while I'm doing this, Lydia replies.

Lydia turns the wheel sharply and the diplomatic car lurches into the space vacated by the car to their right. The next in the queue, a purple Innoson, is also trying to take that space but Lydia cuts across it, forcing it to brake abruptly. Lydia glances up and sees the occupants jolted into awareness of their surroundings, looking back at her, outraged and perplexed by her unorthodox maneuver. She can see them starting to berate her, their silent faces staring out through the windshield mouthing *What the fuck are you doing?* It's a fair question but she hasn't time to apologize, she needs to concentrate on the road.

Because of the weird angle she's taken, Lydia is forced to cut the corner: the diplomatic car bumps as it hits the curb and she remembers just in time to check there are no cyclists or pedestrians in the way. In the places back home where she used to drive there was never anyone around so she never had to worry about that stuff. At least she's judged the height of the curb correctly and doesn't break the axle. The wheels hit the surface of the next street and Lydia steers sharply to ensure she doesn't crash into the car waiting at the crosswalk. She glances in the rearview and sees the purple Innoson moving up to the junction, its Smartsteer having deemed it safe to do so, and the gap she just used is closed. The cops can't follow.

Yes! thinks Lydia.

What? Madison replies.

I told you not to talk to me. Distantly she can hear sirens: the cops will be deploying other units, of course. She wonders if they're allowed to do manual high-speed pursuit, or even know how. Halifax cops weren't trained for it, they just had a pursuit setting on the Smartsteer, which the police preferred because it meant no one was directly responsible if they ran anyone down. It might be different in America—but even so, they won't have seen anyone drive like her before. Also the streets here are all *really* straight and going fast down these should be easy. She's literally on Easy Street.

Thanks to the traffic jam clogging Broadway, the road ahead is clear. Lydia has only a rough idea where the embassy is—she's been there only a few times and never had to pay attention to the route. She knows she needs to make a left turn but she's not sure where. More sirens are sounding—cops heading for the street she's driving down. She looks up ahead and sees a gap in the traffic coming the other way and she watches to see if it lines up with the next junction. Back in the day, one of her favorite things to do was to take corners without slowing down or losing control—but the thing about corners is they don't move, and traffic unfortunately does. She needs to be decisive: either make the turn or keep going. The worst thing she can do is hesitate.

She arrives at the junction and there's a truck coming the other way but she judges the gap is plenty big enough. Trucks are meant to drive slowly and carefully, make sure stock isn't damaged—she thinks she read that somewhere once.

Lydia turns the wheel hard to the left—it's not a smooth action, these shitty emergency wheels bend slightly when you turn them too hard and the steering column resists sharp movements, and she has to hold it longer than expected to make the turn. The wheels skid and the car drifts into the other lane, but Lydia steers back to compensate before they hit anything. Despite the limitations of the controls the car itself is a classy product and a good weight for this sort of driving, neither so heavy as to be sluggish nor so light as to risk overturning.

Madison isn't speaking, but Lydia's aware of a furious muttering radiating out of her. She is not happy. But Lydia didn't expect her to be.

Lydia can see Central Park up ahead. More sirens echo around the streets, coming from somewhere she can't see. She comes to a box junction, throws the wheel to the right, then accelerates to eighty. This isn't necessarily the quickest route to the embassy but her aim is to drive in an unpredictable manner, and she's certainly achieving this if nothing else.

She'd love to stick some tunes on. Doesn't feel right driving without music. She could tell the sys to hook up to her scroll and find one of her old driving playlists. But she doubts Madison would appreciate it, and it might undermine confidence in her driving skills.

I know I said don't talk to me but I need you to give me directions, says Lydia.

You don't know where we're going?

I vaguely know where we're going, says Lydia, making another turn. She sees this street is free of traffic and drives straight up the middle before turning again onto Fifth Avenue. A cop car swings out of a side street and tries to cut them off, but Lydia goes up on the sidewalk before turning sharply.

Next left, says Madison.

Lydia takes the next left. A barrier announces this street is closed for resurfacing: she drives into the barrier, knocking it aside. This is not purely because she enjoys driving into things, though she *does* enjoy it: the noise of the collision ensures the construction drones immediately notice and retreat to the side of the road, making it easy to steer around them.

This is fun. She feels like she shouldn't be having fun doing it, which makes it even more fun.

Keep going, says Madison. *It's on this street.*

Lydia is both relieved they've almost made it and disappointed it's almost over. *Just tell me when I need to stop.*

Cops are approaching in the rearview. Surely they've guessed where the car's heading? Yes—up ahead she sees more cop cars, three of them bumper-to-bumper, blocking the road. Lydia recognizes the street now and knows the embassy is just beyond the line. They're so close and yet they're about to be boxed in again. What can she do? Is the sidewalk clear enough or wide enough to drive down?

Turn right, says Madison. *Now.*

Lydia doesn't understand this instruction, yet she has complete confidence in it. She believes it's the right thing to do, and that the logic behind it will become clear.

This confidence lasts just long enough for her to turn the wheel, then she wonders how the hell this helps them reach the embassy. Is Madison thinking they can approach from the opposite direction? The cops will have thought of that—surely they'll block that route too?

Now left, says Madison.

Lydia feels the confidence return as she steers left, glances over her shoulder to see if they're being followed, and very nearly crashes into a cleaning truck.

Down there, says Madison, pointing at a ramp that leads into the basement of a gray office building coming up on their left.

A cop car speeds towards them from the opposite direction. In moments it'll cut off the route to the ramp. Lydia swings the car across the street towards the building, cutting it a little too fine and grazing the wall of the entrance with the right-hand side of the front bumper—

Careful!

Lydia rights the car and the ramp takes them below street level and she slows right down because there's a hairpin bend coming up and she doesn't want to smash into the wall. Where the hell are they? How come Madison knows about it? More urgently, what about the shiny, yet rough-textured, dark gray wall up ahead that entirely blocks their way? There's no way Lydia can get back around that hairpin, reversing is *not* her strong point. Flashes of red light up the tunnel and a siren echoes around as the cop car drives down the ramp behind them. Why did Madison lead them into this underground dead end?

Don't stop, says Madison. *Keep going.*

As with Madison's directions, Lydia finds this assurance completely overrides her own instincts. She knows they are driving towards a solid surface but there's an absolute conviction in Madison's voice that this will be fine. It's almost scary how, in this moment, she trusts Madison over and above the evidence of her own senses.

Lydia takes her foot off the brake—they have not yet quite stopped moving—and instead she accelerates.

Careful, says Madison. *We don't want to hurt it.*

The dark gray wall parts easily as the car makes contact—it seems to have a thick viscous consistency—but Lydia can see its edges remain stuck fast to the bodywork, forming a seal. The car passes through and nothing else passes through with it, not even an air molecule.

It's like a perfect air lock, says Lydia.

Very good, says Madison: she seems impressed by Lydia's description. *Yes, it's a version of the technology we use on air locks. Usually they're transparent, but this breed enables greater privacy.*

The car completes its journey through the wall and Lydia sees they are in a branch of Hertz car rental, which is something of an anticlimax. Or at least, the signage says it's a Hertz: notably there are very few cars here, maybe four or five, and the place doesn't seem to be staffed. Lydia pulls into a parking space and turns to look at the wall they just drove through.

The wall has closed up behind them. Dully, Lydia can hear the siren through it.

Don't worry, says Madison. *The membrane won't let them through.*

Won't let them?

It parted for us because I told it to. They won't be able to talk to it.

It's alive? Lydia gets out of the car and walks towards the wall. It looks like a huge slab of jelly candy. She reaches her hand out and touches its surface: it's soft and a little warm, but absolutely does not give way under pressure.

Madison gets out of the car and walks towards Lydia, carrying the evidence box. *Careful. They can sting if they decide they don't like you.*

It seems OK, Lydia replies. In fact she feels a faint vibration coming from the wall, like the purr of a cat. *Can I talk to it?*

Potentially, yes—but you'd have to learn their language. It's very different from ours.

Wow. I never knew you had anything like this.

One has to be responsible with one's technology on other planets.

Lydia listens out for a moment. *I can hear the cops talking on the other side. They're bloody furious. Ha-ha.*

We need to go.

Go where?

TECHNICALLY ON ANOTHER PLANET

This defunct branch of Hertz car rental is the property of the embassy, and is connected to it via a short foot tunnel. While the diplomatic status of the former is ambiguous and hinges on whether one could argue it to be "part" of the embassy, the latter is most definitely safe ground.

We felt it wise to have a secluded entrance, says Madison, *for more discreet comings and goings.*

Why leave all the Hertz signs up?

The what signs?

These, says Lydia as they pass one on their way to the foot tunnel.

Oh, the ambassador liked them. Thought they added a nice authentic feel to the place.

Fair enough.

The tunnel takes them into the embassy basement and past the kitchens: a warm dusty smell drifts from a nearby door. Now they're on Logi soil and Fitz's head cannot be taken from them. Lydia feels relieved, for Fitz more than herself—she knows she'll be in very deep shit when she steps out of the embassy, but at least no one will be able to do horrible stuff to him anymore.

Lydia wonders if she could claim asylum on Logia or something. It'd be lonely, she'd be limited in how much time she could talk to people each day, and she'd more or less lose contact with everyone on Earth, including her family. And anyway the Logi probably wouldn't let her go there. There's no reason they should see her as their problem.

They ascend the stairs into the high-ceilinged lobby. Whereas

Fitz liked the residence to have a broadly Earthlike aesthetic—for him, that was part of the point of living here—the embassy is a dizzying culture clash, with insanely deep-pile carpets that mimic the spongy floors of homes on Logia, and walls decorated with strangely colorless paper—not even really white or gray, if you stare at them they seem to have no depth, like you're looking into mist. Apparently the Logi see them very differently. Fitz told her once he saw skies filled with birds.

A staff member rushes over urgently to speak to Madison. He seems aghast by what's happened and for the first time Lydia senses they may not be hailed as heroes after all. She'd assumed Madison was carrying out orders, with clearance to resolve the situation by any means necessary. But perhaps she's gone off-piste too.

Madison turns to Lydia. *The ambassador wants to see us.*

Us? Not just you?

Us.

Whenever Fitz came to the embassy he didn't need Lydia, so she either didn't come with him at all or waited in the reception room just off the lobby. Her only previous meeting with the ambassador wasn't even at the embassy, but at the Met Gala earlier this year. When they were introduced he seemed unaware Fitz had a new translator, and asked what happened to the old one: then he and Fitz had a conversation Lydia was not privy to, and the ambassador moved on to another group without speaking to her again. She's sure he won't remember her.

The ambassador's name is Temple. He's quite short (by Logi standards, which means he's a little taller than Lydia), and Lydia assumes he's quite old, though she always finds it hard to tell: maybe he just moves and speaks slowly. He wears a thick robe that looks like a dressing gown and a shapeless hat that resembles a shower cap. Lydia will have to be careful these observations don't leak out at any point. She offended an important trade negotiator back in London during a work experience placement in a very similar way: he had no scalp spikes and preferred to converse with his eyes closed, and Lydia couldn't help thinking about how his head looked like a dirty tooth.

Take a seat, please, says Temple without looking up from the copious paperwork on his desk. When you see the desks of high-ranking officials on media, they're always really neat and have, like, *one* document on them and a lamp, and the document is probably just for show anyway. Lydia notices that to one side of Temple's desk there's a wheeled office chair, a copyright-free printed thing like the ones in schools and public buildings everywhere, which is incongruous in the tasteful surroundings: Probably Temple doesn't know humans would see it as basic and inelegant, and even if he does he probably doesn't care. However, it is clearly there for human use and Lydia pulls it into position, then sits.

Madison takes one of the other chairs, which has a slightly convex back, and places the box on her lap.

Is that the head? Temple asks, allowing Lydia to hear. She's rarely experienced three-way conversations like this: if she's not required to translate, she doesn't need to know, so she's not looped in.

It is, says Madison. She starts to open the box—

Please, not here, says Temple. *I don't need to see it.*

Of course, says Madison, folding it back down.

The police are livid, Temple says.

We didn't expect them not to be, says Madison. Lydia wonders if she is included in this "we."

They're literally outside right now, demanding we give them that box and hand her—Temple points at Lydia—*into their custody.*

What have you told them?

I told them I had to speak to you first. But it's going to take a great deal of work to smooth this over, you know.

It is, but they're the ones who need to do it. What happened to Fitzwilliam is an outrage and they allowed it to happen.

I agree, but—

You think we were wrong to take it back? You want us to return it?

Not wrong *as such, but there were more amicable ways of doing this. This has created quite a situation.*

Yes, says Lydia, *we noticed that when we were driving over here.*

A ripple of amusement emanates from Madison, which she swiftly suppresses. Temple turns his attention to Lydia. *The monitors are arriving tomorrow. This is not an ideal situation for them to find us in.*

No, I see that.

I'm not clear what we're supposed to do with you now.

If I may, Madison interjects, *Lydia deserves our gratitude. She's been the target of a sophisticated effort to manipulate her against us, and not only has she resisted it, she's uncovered possible direct police involvement in it.*

Temple leans back in his chair. *Do I understand you correctly? You're suggesting the NYPD conspired to manipulate this translator against us?*

Not necessarily all of them, Lydia interjects. *But someone there must be involved in this, I'm sure of it.*

Tell him what you told me, Madison says. *The whole thing.*

Lydia looks to Temple. He gives a gesture Lydia recognizes as "open mind"—a steady unclenching of a fist accompanied by a studied, calm silence that awaits a response. She tries to keep her account as concise as possible, partly because the longer it goes on the less sober she'll be, partly because the more detail she puts in, the madder she sounds.

This is very serious, says Temple, *if true.*

You don't need to tell me it's serious, I've been living it.

I went with her to the places where she was deceived, says Madison. *Her reactions were absolutely in earnest, I can vouch for them. And then there's this.* She points to the box.

Temple shudders and looks away. *The one thing missing from your story is who. All you have is an unspecified number of unidentified employees of the NYPD.*

Yes, says Lydia, *I'm very aware of that.*

I think there's something we can try, says Madison.

This surprises Lydia. *Is there?*

Madison taps the top of the box.

Temple has given his permission to go ahead with Madison's proposal, provided they find a different room to do it in and don't tell him the details. Lydia can't really argue with either of these points. So a meeting room has been requisitioned and the box has been placed on the tall circular table in the center of it. Lydia clambers onto a chair and kneels on it so she can get a better view of what's going on.

Madison opens the box and starts to lift the contents out. Lydia braces herself.

The shock of seeing Fitz's head in the tank is dulled on a second viewing, but Lydia now realizes how many of the details she blanked out upon seeing it earlier. She paid little attention to the clumsy way his neck has been sealed, for instance—it looks like molded plastic and glue. She sees the slackness of his unmasked face through the distorting prism of the fluid. And she can see the cauterized blood under the helmet, where his head has been sliced into and patched with electronics. She wonders why that was necessary: perhaps to stimulate the brain into activity.

Madison busies herself with checking over the components that hang on the side of the tank, seemingly detached and unaffected. But then she suddenly says, *Excuse me,* turns away and hurriedly leaves the room, and Lydia senses the wave of upset and revulsion, and realizes she was just trying to act detached and unaffected.

Lydia is left alone in the room with Fitz's head.

"You poor bastard," she says. She's never spoken aloud to him before. Even the best translators sometimes succumb to their instincts and speak aloud to Logi—she did it a few times when training for the job—but she never did it to Fitz. "Did you ever notice that? Depends what the last one you had was like, I suppose. You always said how brilliant she was. I hope I wasn't too crap by comparison, anyway."

Madison comes back into the room, composed once more, saying, *Sorry about that.*

It's OK, Lydia says.

I don't think there's much chance of me managing to operate this. Can you try?

I'm no expert with this stuff.

But you've used things like this before, whereas I haven't.

Lydia's about to protest that, actually, she hasn't used things like this, but realizes Madison's definition of "things like this" is "any digital technology." Madison rotates the tank—which means Lydia can no longer see Fitz's face, but has a better view of the spots where his head has been opened up, so swings and roundabouts really— and pushes it across the table towards her.

The interface on the screen is not very user-friendly—it's not based on off-the-shelf software and was plainly never designed for anyone other than its operator to use. It has its own power source and can connect to any pair of glasses, which supply it with a mic and phones. Like any such interface, it keeps a log of all connections and Lydia manages to locate it—but she's unsurprised to find it's been wiped, either by its operator or by someone at the NYPD. She searches through it, trying to find any clues anywhere in its records—but it's a very basic device and there aren't many places to look.

Do you think you might find something, you know . . . Madison points directly at Fitz's head. *In there?*

Lydia glances at the head. *You mean try to make contact with him? Would that work?*

I've no idea. No one's ever attempted this kind of ghoulish technology before. But if someone's been speaking through him, perhaps they left some traces?

It seems possible, at least. *But why do I have to do it?* Lydia asks. *You can talk to him better than I can.*

Why do you say that?

Because I'm not one of you, am I?

But you spoke to him more than anyone. He was terribly antisocial, and you saw him every day. You know him much better than anyone else.

Lydia's not sure she really knew him at all, yet she thinks Madison might be right. She works out how to turn on the power to the head and the tank glows very slightly—it seems power flows directly through the liquid, taking the place of the energy the body would usually supply. She feels it the moment she throws the switch—it's not Fitz as he used to be, it's a weak yet recognizable version of him, like a recording of a recording of a recording, growing a little fainter and more corrupted each time. It really is like his ghost has stepped into the room, unable to communicate but letting her know: *I'm still here.*

Lydia's mind connects to what's left of his with no effort, and she queasily becomes aware that he *is* in some sense alive. Previously she'd thought the machine merely plugged into the language centers of his brain and bypassed everything else, but the rest of the brain is in fact awake, just heavily suppressed so it can't take any action. He knew what was happening to him and could do nothing about it.

She's getting nothing coherent from the contact. Just this horrible uneasy feeling. It's like talking to someone who's asleep and having a nightmare, whimpering the occasional half sentence in reply. If she keeps listening, it's possible something useful might surface—but it might not. There must be a way to adjust the settings and release him from this suppression so he can tell them who was responsible, but how? Her hand hovers over the interface, trying to make sense of it—probably the user was never intended to do anything other than plug in and talk through it, but it must be possible to tweak the settings. She finds a series of toggle switches and experiments with turning them off and on—

Lydia notices she's lying on her back on the floor of the meeting room and she wonders why. Her head hurts a lot and there's a wetness on her top lip which turns out to be blood leaking from her nose.

She opens her eyes and sees Madison standing over her. She blinks and tries to speak to Madison—but her head throbs like someone's injecting scalding hot coffee into it. She winces, waits for it to pass.

When she opens her eyes she can see Madison gesticulating. Lydia can tell the Logi is talking but can't hear her. She just shakes her head at Madison and shrugs.

Madison seems to understand there's a communication problem, and she helps Lydia up. At this point Lydia becomes aware she has also vomited down the front of her shirt, and dully wonders where the hell she's going to get a clean one from: all her clothes are at the residence. The details of her dire situation come back to her as Madison helps her into a chair (which is too high, as usual). Madison points at her, turning her hand in a circle, which Lydia recalls means *stay here,* and then leaves the meeting room.

Lydia tries to collect herself as she comes to terms with the possibility that she may have destroyed whatever it is that enables her to speak Logisi. If so, she's finished. This was her life, her one useful thing, and she's broken it, and her one chance was maybe to go to Logia and it was probably a stupid idea but now it's definitely not going to work, not now that she's broken her brain—

Madison returns, accompanied by a man with a warm manner, unruly graying hair and a dark suit with a bright green shirt underneath, who looks to be in early middle age. He introduces himself as Ivan, and explains he's the senior translator here at the embassy. Lydia's never met a working translator as old as this before: usually they burn out, go into teaching, change careers (e.g., become drug dealers) or just retire. "Maddie here tells me you've had a shock, is that right?"

Despite everything, Lydia laughs when she hears Madison referred to as *Maddie.* She thought she was the only one who used nicknames.

Ivan looks more concerned, asks Lydia if she's OK.

"I'm not great, to be honest with you, Ivan."

Ivan nods, glances at Madison, then turns back to Lydia. "She wants to know if you found anything out?" From his tone it's clear Madison hasn't explained to him what they were doing, and it's only now that Lydia thinks: *Did* I find anything out? After she tinkered with the settings there was a howl in her mind. Just pure unfiltered pain, worst thing she's ever felt in her entire life, and then she passed out. She explains this to Ivan, who relates it to Madison.

"So you're saying there was nothing?" Ivan says on Madison's behalf.

But no, there was: amid the pain, something else. Lydia recalls how she could usually tell who Fitz was talking about without him using their name, because there was an emotional flavor to how he spoke: it tasted of his precise opinion of that person. And through the pain she could hear Fitz speak of the person responsible for his torment, and Lydia knows exactly who it was. He was trying to tell her before, at the residence, when she thought she was talking to his ghost—but she couldn't hear him. Suddenly she could, and it all came out in a torrent.

While Ivan explains this to Madison, Lydia realizes there's something she has to do, right now. She stumbles down from the chair and over to the tank, and she cuts off the power. Then she takes the helmet off Fitz's head, tears the wires out and smashes it against the table until it breaks.

CLOSING

Lydia paces the reception room. They don't have time for this bollocks. He could be leaving the city; he might already have left. Her instincts tell her he won't have done, but recent events have shaken her trust in her instincts.

She's also desperate to get all this over with so she can get to a neurologist and find out if what's happened to her is permanent. She still can't hear or speak to the Logi and she's scared. She's never heard of anything like this happening before, they didn't mention it at LSTL.

On the bright side, Ivan has managed to find her a clean shirt, a polo with blue and brown horizontal stripes. It's not the kind of thing she'd usually wear because she'd assume the stripes would make her look fat, but she rather likes it.

She's cheering herself up looking at the footage people have posted online of her drive through Manhattan, and pulling clips in the hope she can make a supercut of the whole trip from beginning to end, when her glasses tell her she's got a call from Marat at the agency. She answers it.

"Is it important?" Lydia asks. "I'm sort of busy here."

"What the *hell* is going on?"

"Oh, god—it's a long story, and I don't mind telling it to you, but right now—"

"I've had the NYPD here—they say you *robbed* their evidence store?"

"No no, Madison was told she could take it, but they were dragging their feet and—look, I was just doing my job."

"It's not your job to drive a diplomatic car at a hundred through the streets of Manhattan."

"That's not true—I never went above eighty. Maybe eighty-five.

Look, you're *always* telling us our first duty is to the Logi. Not to the cops. So I did what I thought was right. Sir."

Marat sighs. "There'll be an investigation—"

"Another one? Oh goody gumdrops."

"But that's not why I called."

"So that was just small talk, was it?"

"I need you to accept a change of assignment. Could you stop laughing, please?" he adds impatiently.

Minutes later, Lydia and Madison are leaving the embassy via the front door. Two cop cars are parked on the street, leaving a space just big enough for a diplomatic car between them (not the one Lydia drove here, because that one needs repairs), and Lydia notices a third cop car parked on the opposite side. The way from the door to the diplomatic car is lined with cops standing at a distance specified in the communications between the NYPD and the embassy. Every one of them turns their head towards Lydia and Madison, and every pair of eyes watches them from behind those dickhead aviators.

The situation is this: Madison is immune from prosecution for her actions. The evidence is on Logi territory now, the NYPD can't force her to return it and, given the fury over their failure to protect the body, have accepted that any protest over this would not be looked kindly upon. Lydia is *not* immune, and while they can't prosecute her for aiding the removal of the evidence, since she was working at Madison's behest, they *can* get her for dangerous driving. Yet she cannot be prosecuted for this while actively employed by a member of embassy staff, and the cops at NYNU overstepped their authority by arresting her. So Madison instructed Ivan to call Marat and offer Lydia a temporary secondment to work as Madison's translator. Lydia accepted, meaning she's free to walk out— provided Madison is with her.

Of course she cannot work as Madison's translator at the moment because she can't translate. But the NYPD doesn't know that.

And for their current purposes it has to be Lydia who goes to this meeting.

She wonders if they might be able to stop on the way and pick up something for her headache.

All the way there, Lydia checks they're not being followed or watched. The embassy made it clear that any police observation or interference in Madison's business would not be tolerated: a little talk of moving the embassy to Chicago got the mayor's office on their side. But Lydia still doesn't trust them to stick to it.

Their destination is a house in the Meatpacking District: Like a lot of the houses on this street, it was clearly a shop or restaurant at some point. The commerce in this part of the city died off long ago, leaving row upon row of eccentrically laid out living spaces. Lydia and Madison have come without prior warning, and they have to hope he's still here.

This would all be so much easier if they could just give his name to the police and let them do the rest. But giving his name to anyone might throw away their last chance to resolve this.

Lydia rings the doorbell. They wait.

Just as she's about to ring again, a voice comes over the intercom. "Hello?" Lydia can hear the uncertainty as Anders speaks. He'll know it's her. She wonders if he knows anything about how events have progressed since this morning. Hopefully he's been lying low and has had no contact with anyone.

"Hi, I'm here with Madison from the Logi embassy?" says Lydia, adopting a bright professional tone she never normally uses, ever. "She'd like to apologize for not having been in touch sooner, but everything's been a bit up in the air since, you know."

"Oh yeah, yeah. I was so sorry to hear about that."

"Thanks, yeah, it's been a tough week—but we don't want it to get in the way of plans for your event, because we really feel it would be a great tribute to Fitz if it all went ahead."

A pause. Will he take the bait?

"I'm glad to hear that," he says.

"So if we can come up—"

"Sure, sure."

The door slides open. They step inside.

Anders is upstairs. The décor preserves some original features of the shop it used to be—there's a vending machine over there, a display stand for shoes by the window, a sign pointing the way to the customer service desk hanging from the ceiling . . . actually, Lydia wonders if these are all original features of the shop, or if they're original features taken from other shops.

As Lydia and Madison cross the floor towards Anders, he rises from the giant (about two meters in diameter) beanbag that lies next to the window and invites them to take a drink from the vintage vending machine. Lydia declines, and there's nothing Madison can drink anyway.

"Anything else I can get you?" he asks, walking to a cocktail cabinet and gesturing at its wares.

"We're good, thanks." Lydia reminds herself not to take her eyes off him. She wants to record everything he does and says. She also reminds herself to smile. He'll surely suspect something might be amiss here—it's getting on for early evening, an odd time for a professional appointment—but it would be more suspicious if he told them to go away. "Sorry for dropping in on you unannounced like this—"

"No no, it's fine," says Anders, mixing himself a highball.

"We were just running a little early for the theater, and Madison suggested we take the opportunity to speak to you."

"Oh?" he says, before sipping his drink and turning to address Madison. "What are you going to see?"

Lydia leaves a brief gap as if translating for Madison and listening to her response, while in fact using this time to bring up Shows Near Me on her glasses, inwardly cursing herself for not doing this on the way here. At least by not talking to Madison she's able to keep a clear head. "*A World Of No,*" she says.

Anders nods. "I found it an excessively *obvious* interpretation of the novel, but the songs are good. See what you think."

"Interesting. And"—Lydia puts a hand on her heart—"speaking for myself now, please let me apologize for my behavior last time we met."

Anders turns to Lydia. He's obviously still furious about it, but he waves a magnanimous hand. "Water under the bridge. So," he says, turning back to Madison, "my event . . . ?"

"Yes," says Lydia. She looks around. It's just the three of them here. There's no reason not to pull the trigger on this, and she should do it while she has the chance. "Specifically what we'd like to talk to you about is, er, we uncovered one of Fitz's last projects while going through his paperwork, and it's very interesting, and we think it could be a great addition to your event."

"Right."

"Yes, in fact, it's a very surprising project. It's a veearr."

Anders pauses. "That *is* surprising."

"No one knew anything about it until now," Lydia continues. "Did you know?"

Anders slowly turns back to Lydia and smiles. "Why would I know? I'd never met him until the last night of the festival." He turns back to the cocktail cabinet, puts his drink down and drops more ice into it. He kneels, opens the hatch and searches through the bottles stored inside. "I'm not sure it'd be the best fit for my event, I'm afraid."

"You did say you were hoping it would be pan-cultural," says Lydia.

"But with the emphasis very much on performing arts." Anders moves a bottle aside and reaches to the back of the cabinet. "Theater, music, poetry, dance—" Then he spins around, a small pistol in his hand. He fires it and it makes the loud, hollow *thok* noise printed guns usually make. Lydia shouts *Look out* to Madison, forgetting she can't do that anymore, and throws herself aside, landing on the beanbag. Her headache comes roaring back.

Anders is a poor shot and his bullet embeds somewhere in the shoe display: he swings his gun around and finds Lydia again, but she rolls aside and his second shot buries itself in the beanbag. Lydia lashes out with a foot and connects with Anders' shin—he cries out in pain and loses his aim—

And Madison's arm arcs down, striking a precise blow between Anders' elbow and his wrist, and Lydia's pretty sure she hears his bone break before he drops the gun. The pitch of his howl increases, supporting this theory. He gathers his wits and realizes all he can do now is run for it, so he lurches away, trying to pass Madison—but she just sticks out her arm and sweeps him back onto the beanbag. He instinctively puts his broken arm out to break his fall—and he screams even louder, and doesn't stop.

Lydia gives Madison a thumbs-up, amused that Madison's main role in all this has been to act as her hired muscle.

Madison points at the floor. Lydia looks in the indicated direction and sees the gun lying in the jaws of a (fake?) bearskin rug. She scrambles to pick it up before Anders recovers, but as she points the gun at him she realizes there's no danger of him fighting back. He's still whimpering on the beanbag, his face screwed up against the pain—and, she suspects, also because he's reluctant to confront the situation. But she needs him to confront the situation.

"You really fucked this up, didn't you mate?" she says.

"She broke my arm," he replies. "You have to call me an ambulance."

"Do we? I mean you *did* just try and kill us, you remember that?"

Finally he opens his eyes and looks at her. He's weeping, snot runs from his nose and there's spittle on his lips. "Are you gonna kill me?"

"I won't lie to you, Anders," Lydia says, weighing the gun in her hand (she's never held one of these before—it's so *light*). "I feel like I want to."

Anders lets out a despairing moan and cries some more.

"I mean, I saw what you did to my boss's head."

"*I* didn't do that. I swear. I wouldn't know how."

"OK, I believe you—but that wasn't the part that really caused him pain, you know? It was what you did to him every day. He knew it was happening, you know that?"

Anders mutters something about how sorry he is.

"And we haven't even got *started* on how you used him to lie to me, and the almighty shitstorm you tried to cause, using me as—"

"It wasn't my idea."

"Was it not?"

"No—Booth just hired me to narrativize it."

Lydia feels like breaking his other arm. "Booth hired you to *what*?"

"They had the basic elements, like the game, and they found me the suicide girl to set up as the killer. It was my job to come up with the story and make the connections and lead you to them."

"Why you?"

"Well, as I mentioned, I have a background in devised theater, and—"

"Wait—those other people I met, Ondine and Marius, and Todd—were they *actors*?"

Anders nods.

"But Booth's real?"

"You know she complained about some of the detail? Said it was getting too convoluted?" He emits a short laugh. "I couldn't make it *too* easy for you, could I? You wouldn't believe it. Also I had to make a *lot* of it up on the fly, like, I had to react to what you were doing, and I had to work with whatever was available so some things just fell by the wayside—"

"You're saying this was just a job?"

"Yeah. I mean I was able to bring something of myself to it, but—"

"But Booth was working with other people, yeah?"

He goes quiet.

"You said 'they' before—'they' had the basic elements. Like, she didn't make the game, did she? There's a whole group behind this, and they've got people on the inside at the NYPD, right?"

Anders remains quiet. It occurs to Lydia he may have a line to the cops on a shortcut and they may already be on their way. She might not have long. She crouches next to him.

"You know you're absolutely fucked, don't you mate? I bet they told you no matter what happened, as long as you kept quiet, they'd make any trouble go away. But the problem is you've not kept quiet, because you just told me you did it and other people were involved—"

"I didn't say that."

"Afraid you did. Did you think they'd have swooped in to save you by now?" Lydia glances up to the window. She doesn't know if they're on their way but they're not here yet. "No sign of them, is there? Because they're in serious shit with the embassy so they've hung you out to dry. They'll circle the wagons and leave you out in the cold." She knows she's mixing metaphors here, but on the other hand Anders is just the sort of person who'll be wound up by that so it's all to the good. "It's so easy to paint someone like you as a random nutter. They don't care about *you*. They'll deny everything, cover their tracks and leave you to take the fall."

"But the head—I couldn't have stolen it, I couldn't have adapted the helmet, I don't have the skills—"

"Yeah, I've got a feeling your accomplices will conveniently never be found. Doesn't matter who you tell. Unless of course it's us."

He looks puzzled. "You?"

"We're looking into this on behalf of the embassy. They're not gonna trust the cops to pursue it after all this. They're gonna push for everyone involved to pay, right? So the cops aren't the ones you want to cut a deal with." She doesn't have the authority to offer what she's about to offer, so she hopes the Logi honor it. She nods in Madison's direction. "*She's* the one you want to cut a deal with."

Anders goes quiet. He sobs a little more, then collects himself. "What do you want to know?"

"The names of everyone you know who's involved."

"And after that, will you take me to a hospital?"

"We'll take you to the embassy and get you a doctor."

"I need to go to the hospital."

"If this is as big as you're saying it is, you'll be much safer at the embassy—that's the deal. So are you going to talk or not?"

They talk in the car, just in case he passes out from the pain and she doesn't get to talk to him for a while. He slumps in the backseat and Lydia turns to face him.

Anders explains the whole operation from his point of view

but he doesn't actually know a lot of names, which figures. Apart from Booth he spoke to some of the developers of the translation helmet. His police contacts were two of the cops stationed outside the residence, and he thinks the other two were involved.

"But someone must've made sure they got put on that detail," says Lydia. "And then there's the sabotage of the manhunts, and the theft from the morgue . . . could they have done all that?"

Anders shakes his head. "Doubt it. And even if they could, I could tell they weren't calling the shots. Decisions were coming down from someone else."

"So who killed Fitz?"

"All I know is it wasn't part of the plan."

"What? How can it not have been part of the plan?"

"The plan was already in motion, it was accelerated after he was murdered. They were gonna position a different Logi as the guy behind it all, I don't know who, but they saw an opportunity and took advantage and changed the plan. That's why they needed me, they needed a new narrative *fast*. I don't even know if *they* know who killed him."

"Seriously?"

"Look, if they told me who killed him I'd have factored that into the story. That's why I had to link Jene into everything, we needed a martyr who wouldn't be able to confirm or deny any of it. I think if they knew the real killer, they'd have made that a part of it, kept it all watertight." He smiles. "I did OK, didn't I? It all hung together and had an emotional realness, I think. How was the girl who played Ondine? I wasn't sure she was right for the part. . . ."

But Lydia has stopped listening. If they didn't kill Fitz, who did? And why?

SEVEN

SEVEN

BOOK OF EULOGY

Lydia awakes in one of the embassy's guest rooms to find all her things have been brought from the residence, including her clothes. Once she's dressed, she goes in search of some breakfast. When a Logi passes her in the hallway, she tries to speak to him—and gets a blinding headache for her trouble.

She goes in search of breakfast and painkillers.

@THE_HAPPENER / D-DAY—Logi delegation to land in NYC today and make demands over attaché killing—we exclusively reveal their agenda! / TR54

@ SWALLOWDOWN / AN EYE FOR AN EYE—The STARTLING Logi demand for a high-ranking politician to be SACRIFICED to satisfy honor! / TR22

@FACTS4FRIENDS / WAR BREWING?? Ships sighted on dark side of Moon / TR17

Last night when they got back, Ivan interpreted for Lydia as Madison explained what would happen next. The embassy wouldn't let it be known that they were holding Anders just yet: they wanted to hear the NYPD's version of events first, as any lies they told might be, in themselves, revealing. It was, Madison said, already the most serious diplomatic incident since the embassy was established and it could get worse from here. They held all the cards, and their demands would include immunity from prosecution for Lydia, for everything, including the driving offenses. This was nonnegotiable. Until this was agreed (and it *would* be agreed) she would stay at the embassy, ensuring her safety.

Despite this Lydia found the conversation depressing. She'd never before had to sit and listen while someone translated for her. She felt like she'd been kicked out of a VIP club. They've said they'll get medical help for her soon, but does anyone even properly understand how her brain does what it does? How are they supposed to fix it?

Furthermore, as she pointed out, they still didn't know who killed Fitz. Madison seemed confident this would all come out in good time: there was probably evidence that had been suppressed. Either way it wasn't Lydia's job: she'd already done more than enough, Madison said. Lydia supposed there was no good reason for her to remain at the center of all this, but couldn't help feeling rejected anyway.

They've given her something pseudo-important to do, which is clearly to get her out of the way while they welcome the monitors from Logia (who have landed and are on their way from Newark now, apparently) and negotiate with the various authorities here on Earth. Madison explained to Lydia that the Logi produce a Book of Eulogy for everyone who dies: Anyone who wants a copy can ask for one, and a further copy is stored at a memorial library. When Lydia heard this she expected to be asked if she wanted to put an order in for one, but instead Madison asked her to contribute some writing or artwork to it, as Fitz was so fond of Earth and proud of his work here. She added, rather pointedly, that they had never asked a human to make such a contribution before, the implication being that Lydia ought to feel honored.

Lydia didn't want to address Madison's change in attitude towards her, certainly not via a translator. She's not sure if she's won Madison's respect via her own strength of character, or it's just that Lydia was the only human she felt able to trust over all this business, but they seem to have some kind of weird bond now. If she ever recovers her ability to speak Logisi, she'll raise the subject. Maybe.

In the meantime she has to think of something to write about Fitz, the problem being she is not a writer and has never pretended to be. By lunchtime she has a doc containing two pages of bits that don't connect up, some anecdotes which might be inappropriate, and four different unsatisfactory opening lines. She keeps worrying she's strayed into some awful stereotype, and everyone will read it and cringe and regret asking a human to do this, and probably rip out the page and burn it. (How many people will read this, anyway? Just his family and friends, or do people often swing by the death library to read random testimonials of the deceased?) Can she really claim to know Fitz? She worked for him for just over ten months, and though she felt a closeness with him, he rarely told her much about himself. Maybe she should say he was a good listener?

Idly searching for inspiration, she looks up Fitz's page on the embassy's hilariously basic English-language site—it's one of those ones that lifts out of your scroll and looks like a book, which was really popular when Lydia was at school but you never see it these days. There's a short biography of Fitz and a few translated posts from him—it hasn't been updated in ages; she remembers reading all this stuff when she was assigned this job after graduation. She hasn't properly looked at it since then—occasionally she'd glance at it to see if it had been updated, discover it hadn't, message someone at the embassy to suggest they take some action on the matter, then forget about it. She swipes down the page, and down again—

And then, buried at the bottom of a page, is an image that stops her in her tracks: a photo of Fitz in his study, sitting on his sofa.

Lydia hurries downstairs, and as she arrives in the lobby Ivan rushes past, heading for the ambassador's office.

"Hi," says Lydia, "you might know this—"

"Sorry," Ivan replies. "The monitors just arrived and we're getting pushback from the cops and need to get a senator involved, so it's all hands on deck. Sorry." And he strides on.

Lydia looks around. She can't talk to any Logi here directly, and all their translators are busy. There's no one here to help her, but she can't afford to delay. She heads for the office where the embassy's personnel files are kept.

CLICK

As Lydia leaves the embassy she's very aware the police haven't yet agreed not to arrest her. She figures they won't want to rock that particular boat while everything's still so delicate, but keeps an alert running on the feeds so if talks break down and the cops decide she'd make a useful bargaining chip, she'll be warned and can try to get back to the embassy before they catch up with her.

Alone, Lydia takes a diplomatic car to the residence. If she does have to make another dash for sanctuary, at least she might get to drive at high speed through Manhattan again. This thought cheers her up.

Lydia arrives at the residence before the people she's agreed to meet because she wants to see everything for herself one more time. She half hopes to find Madison in the study: she has no reason to believe she'll be here but who knows, maybe she was sent to fetch some significant evidence. But the house is empty. She steps inside and looks up at the canvas, which right now shows a field of stars. She wonders who was last here to make it look like that. Maybe it's the default?

The doorbell rings. Lydia glances through the study window and sees Rollo standing on the doorstep with Dion. Lydia glances up and down the street and it seems like it's just the two of them. There's one police car in front of the house: she tells her glasses to run a comparison of the street with other images from the past few months, and all the cars currently out there seem to belong to residents.

Lydia releases the catch on the door, opens it and greets them.

"I was surprised to hear from you," says Rollo.

"I'm sure you were."

"I hear you're involved in some serious allegations against the department."

"This isn't about that," says Lydia, neither confirming nor denying this. She turns to Dion. "I'm afraid Madison's not here yet—but thanks for coming."

"Sure," says Dion with a flicker of a smile. "Don't worry about it."

"Are you OK?" Rollo asks Lydia, with genuine concern: she told him about her injury but not the circumstances.

"Minor head trauma," Lydia replies. "Doctor said I should give it a rest for a few days." She'd kept her lies simple when arranging the meeting, telling Rollo that Madison requested it and as Lydia wasn't fit and all the translators at the embassy were busy, Madison had asked Dion to attend. Lydia tried not to be too insistent on this point, to avoid arousing suspicion, while also making clear that Madison would expect Dion to be here and Rollo's cooperation would be noted and appreciated, which would go a long way at this sensitive time. She also dangled the carrot that this information would help resolve the increasingly tense situation between the embassy and the NYPD. She's just hoping no one questions what she's doing here, given she isn't in a fit state to translate.

"And Madison has new information about the case?" asks Rollo.

Lydia looks for a reaction from Dion, but doesn't see one and doesn't want to stare. "She does, yeah. I think, er, one of the embassy staff might be a suspect? But I'm not sure. Shall we wait for her in the study?" She gestures for them to go first, because she wants to watch Dion's reaction when she walks in—and yes, Dion does glance at the canvas for a moment, then stands with her back to it.

"Sorry she's late," says Lydia. "There's a hell of a lot going on today."

Dion remains silent and looks towards the window.

Lydia steels herself. "When you were here last time, you didn't mention you were Fitz's translator before me."

Dion takes a moment to realize she's being addressed. "Oh. Yes."

"See, I didn't know that."

"I didn't know you didn't know that."

"I had to go looking in the personnel files at the embassy. Seems like an obvious thing to mention when you meet someone for the first time, that they used to do your job."

"I assumed you knew," Dion says. "Didn't Fitzwilliam ever mention me?"

"Sometimes," says Lydia. "But never by name, it was always 'your predecessor.' He said you quit because you burnt out, yeah?"

Dion nods uneasily. "The work was taking its toll."

"But you can manage the police stuff?"

"Yeah, it's less full-on, y'know. Sometimes whole days can go by without—"

"So it was your choice to leave?"

"Yeah." Dion's eyes dart to the door and back. Rollo has sensed the edginess of this conversation but doesn't understand it.

As Lydia hoped, the canvas has changed. She gestures at it. "Funny, I never saw it look like that in all the time I lived here."

Dion turns to look. The image on the canvas is that same pastoral scene that was there when Madison repaired it. "Right."

"Except once. When we fixed it after it got hit by the bullets that missed Fitz. Which means it looked like that when he died. And if you look at his staff page on the embassy site, there's a picture of him in his office, and you can see the canvas behind him, and it looks like that again. That picture's been on the site since before I started here, so I thought—maybe it's an image he associated with that time? But then I realized the image didn't necessarily come from him, because he wouldn't have been alone. He never *droned* photos, he always got other people to take them. So there was someone else in the room, behind the camera."

"So?" says Dion—a question to which she knows the answer.

Lydia takes a step closer to Dion. "You took the picture."

Dion blinks. "I don't remember."

"You did, I checked the metadata—Dion Dalton. And it makes sense." Lydia glances at Rollo, who's watching all this unfold in puzzlement, then she turns back to Dion, confident she has her predecessor on the ropes—

And then the front door opens.

"Who the fuck's that?" says Lydia, turning in the direction of the noise.

"Madison?" says Rollo.

"Oh. Yes, probably," says Lydia, wondering if she should try to maintain her ruse or press ahead with her accusation—of course it depends who's actually out there—

And then, to Lydia's amazement, Madison walks into the study.

"Hello, ma'am," Rollo says to Madison. "Ms. Southwell told us you wanted to meet here?"

Dion translates Madison's reply: "You've been misinformed. I came here to collect some documents. You shouldn't be here at all, given the delicacy of the present situation. None of you," she adds, ensuring Lydia is included.

"My apologies, ma'am." Rollo looks to Lydia. "So that was bullshit, what you told us?"

"Well—" Lydia says. "About her wanting to meet you, yeah, but the other stuff—"

"In fact, we've been looking for this woman," Dion continues, translating for Madison, pointing at Lydia. "She absconded from our embassy after we discovered evidence *she* killed Fitzwilliam."

"What?" Lydia turns to look at Madison. "What are you talking about? You didn't—" But then she realizes what's happening and turns to Dion. "No—that's not what she just said. You're lying. *You* killed him. I was literally just about to say—"

"Dion has an alibi," says Rollo. "We checked her out because of her connection with the victim—she might've known how to get past security and he might put his guard down with her. But she was on duty at the station when it happened, we got witnesses and records."

"And these witnesses would be your colleagues? They're *in* on this. They fixed the records at the station just like they fixed the records here. They're covering for her."

"That's a very serious accusation."

"You need to arrest her *now*," says Dion calmly to Rollo. "You'll make the situation a lot worse if you let her go." Suddenly she's in control. She can tell everyone whatever she wants. Lydia tries to speak to Madison, tell her what's really happening—but nothing comes out and it feels like her brain's being flossed with barbed wire.

"OK," says Rollo, pulling a length of cuff tape from his belt. "Face the wall and put your hands behind your back."

"You're arresting me just because she said so?" asks Lydia.

"If Madison says there's evidence—"

"I don't mean Madison"—Lydia points at Dion—"*her*! She's lying! That's not what Madison said!"

Rollo loses patience and shoves Lydia's shoulder, turning her against the wall. "Hands out. Now."

Lydia turns her head and sees Madison, still standing in the doorway, staring back at her, tilting her head a little to one side. What does she think is happening? What if she *does* think Lydia killed Fitz? What if she *has* found something?

Rollo wraps the tape around Lydia's wrists. From the corner of her eye Lydia sees Dion moving across the room, towards the door. She's probably "explaining" to Madison what's happening and then she'll make some excuse for leaving. If Dion walks out of the residence, that's it—she'll skip town while Lydia's being questioned and no one will see her again—

Then Madison puts out an arm, blocking the doorway. Dion tries to duck—

And Madison blocks her with the other arm. To her relief Lydia realizes Madison knows Dion's been lying to her. She's going to be saved after all—

Then Dion draws a gun and points it at Madison. Madison slowly withdraws her arms from their position across the door—

But Rollo reacts quick, drawing his own gun and shouting for Dion to drop hers.

Dion does not drop her gun. Instead she swings it around and points it at Lydia.

There was a split second just now when Dion's gun wasn't pointing at anyone, and if Rollo had fired at that moment and taken her down, no one would have got hurt. But he missed his chance and now Lydia's at her mercy.

"He'll shoot you the moment you shoot me," Lydia says. "You can't get out of here."

Dion doesn't answer. Lydia considers the very real possibility that Dion just wants to kill her, and isn't thinking any further than that.

"You didn't want to quit this job, did you?" says Lydia. "Fitz made you leave."

Dion keeps pointing the gun. She nods.

"Why?"

Dion bites her lip. "I intruded."

Lydia tries to remember if this is something she was taught at LSTL and has forgotten. "Intruded?"

"I . . . found I could go deeper into his mind. Where he didn't want me to go."

"That's not possible."

"They don't tell you it's possible at the school because they don't want you to do it—only a few of us can."

"Oh my god. They said you were one of the most talented translators they'd ever had."

Dion smiles. "Did they?" The smile quickly collapses. "I tried to resist, but I kept getting occasional glimpses, just by accident and . . . I had to know more, I got obsessed with what was in his mind, it was driving me insane. I knew how to get in and out without him noticing—"

"And then one day . . . he noticed?"

"I said something he'd only ever thought, and he was . . . pretty shocked. He said he wouldn't tell anyone I did it, as long as I quit the agency . . ."

"And you went from there to the police." Lydia glances at Rollo, whose gun is still aimed at Dion. "Did you know she can do this?"

"I . . . ," he says. "No."

"Has she ever used it in police work?"

"That would be illegal."

"Yes it would—*has she*?"

"I . . . know she's been used sometimes on . . . special cases—but no, I don't know anything about that, I swear."

Lydia turns back to Dion. "So why'd you kill him?"

The coldness leaves Dion's expression, and all of a sudden she just looks tired and sad. "I . . . I needed his voice back."

This makes no sense to Lydia. "OK . . ."

"I wanted Fitz to take me back—let me work for him again. Their voices—his voice especially—it's the only real truth and I didn't know how much it was holding me up until it was gone. People are just . . . impossible."

"And he said you couldn't come back?"

"He said yes, or he'd see, or something like that . . . But I could tell he was lying, he was scared of me. I don't—I don't know what came over me . . . I remember the moment I shot him, but before that it's all hazy . . ."

Lydia nods. "You were drunk."

"I don't get drunk. It's one of my skills."

"You were jealous of me, then? If you can't have his voice no one can?"

Dion's manner has completely changed now. She's pleading. "After it happened, I went to the station and I was going to just confess. I told Sturges and he said he could make it OK and all I had to do was keep quiet about it—"

Rollo looks alarmed. "Sturges?"

"He said I was too valuable to the department, he couldn't let me go down—said he'd protect me—"

"You know what they *did* to Fitz?"

"I didn't know they'd do that, or they'd turn it into this whole thing about the game . . . I thought they'd just pin it on someone else. And then it all started unraveling. . . ."

Lydia quells her anger and says, "I understand." If she was talking to a Logi she'd never get away with saying this, because she's saying it like it's OK and she sympathizes. In fact she finds what Dion has done unforgivable on every level—in terms of the act itself, what it enabled and what it put her through. A Logi would be able to taste the contempt, the hatred. Really, Lydia's just saying this because she wants Dion to put the gun down.

Dion nods, then starts to raise the gun to her own head. In this moment Lydia's only thought is whether Dion has said enough, in the presence of a police officer, for the case to be considered closed and herself to be cleared and Sturges to go down. That's all she cares about, not that Dion is about to kill herself. Later she'll feel a little bad about this, but in the moment she just wants this to be over.

The gun doesn't quite reach Dion's head before it falls from her hand. Her nerve has failed. Rollo swiftly kicks the gun away and orders Dion to turn so he can tape her hands.

Lydia looks up at Madison and tries to say *thank you,* but can't.

AUTUMN

I finished it, Lydia tells Madison, entering her office with a slim manila folder in hand. *If it's not too late.*

No, it's not, Madison replies, looking up from her desk. *It won't go to press until the morning of the funeral. It's considered inappropriate to do it any other way.*

Lydia's speech is recovering—it started to come back a couple of days after Dion was arrested—but she still finds there's a slightly grating quality to Madison's voice, like listening to a very, very compressed audio file. She can't cope with this for long, but there are things she needs to say, and she doesn't want to say them through a translator.

Are you going to the funeral? Lydia asks.

Me? No. He and I never saw eye to eye. It would be hypocritical for me to go. Besides, they can't afford for everyone to take two weeks off to do the whole round trip. Someone's got to stay here. Have you decided what you're going to do yet?

To be honest I'd resigned myself to not being able to translate anymore, so I just assumed I'd have to go home and . . . whatever. It never occurred to me I might have options. She's been living in the guest room at the embassy and recuperating in between giving evidence. It's the safest place for her to be: since the whole fake conspiracy was exposed she's received threats from groups who want to believe that it was all real and she broke ranks to discredit it. She's made public statements to the contrary with a high truthiness rating, but to no avail. Meanwhile Mum is talking about moving to New York because she thinks it might make her worry about Lydia less.

I might have to keep on working for you guys just because I need your protection, Lydia says.

But you'd rather not?

It's not that—I want to. In fact, more than ever Lydia feels she wants to be a part of all this. *But I'm concerned about the mental health implications. I feel like doing this job sent Dion mad in the end.*

Lots of people do your job and don't go mad.

Lydia nods. *Well, they say I don't have to decide until the new cultural attaché is appointed.*

I wondered about applying for the role. I don't know if that would make you more or less interested in staying on.

Lydia can't hide her surprise. She literally can't. *You?*

Going through his paperwork made me think there are things I could do with it.

Lydia nods. *Well, thanks for the heads-up.* She hands the manila folder over to Madison. *Oh—would I be able to get a copy of the book? Fitz's memorial book?*

Of course, Madison replies. *It'll be in Logisi, you realize.*

Oh yeah, I get that. Lydia's own tribute has already been translated: she got someone from the typing pool to do it for her. She'd like to learn to read it properly. LSTL only gave her a basic grounding in the written language. Maybe she'll try to teach herself.

May I read this? says Madison, opening the folder to find two sheets of paper.

Of course. Lydia was half hoping she would and half hoping she wouldn't; but it's absurd to object. They sit in silence while Madison reads the story of how Fitz caught her when she fell from the balcony at the theater; his strength, consideration and graciousness.

Lydia looks out of the window of Madison's office, sees autumn trying to break through the last of the summer heat and listens to Fitz's voice telling her she's done a good job, not just of the tribute but of finding the truth, even if she often wishes she hadn't found it, even if she often wishes someone else could've found it and she wouldn't have to know. His voice tells her she can't change it now, and that another person would not necessarily have done the same in her place.

She knows the voice is really her own. But it tells her things she needs to hear, things she can't rely on others to tell her. So she goes on listening.

ACKNOWLEDGMENTS

I can remember exactly when I thought of the idea for this book—it was on 7th February 2020, during my last trip to the cinema before the UK was locked down to protect against COVID-19. The film was *Parasite,* and it was followed by a Q&A with director Bong Joon-ho and star Song Kang-ho, accompanied by translator Sharon Choi. It got me thinking about the future of translation as a job, and whether technology would ever replace it entirely, and what circumstances might make that impossible. I pitched the novel a month later.

I then spent much of the next year shielding from the pandemic on medical advice, and my family were often in the house with me all day, doing their work and schooling online, unable to go out and see anyone else. Writing a book is always an intense experience and this made it even more so. So I'm incredibly grateful to Catherine Spooner, Gabriel Robson Spooner, and Jago Robson Spooner for giving me the space to do it under circumstances that were very challenging for us all.

Thanks also to my editor, Lee Harris, and to everyone at Tordotcom; to Henry Sene Yee for his wonderful cover; to Mark Clapham, James Cooray Smith, and Lance Parkin; and to Mum, Dad, and Helen.